DEFENDER OF THE WALL

BOOK ONE IN THE
DRAGON OF THE NORTH TRILOGY

BY

CHRIS THORNDYCROFT

Dragon of the North Trilogy Book 1: Defender of the Wall
By Chris Thorndycroft
2025 by Copyright © Chris Thorndycroft

All rights reserved. This book or any portion thereof may not be reproduced or used in any manner whatsoever without the express written permission of the publisher except for the use of brief quotations in a book review.

https://christhorndycroft.wordpress.com/

For Maia for her constant encouragement and my parents for their unwavering support.

Place Names

Latin	British	Modern English
Britannia	Albion	Britain
Mona	Ynys Mon	Anglesey
	Din Eidyn	Edinburgh
Eboracum	Cair Eborac	York
	Din Eil	Eildon Hill
Trimontium		Newstead
	Aber Teu	River Tweed
Cilurnum		Chesters, near the village of Walwick
Cambloganna		Castlesteads
Vindolanda		Near the village of Bardon Mill
Cataractonium		Catterick
Segedunum		Wallsend
Banna		Birdoswald
	Din Peldur	Traprain Law
Brocavum		Brougham
Onnum		Halton Chesters
Vercovicium		Housesteads
Brocolitia		Carrawburgh
	Aber Tina	River Tyne
Banovallum		Horncastle
Bremetenacum		Ribchester
	Din Guaire	Bamburgh
	Aber Clut	River Clyde

Prologue

"Maelgwn, the great king, was reigning among the Britons in the region of Gwynedd, for his ancestor, Cunedag, with his sons, whose number was eight, had come previously from the northern part, that is from the region which is called Manaw Gododdin, one hundred and forty-six years before Maelgwn reigned. And with great slaughter they drove out from those regions the Scotti who never returned again to inhabit them." – Historia Brittonum

445 A.D.

Time was running out.

A dull dawn was breaking over the island of Ynys Mon. Cunedag sat astride his white mare and watched the boats being unloaded. They were flat-bottomed things suitable for crossing the turbulent straits between the island and the mainland but there had still been the need for a local guide to navigate the strong currents and shifting sands. A small window of time had allowed him to ferry his men and supplies across at slack tide while the cavalry swam. It was a massive operation carried out within a few hours, but they had made it across and now Manawydan, ruler of the sea, was filling up the straits with his thundering swell once more.

The older he got, Cunedag thought, the more precious time seemed to be. He pulled his fur-trimmed cloak around him against the chill of the morning that seemed to seep into his old bones. He had commanded warriors for almost all his life. He had fought in more wars than the gods had any right to visit upon a man. He had seen Rome's control over Albion crumble and slip from its shores. He had been there when the last legions had left, experienced the chaos that had followed and played a part in building the first kingdoms that had risen from its ashes. Now, his own time in this world was coming to an end.

There were some cheers as one of the hunting parties he had dispatched returned with a boar carried between a bundle of spears. *A good omen.* Ynys Mon was plentiful in game and would feed them well now they had established a foothold. Cunedag glanced at the rising ground beyond the beach, topped with tangled trees over which a silence seemed to hang. *No sign of the enemy*, he thought. *But they know we're here.*

The hunting party were accepting congratulations as the boar was strung up by its hindquarters and the cookfires were banked to provide heat enough to roast the meat. Osmael, Cunedag's sixth son, approached him after conversing with the returning party.

"Any sign of the enemy?" Cunedag asked him.

"They spotted a band of Gaels on a ridge deep in the forest," Osmael replied, removing his helmet and running his fingers through his dark hair. At thirty-nine, Osmael was in his prime. A good fighter and a better leader. Not once had Cunedag regretted making him his *penteulu*; commander of his warband. "They ran from a mere hunting party, so they were likely just scouts."

"Sent to spy on us," said Cunedag. "They knew of our coming long before we set out. Strange that there is no warband here to greet us. Do you think we present too much of a challenge for open battle? Have we really whittled Beli down to such a small force?"

"It's possible, Father," said Osmael. "But if we have learned anything from the Gaels, then it is to not underestimate their trickery. They will be regrouping as we speak. Messengers will be riding between every hillfort on the island. Beli will be biding his time and laying his traps for us."

"Then we must be ever cautious," said Cunedag. "Where is Enniaun?"

"Arguing with Etern, as usual," said Osmael.

Cunedag swore. "What is it this time?"

"Horse fodder. Some of Etern's men accused Enniaun's of stealing thirty sacks of barley as they came off the boats. I've had the quartermaster resolve the matter, but you know Enniaun and Etern. It's gone beyond a matter of horse fodder."

They rode down the beach towards the cluster of hide tents that had been erected in the shadows of the beached boats. Warriors who sat by the cookfires stood to attention as Cunedag rode past, bowing their heads in respect to their king.

Four of Cunedag's eight remaining sons were with him for the invasion of Ynys Mon. There was Etern, who was his second born and heir to their homelands in the north beyond the Wall now that his firstborn, Tybiaun was dead. Ruman, was his thoughtful and scholarly third son. Osmael, his loyal and mild-mannered penteulu. And then there was Enniaun, his seventh; an infuriating, impetuous lad whom Cunedag couldn't help but feel great affection for. In fact, Enniaun had long rivalled Osmael as his favourite but had never been considered for the position of penteulu due to his bull-headed nature and impulsiveness.

Cunedag's other four sons were on the mainland, ruling their portions of the territory they had reclaimed from the Gaels. It had taken eight long years to drive them from the mainland. Now, only Ynys Mon held out against them; the last retreat of Beli mac Benlli, war chief of the Gaels. Eight years since Lord Vertigernus, head of the Council of Britannia, had sent Cunedag and his nine sons to reclaim the lost lands. It had taken far longer than he had ever thought. May Modron, the Great Mother, grant them victory in this final battle!

Cunedag dismounted, knocking aside Osmael's offered arm as he attempted to aid his aging father down from the saddle. The day he became too old to get off a bloody horse, Cunedag maintained, was the day he'd let one of his sons succeed him.

He entered the tent to find two of them almost screaming in each other's faces, both trying their damndest to tower over the other. He was put in mind of the fights his sons had had when they had been children. Little had changed but for their size and the fact that they all now carried weapons by their sides. Modron forbid that they should ever use those blades against each other!

"Your men overstep their mark again and again, Enniaun!" Etern was yelling. "I've a mind you deliberately set them against me to provoke me!"

"Or maybe you're so ashamed that my teulu outshines yours on every battlefield that you seek the smallest slight to feign outrage," said Enniaun. "What's the matter, Etern? Worried that your light has been eclipsed in Father's eye?"

"Have a care, Brother," Etern snarled. "Whatever glories you win on the battlefield won't make you Father's heir. Just remember that I will be your king once he is gone."

"I am not yet under my cairn, Etern," Cunedag snapped. The bark of his seasoned voice made everybody in the tent jump.

"My apologies, Father," Etern said. "I meant no disrespect."

"You just meant to establish your dominance over your siblings prematurely," said Cunedag. "But I am still king. I am still *Pendraig*."

The title had been given to him by the Britons in the lands they had reclaimed from the Gaels in reference to the red dragon banner that was Cunedag's battle standard. The sons of Cunedag were known in these parts as 'the dragons of the north' and he, as their father, was the 'chief dragon'.

"And long may you reign, Father," said Ruman from where he lounged on some stacked sacks of grain, eating an apple, a codex of some ancient chronicle in his lap. His two brothers glared at him, knowing that he was too cunning to support either of them, at least in Father's eyes. Ruman was always the thinker, but knew he was never in the running to succeed their father. That had always been Tybiaun until his tragic death earlier that year. Since then, Etern had made much noise about being the next in line which contributed greatly to the antagonism between him and Enniaun, their father's favourite.

Enniaun, a handsome but arrogant youth, had just turned twenty when Vertigernus had made his offer of ruling Venedotia to Cunedag and had been eager to prove himself in battle. So far, he had done well, slaying many Gaels, but he was the only one of Cunedag's sons besides Osmael, the penteulu, who had not been given a territory of his own on the mainland. With Ynys Mon still to conquer, there would be land aplenty for all Cunedag's sons and the feeling was that Cunedag was saving the final jewel in his territorial crown for Enniaun. It was time to finish this war so Enniaun could be given a position of power and a kingdom to rule, and the lad knew it.

"We are on the cusp of what might be our final battle," Cunedag reprimanded his sons. "And you think to waste time arguing over horse fodder and old grievances? Have we not enough Gaels to wet our blades in that we must fight among ourselves?"

"Apologies, Father," said Etern. "I would not quarrel with my own brothers, but Enniaun has ever sought new ways to incite me."

"Then learn to endure his barbs for the greater good!" Cunedag snapped. "We cannot afford distractions now. Enniaun, you will make peace with your brother."

"Always, Father," said Enniaun. "A simple misunderstanding, I assure you."

"If you will not set aside your differences for me," said Cunedag, "Then do so for the memory of your mother, may her shade be at peace in Annun."

The invocation of their late and much-beloved matriarch made both of them hang their heads in shame.

Cunedag left the tent and went outside. Other hunting parties had returned, and meat was being prepared for roasting. His mood was even more sour than it had been previously. He supposed he should be thankful that the quarrels between his sons were not as bad as his quarrels had been with his own brothers. But the world had been different back then. The Romans had still ruled Albion. Now, the stakes were much higher. His sons had the luxury of youth to waste time on quarrels. At sixty-seven, he was lucky to still be among the living, especially after a lifetime of little else but war. He hoped this would be his last campaign. He didn't feel he had many left in him.

And this damned war had lasted so long that he wouldn't live to see the kingdom he had created on the mainland flourish. All he could do was to ensure that his sons did. But to do that, he had to smash the Gaels and their leader, Beli mac Benlli, for good. And he had to smash them quickly before they received reinforcements from Erin. It was already spring and the sea to the west that separated Albion from the homeland of the Gaels would soon be calm enough for a fleet of hide-covered boats to bring thousands of the bastards to these shores.

Time was running out.

As Cunedag watched the boar being dressed for the fire, his thoughts wandered to the fate of another boar, seemingly several lifetimes ago.

Part I

390 A.D.

*"A chief of lion aspect, ashes become his fellow-countrymen,
Against the son of Edern, before the supremacy of terrors,
He was fierce, dauntless, irresistible,
For the streams of death he is distressed."*
- *The Death Song of Cunedda* from *The Book of Taliesin*
(trans. Mary Jones)

Chapter 1

The boy reined in his stocky white pony and looked about him. He could hear his brother's cry clearly through the dense dampness of the forest. That meant he must be close by. But there was a note of urgency in his voice that indicated terror rather than pain.

They had become separated from the main hunt shortly after they had found the spoor and their father and his retainers had galloped off after it. Cunedag and Brude, brothers and princes of the Votadini, had struggled to keep up, forcing their ponies on through the deepening woodland as the ground sloped down into the glen. They should have followed the group, but Brude had insisted he knew a shortcut that would enable them to catch up quicker and Cunedag had blindly followed him.

Brude was the better rider of the two and had ridden on too hard, leaving Cunedag behind. Cunedag had called out for his older brother to wait but he knew that nothing could stop Brude when he set his mind to something.

Cunedag heard Brude scream again, closer this time, so he knew he was headed in the right direction. He jabbed his heels in and urged his mount on through the springy, bare branches and over fallen, rotting trunks to reach his brother in time.

He found Brude in a small clearing, on his back, thrown from his pony which lay on its side a few feet from him, unmoving. Its belly was ripped open, and the agent of its death was still goring it with its seven-inch tusks.

The boar was one of the biggest Cunedag had ever seen. Its razor back arched as it snorted and tore at the fallen pony, ripping its entrails out in its rage. Cunedag gripped his spear and tried to swallow, his throat sapped of moisture by fear. A boar like this could take down a mounted rider with ease and do the same to him as it had done to Brude's pony.

"Cunedag, watch yourself!" Brude screamed as the boar raised its reddened snout at the new target that had entered the clearing. It squealed with rage and rounded the dead pony to charge, its tusks lowered.

Cunedag's pony reared in fright, nearly throwing him, but Cunedag gripped the reins with his left hand and his spear with his right, squeezing his thighs for purchase on the terrified animal's back for all he was worth. As the boar tried to rake its tusks along the pony's left flank, Cunedag nudged it into a side pass and thrust his spear tip over his left arm and down, into the boar's back.

The beast shrieked its anger and wheeled around to charge the pony a second time. The pony's courage left it and broke into a gallop, jolting Cunedag from its saddle as it fled the clearing.

Cunedag tumbled to the dead leaves, his spear landing beside him as the wind was knocked from his lungs. He struggled to get to his feet, grabbing his spear as his only defence against the enraged boar.

Brude had crawled over to his slain mount, his leg apparently injured from the fall, and was clinging to it as if it would offer some sort of protection. Cunedag hurried over to him just as the boar lost interest in the fleeing pony and rounded on them, its bloodied tusks pointed in their direction.

"Cunedag, it's going to charge!" Brude cried.

Cunedag gritted his teeth and tried to still the shaking in his arms as he lowered his spear tip and jammed the butt into the earth, bracing his foot against it. A cold anger took hold of him. If this bastard boar was going to kill him and his brother, then he would damn well make sure it died with them.

With a snort of challenge, the boar glared at them with its eyes of jet and lowered its head before breaking into a run, the speed of which defied its hulking shape.

Both Cunedag and Brude screamed in terror as four-hundred pounds of muscle, fat and slavering death bore down on them. Cunedag forced his eyes to stay open as he faced down his fate, refusing to look away or try to shut out the nightmare.

He lowered the spearpoint below the dripping tusks and the boar slid onto it, squealing in pain as the weight and power of its charge impaled the beast on the outthrust spear. Only then did Cunedag flinch as he felt its hot, stinking breath on his face, its blood running down the spear shaft to coat his hands in gore as the spear bent precariously under its weight, the beast caught on its crossbar.

The boar jerked and twisted, snapping the ash shaft of the spear and tumbling to one side as Cunedag rolled in the opposite direction, thanking the Great Mother that he had not rolled under it for a beast that size would crush the life from him. He lay panting on the ground as the death cries of the boar receded.

He slowly got to his feet, amazed that he was alive, and helped Brude stand. His ankle didn't seem to be broken but it was already badly swollen. Arms around each other, they went in search of Cunedag's pony.

By the time they had found and calmed it enough to get Brude up into its saddle, the rest of the hunt was crashing through the trees towards them, wondering what had happened to their prey.

"What befell you two?" their father demanded. "Brude, where is your pony?"

"We got separated," said Brude, casually neglecting to mention his 'short cut' that had been his idea. "The boar must have doubled back. It slew my pony and nearly gored me to death."

The hounds were whining at the scent of blood in the air. They were not far from the carcass of the boar.

"Which of you slew it?" said their father once his men had gone off to retrieve the kill.

Cunedag was about to open his mouth, his head giddy at the prospect of winning his father's admiration, but before he could speak, Brude said; "I did."

The magnitude of the lie sucked Cunedag's voice from him. He was unable to speak, scarcely able to believe his ears. Did Brude really mean to claim the credit for killing the boar? Worse; claim that he had saved his little brother's life when it had been the other way around?

"Cunedag found me, but the boar scared off his pony and he was thrown too," Brude continued. "The boar charged us, but I was able to defend us with Cunedag's spear."

"By Modron's tits!" one of their father's warriors cried as the boar was dragged towards them. "Did you ever hear of a lad of seventeen sticking a boar that size?"

"No," said their father, a broad smile widening across his grizzled features. "Never. But my son did!" He clapped his massive hand on Brude's shoulder and Cunedag didn't have it in him to shatter the moment with the truth. It wasn't the beating he would undoubtedly get from Brude that frightened him. It was the look of disappointment that would be in his father's eyes if he ruined the moment. Even worse, he might not be believed. To appear as a liar trying to steal his brother's thunder would be more than he could bear. So, he remained silent and swallowed down the bitter draught of resentment.

The kill was dressed, and the hunters made the customary offering to the Horned God by burying some of the offal. They rode back to Din Eidyn, royal seat of the Votadini, with the boar carried on a litter, the dogs running alongside, their heads proudly in the air as if they had played some part in bringing it down. Everybody, Cunedag thought, wanted to take the credit for his kill.

He said nothing as they rode up the approach to the top of the massive volcanic rock. Din Eidyn crowned its peak; a fortress of dry-stone walls, laced with timbers and topped with a wattle palisade that enclosed the roundhouses of his father's chief fortification.

The boar was roasted and presented at King Etern's table that night in his *lys*; the Great Roundhouse where the nobles of the tribe gathered. Brude, his ankle bandaged, was the toast of the feast and everybody looked enraptured as he embellished his lie for the entertainment of his father's court, mead horn in one hand, his other gripping the crutch he was now required to use to keep the weight off his foot.

Seeing the pride in his mother's eyes and the awed expression of his little brother, Murcho, was almost more than Cunedag could bear. That pride should have been for him! Only their sister, Alpia, two years older than Cunedag, seemed uninterested in Brude's boasts. She knew as well as Cunedag what a bullying braggart their big brother was.

The walls and smoke-stained rafters of the roundhouse were decorated with shields and tapestries. Above King Etern's seat hung the scarlet cloak of Cunedag's grandfather, Padarn. During the Great Conspiracy of 367, the tribes of the highlands joined forces with the Attacotti of Alt Clud and had swarmed south to attack the great Roman wall which stretched from coast to coast across Albion. The Votadini and their fellow tribes of the lowlands – the Selgovae and the Novantae, which had long been allies of Rome – had been pressured into joining them.

This betrayal did not go unanswered and, after a punitive expedition against the north, Padarn was set up as a client king of the Votadini, given an officer's rank in the Roman army, and was required to send one of his sons to be fostered by the governor of Britannia Secunda below the Wall. Cunedag's father rarely spoke of his youth in the great households of the Romans, but the red cloak of his father still hung over his throne like a stern threat from their overlords to the south, reminding the Votadini to honour their old alliance.

The Votadini, like the Selgovae and Novantae, had once been little different from the tribes of the highlands, although, as the closest neighbours to the Wall, trade with the Romans seemed like a better prospect to them than war. When the Emperor Antoninus built a second wall a hundred miles to the north, they had been sealed between the walls in a new province the Romans called Valentia and officially became part of the empire. The Romans had been unable to hold the frontier, however, and had retreated back to the first wall after only twenty years, leaving the three tribes of the lowlands and the abandoned province of Valentia in a curious state of limbo between Rome and the wild, untamed tribes of the highlands.

The boar, deemed ready at last, was carved with the choicest portion going to Brude. The rest was passed around on platters and Cunedag grudgingly accepted a small portion. He ate it but the taste to him was sour.

The following day, when the Great Roundhouse was all but deserted, Cunedag challenged his big brother, finding him alone with one of father's hounds, his bound leg preventing him from being out and about.

"Why did you lie about the boar?" Cunedag demanded, striding up to him, but stopping short of fist range. Brude might be injured, but he was still a formidable brawler.

"Why do you think, fool?" Brude snapped. "To save myself face. How would it look if Father's eldest son and heir to the tribe had to be rescued by his little brother? It would be a bad look. I know it's not pleasant, Cunedag, but sometimes you have to put the tribe first."

Cunedag was briefly stunned into silence by the audacity of his older brother. "I saved your life!"

"And I'm grateful. But I couldn't allow it to be known that you had killed the boar and not me. That's just not the way of things, little brother. I must be held in higher esteem. Hence the lie."

"You lied so you could bask in everybody's praise!" Cunedag snapped. "You stole the affection and praise that was rightly mine! I'm going to tell everybody! I'm going to strip you of your glamour and see that they all know what a lying wretch their next king is!"

He was out of fist range but Brude's crutch, forgotten by Cunedag, wasn't and the blow lashed out like the strike of a viper, catching Cunedag in the left thigh. Pain seeped through the muscle, robbing it of strength so his leg buckled beneath him and he fell to the hardpacked dirt floor. Then, Brude was upon him, heaving himself up and landing heavily on his little brother before he began to pummel him with his fists.

"I'll tell Father how I got these bruises!" Cunedag cried through snot and blood as Brude pinned him to the ground with his left hand, his other raised to threaten another savage blow.

"And I'll tell him your jealously led you to try and take advantage and attack me while I was vulnerable," Brude replied. "Who do you think he'll believe? Who will *everyone* believe?"

He got off his brother and Cunedag scrabbled to get away from him.

"Run off and tell your lies," Brude said as he eased himself back onto the bench. "See how far they get you. But I suspect you'll find that people aren't too willing to listen."

Cunedag fled from the Great Roundhouse and found some quiet, hidden place to be alone with his tears. Whatever Brude did to him, he wouldn't let anybody see him cry.

Chapter 2

The following week saw spring bloom across the lowlands. The wind blew through the rolling green hills and across the moors where the purple heather danced. Cunedag stood atop the palisade of Din Eidyn, looking south. He had done his best to avoid his brother over the past few days, but resentment still burned in his heart.

He frowned as he saw movement in the distance. Horses were approaching from the south. He squinted and counted six riders on the large cavalry horses the Romans used. The sunlight glinted off helmets and the rims of the round shields that were carried on their backs.

"A deputation from beyond the Wall," said one of his father's sentries at his side. "I wonder what they want."

As the riders wound their way up the approach to the fortress, Cunedag watched them in awe. He had never seen Roman soldiers before. Their mail coats, bronze greaves and crested helms made them seem impenetrable in comparison to the warriors of the Votadini, of whom only the wealthiest and noblest wore mail shirts or helms.

There was a flurry of excitement about the fort as King Etern ordered a reception for the strangers. All members of his family were called to the Great Roundhouse while the horses of the Romans were stabled and fed.

The roundhouse was packed with people, all eager to see the newcomers at close range and hear what they had to say. King Etern sat in his high-backed chair, his family dutifully standing on either side of him. The six strangers, their weapons left in the antechamber, stood in the centre of the room beside the firepit. The one with the more ostentatious armour wore a scarlet cloak fastened at the right shoulder with a brooch; twin to the older, more faded cloak that hung behind Etern's chair. This man was an officer.

"I am Flavius Lestinus, *primus pilus* of the Sixth Victrix," the officer said in the British dialect of the south.

The words meant nothing to Cunedag nor apparently to many others in the room for silence followed the officer's pompous announcement. A brief flash of disappointment crossed the man's face before he continued. "We have come from Praeses Paullus Decius Colias of Britannia Secunda. Greetings, Eternus of the Votadini."

"Greetings, Flavius Lestinus," said King Etern, his voice level and devoid of warmth.

Before the conversation went any further, a voice from the doorway to the antechamber spoke; "Does the king think to engage in wordplay with strangers from the south without his most trusted councillor by his side?"

The mood in the roundhouse immediately changed as the ragged figure of an elderly man appeared, white of beard and robe from which hung many ornaments and talismans.

"Don't think to lecture me, Gonar," said King Etern. "I summoned you here along with everybody else. You seek to insult our guests with your tardiness?"

"My bones are old, and it takes twice as long to move them up this hill which, I swear by Taran, increases in size every year."

The two men grinned at each other, and it was clear to all that the antagonism between them was merely the play of two old acquaintances. Gonar strode across the room, ignoring the Romans, to take his place by Etern's side.

"Allow me to introduce Gonar the druid," Etern said to the visitors. "He is a miserable old sorcerer but a good counsellor and a fine poet."

The Romans eyed Gonar with a mixture of distrust and loathing. Cunedag had heard that they despised the druids and had all but wiped them out south of the Wall. Here in the north, the druids still fulfilled their roles as priests, poets, judges and counsellors. And old Gonar had been chief druid to the Votadini since Padarn's day.

"Many winters have passed since we heard from Eboracum," Etern continued. "Not since I returned from there myself, a mere stripling of a man. Now I am a king and grey of hair. What does the son of my former foster father wish of me?"

"You are informed enough to know that your foster father is no longer with us," said the officer. "And that he has been succeeded by his son, whom you knew in your youth."

"I knew him little, and he knew me less than that," Etern said. "We barbarian hostages were little more than a nuisance for the true sons of those who held us captive."

"Your choice of words indicates that you did not warm to your situation during your time in the south."

"My choice of words was not my own," Etern shot back. "Many times did my masters remind me of my *situation*."

"Praeses Colias hopes that your own poor experience will not cause any friction between us."

"Not at all," said Etern. "It is in the past and the old tyrant who called himself my foster father is dead."

"And his son now requires you to honour the same agreement your own father held."

There was a ripple of murmurs throughout the roundhouse as the implication of the Roman's words was understood by some.

"I hope you are not suggesting what I think you are," said Etern, his blazing eyes reflecting more than the flames of the firepit.

"It was understood that this arrangement would continue for as long as peace lasted between Britannia and the tribes north of the Wall," said the officer, with none of the trepidation that would have been shown by those who knew Etern and his rages.

"It was not understood by me!" Etern bellowed. "I was given to understand that my people's debt to Rome was fulfilled the day I was allowed to return to my home a free man. Nothing was said about men coming to claim one of my sons years later!"

Cunedag's eyes widened as he finally understood the purpose of the strangers in coming here. They meant to carry Brude away with them to Eboracum and foster him to the household of the governor as their father had been! He had to admit, the idea had its merits. To be rid of Brude's bullying and swaggering for the next few years was a pleasant prospect. But the bonds of family in the face of an outside threat made him push that thought aside. He might hate Brude, but he was his brother. These Romans *couldn't* take him. Their father wouldn't let them.

"It is unfortunate that this was not made clear to you," said the officer calmly. "Nevertheless, Rome's desire to maintain peace with the northern tribes continues as does the agreement. Of course, times are not as tumultuous as they were in your father's day. Praeses Colias does not require your firstborn. One of your other sons will suffice."

Cunedag felt suddenly sick. *Not Brude, then. Murcho, perhaps?* But he was still so young … no, it would be him, he was sure of it. In fact, the eyes of the Roman had settled on him, as if having finally sought him out. It occurred to him that their arrival at Din Eidyn in his twelfth year was no accident. Twelve was the usual age for fostering. *They've been waiting for me*, he thought. *They've been keeping a close eye on the royal families of the north …*

"We believe your second son has now reached his twelfth year, said the officer, confirming Cunedag's suspicions. "Do you not wish to strengthen ties between our two peoples?"

"None of my sons are going with you to your damned southern towns," growled Etern. "If you cannot trust my word that the Votadini will not wage war on Rome again, then my own time in your clutches was for nothing! I bought my family's right to freedom with my own blood!"

"I'm afraid that to refuse Praeses Colias's offer of continued friendship would be seen as a gross provocation," the officer replied. "He has already accepted sons from the Selgovae and the Novantae. Would it really be wise to become the only tribe not to honour the agreement of your fathers?"

Etern seethed, apparently knowing he was at an impasse. Silence hung in the smoky air of the roundhouse as all awaited the king's response to this veiled threat. Cunedag felt his entire future hanging in the air with it. His mouth was dry as he awaited his father's words.

"I will discuss this in private with my druid," he said. "We must ask the gods what the right path is."

"As you wish," said the officer. "Look to your superstitions but I must warn you, the patterns of clouds or the entrails of birds have no bearing on Rome's demands."

There was a grumble at this insult to their religious beliefs. Most people below the Wall had converted to Christianity, as encouraged to by their emperors, but in the wild north, the old gods and traditions still held sway.

"I will give you my answer tomorrow," said Etern.

The Romans were dismissed, and a small roundhouse was given over for their accommodation. Everybody else dispersed and Etern left with Gonar for private counsel, their faces grim. Only, Cunedag, his siblings and their mother, Ceindrich, remained.

"It looks like Cunedag is to leave us," said Brude, a faint trace of amusement on his face.

"Nobody knows anything until Gonar has put it to the gods," said their mother as she pulled both Cunedag and Murcho close to her. There was fear in her voice and it only increased Cunedag's own fear as he clung to her and his little brother.

"Why do they want to take Cunedag?" little Murcho asked, looking up at their mother with wide eyes. He was only nine and his innocence made Cunedag want to protect him. He would gladly go with these Romans to save his little brother from such a fate. Even though the thought terrified him.

"Because the Romans don't trust us," said Alpia, their sister, venom in her voice. "They want hostages to make sure we behave ourselves."

At fourteen, Alpia was old enough to leave home herself as soon as their father found her a suitable husband though, as many agreed, she would prove a formidable match for any man. She was as quick with words as she was with a blade and their father had made sure she has been trained with spear and bow along with her brothers. She might make a good leader one day, but perhaps a troublesome wife.

"We must be strong for each other whatever your father's decision," said their mother. "Only the gods know what the future holds."

Cunedag couldn't sleep that night and lay awake listening to the wind and the mice rustling around in the thatch above his head. His fate was in the hands of the gods, and he prayed to them, begging to be allowed to stay. Only the wind and the creaking timbers answered him, and they offered no solace. How many nights had he left under this roof?

Early the following morning, just after a breakfast which Cunedag had not the stomach for, everybody reconvened in the roundhouse. The Romans stood before his father, as before, and all awaited his verdict. Gonar stood by his side, stony-faced.

"You leave me with no choice," Etern said. "Rome has ever held the threat of war over its so-called allies. And if the Selgovae and the Novantae have not the spines to stand against you, then the Votadini are all alone." He sighed with the effort of a heavy decision that had already been made. "Last night, my druid asked the gods for guidance, and they gave us their answer. My son, Cunedag, shall go with you."

Cunedag felt as if his world had dropped out from beneath him like a trapdoor, leaving nothing below him but impenetrable blackness. The roundhouse broke into excited chattering. Many were angry but cautious enough not to appear to be directing their ire at their king. It was the Romans who were the cause of this outrage.

"I am glad you see reason," said the officer. "Your son will do you proud, I am sure. Perhaps he will even attain the rank of tribune as your own father did." He glanced at the red cloak hanging behind Etern's throne, recognising it as a twin, albeit a faded and more ragged one to his own.

They were to leave the following morning. Cunedag's world was changing so fast he could scarcely keep up with it. His family assembled in the main enclosure where his pony was saddled and loaded with some meagre provisions. The Romans were seeing to their own mounts in the stables, leaving Cunedag to say goodbye to his family in private.

Gonar the druid was with them and Cunedag found that he was going to miss the old man almost as much as his family for the druid had been his teacher since he had been able to walk, instructing him and his siblings in nature, astronomy and the feats of kings and heroes long dead and remembered through song.

"I wish I didn't have to go," he found himself saying. "I wish the Votadini had never stood against Rome years ago and incurred its wrath. Then they would not ask for such a heavy price."

Gonar placed a comforting hand on his shoulder. "We cannot change the past, lad. All we can do is decide how to deal with the present. Leave the rest to the gods."

"Eight short years," his mother said as she hugged him close, her voice nearly cracking under the strain of staying positive. She was losing one of her children and was struggling to be brave for him. That alone almost made Cunedag weep in her arms, but he forced himself to match her courage. "Eight years and you will return to us a man. Just as your father did."

As for his father, he stood silent, his face showing no emotion. Not that Etern was particularly given to sensitivity, but Cunedag suspected the shame at being forced to give into the Romans made his face even harder that cold morning. "Learn your lessons well," he told Cunedag. "Do as you are told but also bear no insult to either yourself or the Votadini. Remember that you are there under protest and do not let yourself be tempted by their decadent ways. You will see many strange and exotic sights in their towns but always remember that you are a prince of the Votadini!"

"Yes, Father," Cunedag said, his voice hoarse.

"Take care, little brother," said Alpia as she gave him a quick hug. "I'll miss you."

"And I you," he replied, feeling the tears threating to well up in his eyes again at the thought of all that was familiar to him being stripped away.

There was little more than a nod of acknowledgement from Brude and Cunedag knew his big brother was privately thanking the Great Mother that it was not him being taken away. As for Murcho, he seemed to have little understanding of what was going on and Cunedag ruffled his hair fondly, knowing that he would miss him as much as the others.

"Saddle up, young prince," the leader of the Romans called over to him. "It's a four-day ride to the Wall and I want to do it in three."

Cunedag cast a resentful glance at the Romans who waited for him by the main gate. The thought of being placed in the company of these hard, unfriendly men from the south for days on end made him want to run and hide. But he knew he had to honour his father. He could not shame his people by showing cowardice. He mounted his pony and, with a parting glance to his family, he headed towards the open gate.

Chapter 3

The Romans were an infuriatingly jovial lot, talking and jesting as they rode south and Cunedag regarded them with cold detachment. They spoke mostly British with occasional snatches of Latin. Every so often, one of them would break out in song and the others would join in. They were coarse, soldierly songs about women in far-flung places and lost comrades. Their leader, Lestinus, who had done the talking to Cunedag's father, had the best voice.

Cunedag only caught the name of one of the other soldiers and that was a big, surly brute called Beliatus who was the only one of them who didn't smile, even when he was joining in the songs in his deep, tuneless voice. He seemed to regard Cunedag's presence as a personal offence and rarely took his glowering gaze off him. It was when he overheard Beliatus talking with Lestinus that Cunedag understood the cause of his hostility.

"I'm of the Brigantes," said Beliatus, naming a tribe with territories just south of the Wall. "We know the Votadini for what they truly are. No friends of Rome, I can tell you that much. I remember when they joined in the Great Conspiracy twenty years ago. I was just a young lad, newly signed up, but my family suffered Pictish raids, had their homes burned and their livestock stolen."

"The Votadini might have joined in the early stage of the Conspiracy," said Lestinus, "but the grandfather of our young prince here, put an end to that, with Rome's backing of course."

"And we're supposed to trust them just because we once put a client king on their throne?" Beliatus said.

"Peace, Beliatus," said Lestinus. "Why do you think we're escorting this young lad to Eboracum? The alliance with the tribes of Valentia still stands and you will honour it."

"Once a Pict, always a Pict," Beliatus muttered.

Cunedag frowned. 'Pict' was a Roman word reserved for the painted people north of the Antonine Wall – the Caledonii, the Epidii and the Venicones among others – wild people of the highlands who were no friends of the Votadini. That this southerner should lump his people in with those savages burned Cunedag's pride.

A little after midday, they stopped to rest the horses and eat a little of their travelling rations by a small brook that wound its way through the wooded hills. Cunedag needed to empty his bladder and, his sense of status as a Votadini princeling making him reluctant to urinate in front of common soldiers, he wandered a short distance from the camp, following the river as it curved out of view.

As he pissed into the river, he could hear the distant voices of his captors, joking and laughing. The far bank of the river and the gloom between the trees looked far more inviting than spending another moment in their company. Beyond the treetops he could see the distant hills of his homeland from which he was being dragged and a lump formed in his throat. He desperately wanted to fling himself into the icy river, swim for the far shore and run through the forests back home.

A blow landed on the side of his head, sending stars before his eyes and knocking him to the ground. He rolled over, clutching his pounding head and saw Beliatus standing over him, his face red with rage.

"Thought you could give us the slip, eh?" the soldier bellowed. "I'll teach you to sneak off!"

He raised his fist to deliver another blow, but Lestinus had rounded the bend and yelled at him to stay his hand.

"Watch how you treat barbarian royalty, Beliatus! I don't want to have to explain to Praeses Colias why his new foster son came to be beaten black and blue on his journey south."

"He was trying to make a run for it!" Beliatus said.

"I was taking a piss!" Cunedag protested.

"Take your hands off him, Beliatus," said Lestinus.

The great oaf snarled and shoved Cunedag to the ground. "Bloody Pict!"

"I'm no Pict, you ignorant prick!" Cunedag snapped angrily. "I am Votadini!"

"You're from north of the Wall," said Beliatus. "You lot might not paint yourselves blue anymore, but your blood is the same as those that do."

"Soldier!" Lestinus barked. "Go and check on the horses!"

Beliatus slunk off and Lestinus helped Cunedag to his feet.

"Old feuds run deep with men like Beliatus," Lestinus said. "Even twenty years of service in a Roman legion can't smooth out the grudges between tribes. Pay no heed to him. And from now on, boy, you piss and shit within range, got it?"

Cunedag nodded sulkily and they returned to their horses, the brief respite over.

Cunedag had never been farther south than Din Eil, a day's ride from Din Eidyn. The massive hillfort crowning the northernmost of three hills was the royal seat of the Selgovae and stood high above the southern bank of the Aber Teu as it flowed eastwards from the mountains to the sea, forming the border between the lands of the Selgovae and the Votadini.

Cunedag had hoped they would spend the night with the Selgovae for he had once accompanied his father to Din Eil on a diplomatic visit, but his hopes were dashed as they camped for the night in the ruined Roman fort of Trimontium which lay at the feet of the three hills on the banks of the river.

What had once been Rome's largest settlement north of the Wall, was now overgrown with weeds, much like the remains of the road that emerged from the long grass to the north and south of it. Its neighbouring canabae had also been deserted, most of the houses demolished and robbed of building materials. Even the amphitheatre was crumbling and mostly ruined. The Roman fort was a ghost of its former self. The roofs of the barrack blocks had fallen in, and the saplings of eager trees grew through the holes and close to the walls.

They stabled the horses in the colonnaded courtyard of the praetorium, the once luxurious residence of the fort's commander. The former gardens were nothing more than tangled weeds surrounding a cracked fountain full of stagnant water. They were not the first to camp in its ruins. Bones and other detritus were scattered about the villa's interior and the charred remains of campfires had scorched the mosaic floors.

They kindled a fire in the main hall and spread their bedrolls on the hard floor before eating a meagre portion of their rations. Cunedag ate the barley cakes his mother had sent with him while the soldiers broiled salted mutton over the fire and passed around a wine skin.

"Thirsty?" Lestinus said, offering the skin to Cunedag.

He took it and sniffed the nozzle. It smelled fruity and sour. He had never tasted wine before but had occasionally been allowed a small cup of mead or ale at feasts. He tentatively took a swig and gulped it down. The sourness stung the back of his throat and rose up through his nostrils, making him choke and splutter. The soldiers roared with laughter.

"You'll have to get used to *posca*, boy," said Lestinus, grinning as he took the skin from him. "You're a Roman now."

As the road wound ever south, signs of Roman civilisation became more commonplace. They passed through more forts, all ruined and overgrown but Cunedag got the impression, with a touch of homesickness, that they were leaving the untamed north and entering the dominion of the Roman Empire, vacant but for the wind and ghosts though it was. The humour of his companions grew as they neared their destination and even Beliatus's disposition seemed to improve. They camped in the ruins of another deserted fort the following night and, at the end of the third day, as the sun was setting over the hills to the west, they saw the Wall.

Cunedag had heard tales of Hadrian's Wall all his life, but nothing could have prepared him for the sight of it. For as far as the eye could see to the east and west, it snaked over the hills like the spiny ridge of some ancient serpent. The sheer manpower and time involved in its construction confounded Cunedag and he felt a resurgence of fear in his gut. Over the past three days, he had grown accustomed to his Roman escort, even warming to Lestinus a little, but the sight of the frontier built by the people who he would be living with for the next eight years, daunted him.

This was the wall the northern tribes had hurled themselves against during the Great Conspiracy. This was the wall which had stood for over three-hundred years as the northern boundary of the Roman world, a clear dividing line between the civilised and the uncivilised. Once he was upon the other side of it, he would no longer be considered royalty. He would be a barbarian, and a hostage at that.

They approached one of the milecastles that guarded the gateways at every mile interval along the Wall. After Lestinus hailed the sentries and stated his rank and business, the doors to the gatehouse straddling the road were heaved open and, as they passed beneath the stone arches, Cunedag knew he was passing from one world to another. The soldiers were gleeful at the prospect of a hot meal and a warm bunk after three days on the road and Cunedag had to admit that such amenities appealed to him too.

They ate with the auxiliary soldiers of the Sixth Victrix legion garrisoned at the fort and Cunedag's companions seemed to be among friends, sharing stories that had passed along the Wall and news from patrols and traders that had gone north. The tales were vulgar and the laughter raucous. Cunedag listened in silence as he dipped his crust of bread into his stew. To hear his homeland spoken of as if it was the arsehole of the world was something he was going to have to get used to, but he wasn't sure he would be able to.

They were given a spare barrack room to sleep in and, despite his exhaustion, Cunedag lay awake in his top bunk, listening to the snores and farts of the soldiers, wondering if his father had been as scared as he was when he had been taken south. Had they taken him to this very milecastle? Perhaps he had slept in this very barrack room? He realised that he knew absolutely nothing about his father's time with the Romans. *Why didn't you warn me, Father?* he wondered. *Why didn't you prepare me?*

Now, he would never receive his spear from his mother on the Moon of the New Warriors ceremony during which the women painted the bodies of the boys who had reached sixteen winters and presented them with their spears in a ceremony that would initiate them into manhood. He would miss the rites of passage of his own people and instead be inducted into Roman customs that were wholly alien to him.

It took them another three days to reach Eboracum, the capital of Britannia Secunda and headquarters of the Sixth Victrix. If Cunedag had been impressed by the Wall, then the sight of a large Roman town completely stole his breath. It was massive. The walls and towers of the legionary fortress were the first thing they could see, dim and purple in the hazy distance; a rigid and solid statement of Rome's domination that hung over the smoky little taverns, brothels and shops of the canabae that clustered around its walls.

They did not enter the fortress, for which Cunedag was glad, but instead crossed the river to the colonia on the other side. There, the residence of the governor or 'praeses' of the province stood, overlooking the sluggish waters that teemed with trading and fishing vessels. Cunedag looked around with awe as the buildings rose around him, colonnaded, tiled and painted in vibrant hues. There were statues too, figures worked in stone and bronze that were so lifelike they resembled giants frozen in time.

There were people everywhere; beggars, children, sellers of hot food, men and women in fine robes, poor people in tatty tunicas. All cleared a path at the bellowed orders of Lestinus. None paid Cunedag a single glance. Barbarians in breeches with Celtic brooches on their cloaks were not uncommon, even in the towns, he learned, where the native culture of the conquered lived shoulder to shoulder with the Roman culture of the conquerors.

Before long, they were riding in through the gates of the praeses' residence and Cunedag's home for the foreseeable future. Iron gates clanged behind him like the slamming of a cell door. Slaves hurried from the main residence to take the horses to the stables and conduct their riders indoors. Soon,

Cunedag found himself standing in a tiled atrium, Lestinus and the other soldiers standing behind him as if he were being offered up as a sacrifice.

A family in flowing robes emerged from another room. There was a man who looked to be the same age as Cunedag's father, and a pretty but rather severe-looking woman whom he assumed was the man's wife. Three youths looked on him with mild curiosity: two boys and a girl.

"*Salve*, Cunedag," said the man. "I am Decius Colias, praeses of Britannia Secunda, but you must call me 'Domine'. You know that much about our customs, I trust?"

Cunedag nodded. He supposed he was supposed to throw in a 'yes, Domine,' but didn't feel like being too compliant. He was here under protest, after all, but Colias seemed to allow him a little leniency on his first day.

"This is my wife," Colias said, turning to the severe-faced woman. "Domina Fulvia and my daughter, Vala."

The girl was pretty but plump, a little younger than him, and regarded him with a haughtiness which made him dislike her as much as he disliked everything else about this place.

"And these," Colias said, indicating the two boys, "are your fellow foster-brothers. This is Morleo of the Selgovae and Canaul of the Novantae. I'm sure you will get along famously."

Morleo looked to be of a similar age to Cunedag and had the friendlier disposition of the two boys. Cunedag thought he remembered him from his visit to Din Eil several years ago but couldn't be sure. Canaul was older, perhaps fourteen or even fifteen and had a surly look to him. Neither boy said anything to him and Cunedag returned the favour. They might all be fellow barbarians of the lowlands beyond the Wall, dragged here as hostages, but that didn't mean they had anything else in common.

"Canaul joined me two years ago," Colias went on, "and has proven himself to be a worthy Roman, when it suits him.

Morleo only arrived two months ago. He is also twelve, like you. You must both look to Canaul for an example. You will be given the education of wealthy Roman boys before your military training will start. Canaul will begin his next year, so you must make use of him while he is available to you. You really are quite lucky. A Roman education and military service instead of whiling away your youths in some muddy tribal village, eh?"

Cunedag said nothing and thought he could detect the same resentment at Colias's words in the faces of his fellow hostages that he felt in his heart. These people sought to make them Romans, to strip away their culture and impose their own on them so they would become friendly and docile tribal leaders when they were returned to their homelands. Remembering his father's words, Cunedag privately swore that would not allow himself to forget who he really was.

Chapter 4

Their quarters consisted of a single sleeping cell fitted with bunks and a larger room in which they ate their meals and received their lessons. Their tutor was a white-haired old tyrant called Catullus who revealed to Cunedag on his first day that he had taught his father and had little pleasant to say about him.

Catullus taught them Latin, astronomy, geography and history, the retention of which were aided by frequent application of his birch rod. Cunedag despised these lessons, and he despised their tutor. To be made to sit and write letters on wax tablets and listen to lengthy passages from Virgil and Livy was an entirely new experience to him. Gonar's lessons had always been delivered out under the open sky or in the wooded glens and he had spent his free hours running wild, playing games, and hunting game, not cooped up in walls of stone.

The afternoons were his salvation as they were taken to a field on the other side of the river under a heavy guard, where they would practice their horse riding and javelin throwing under the tutelage of a retired centurion from the Sixth Victrix. Cunedag found these lessons much more to his liking. He was a skilled rider for his age and was even better than Canaul, much to the older boy's resentment. He got on well with the mild-mannered Morleo and considered him a friend, but Canaul was an ever-present threat, sullen and disdainful of his fellow hostages whom he saw as belonging to inferior tribes to the Novantae.

It was curious that the biggest insult to Cunedag's honour came not from his Roman captors but from a fellow hostage. Canaul was in a particularly sore mood one afternoon after being outmatched by Cunedag once again on the training field and, when they were cleaning their weapons in the armoury, made a comment to Cunedag on his ancestry.

It was a small barb concerning his grandfather, Padarn, who, Canaul claimed was the greatest traitor north of the Wall for failing to support the Great Conspiracy and throwing his lot in with Rome. It was due to his cowardice, Canaul maintained, that they and their fathers owed their current predicament. Generations of hostages due to one man's betrayal.

Cunedag knew that Canaul was only lashing out after being humiliated during training but his father's words about not suffering any stain on Votadini honour rang in his head and he was unable to let it slide. With an oath, he launched his fist at Canaul's jaw and knocked the bigger boy sprawling.

Enraged, Canaul got to his feet and then they were swinging at each other like prize-fighters in the arena while Morleo looked on in horror. They both had bloodied noses and swollen eyelids by the time two guards rushed into the armoury and hauled them apart. They were taken directly to Praeses Colias who reprimanded them severely. Once they had been dismissed and Canaul had slunk off to tend to his wounds, Colias took Cunedag aside for a private word.

"I understand it was Canaul who instigated the quarrel," he said. "Something about your Votadini ancestors set you off. You are a prideful boy, Cunedag. Just like your father."

The mention of his father made Cunedag raise his eyebrows in surprise, and he winced at the pain this movement caused his swellings. Colias smiled.

"Oh, yes, your father was quite the brawler, and I can tell you that I was on the receiving end of his rage on more than one occasion. It didn't do him any favours in the long run, and he suffered more floggings than was good for him during his military service. Learn from your father's mistakes, Cunedag, and your time here will be easier. I know that tribal differences are hard things to forget, but that is the beauty of Rome. It unites and pacifies, makes one where there are many. And, just as Rome brings peace to the tribes it colonises, while you boys are under my roof, you are equals."

As Cunedag left Colias's study, he saw Vala coming in the opposite direction and braced himself for the inevitable stinging comment. He had taken a disliking to her from the day he had been brought into Colias's household. She was aloof and entitled, as one could expect from a Roman governor's daughter, and regularly traded barbed insults with the boys on the rare occasions their paths crossed. Canaul in particular despised her and regularly described what he'd like to do to her if their roles were reversed.

Vala looked Cunedag up and down with disgust and he knew he must look a sight with the dried blood caked on his face and swollen eyes.

"I know you boys are barbarians," she sneered, "but *must* you brawl like feral dogs over a bone?"

"I don't see that it's any of your business," Cunedag snapped back.

"Shows what you know. I am a lady of this household, and the actions of its hostages reflect on all of us. Still, your rearranged face might be an improvement once it heals up. Small blessings, I suppose."

Unable to think of a biting reply, Cunedag clenched his fists and watched her sweep away from him, her nose in the air.

Praeses Colias and his family were Christians, and the boys were made to attend mass with them in the town's basilica. As Cunedag watched the Bishop of Eboracum break bread and pour wine, claiming that it was the body and blood of the crucified Christ, he was bemused by this vaguely cannibalistic rite. Privately, he still prayed to Modron, the Great Mother, every night that she would spirit him away from Eboracum and back to his homeland. She never did and it felt like the old gods were silent south of the Wall.

Not long after Cunedag's arrival in Colias's household, the Christians celebrated the feast of Pascha which marked the death and resurrection of the Christ. It was preceded by forty days of abstinence from meat, dairy and alcohol and the last night before this severe alteration to their diet was given over to a huge feast at the praeses' residence to which many local nobles were invited.

The hostage boys were required to attend and were given new tunicas of fine material decorated with patterned strips. Bathed, brushed and feeling like prized ponies to be displayed by their owner, they filed into the dining room behind the rest of the family who were dressed in their finery. Tables groaned with dishes, breads and sauces that the kitchens had been preparing all day. There were oysters, honey-roasted peacock, boiled sow's womb stuffed with ground pork and pine nuts, pates of goose liver, fried ram's testicles and cheeses from the milk of just about every mammal that could be thought of. There were wines and garum sauces imported from all corners of the empire along with figs and olives piled high in bowls, glistening with oil and honey.

"You will be exposed to many other faiths when you begin your military careers," Colias said to Cunedag and his fellow hostages as he twisted apart the leg of a honey-glazed pigeon. "Alas, the common soldier's mind is a simple one and given to idolatry. Worship of Jupiter, Mars and Minerva are popular in the legions still, as are the cults of Mithras and Sol Invictus. But do not let yourselves be led astray from the true path. Only through worship of God can you enter His Kingdom of Heaven."

Cunedag barely heard him as his attention was so taken up with sampling the strange and exotic dishes served to him by slaves, barely knowing what he was eating. Some of it was surprisingly good, despite appearances, while some of it turned his stomach and he washed away the taste with gulps of wine which was of a good quality and far more palatable than the posca Lestinus had given him.

"I don't know why the emperor allows such open worship of idols," said Domina Fulvia as she popped a honeyed fig into her mouth. "If he would but order the temples to be closed, these false gods would wither and die and people's faith in them too. Take the upcoming festival of Quinquatria. The soldiers will be descending on the colonia to have their weapons and shields blessed at the shine of Minerva again, one assumes."

"Protective blessings have long given peace of mind to the soldier," Colias said.

"Idiotic superstitions!" Fulvia snapped, with a dismissive handwave. "All they need do is pray to the one true God. He will provide all the protection they need. The longer Emperor Theodosius allows these silly things to go on, the weaker we are in the face of our enemies for how can we stand against the barbarian hordes when we allow such barbaric practices within the empire's boundaries?"

"But so many people believe in these gods," said Vala. "What right does anyone have to stop them worshipping them? For centuries, our ancestors worshiped the old gods, both British and Roman."

The young girl's words caused an embarrassed silence and some wry looks around the room.

"Those were dark days, Daughter," said Fulvia. "We know better now, and we have the responsibility of helping the less enlightened to find their way to God."

"Although our daughter does have a point of sorts," said Colias. "As I said, many soldiers follow the old paths. It would not do to incite resentment and unrest among the legions. God knows, they are an irascible lot as it is."

"So, we are to be held hostage by pagans?" Fulvia remarked, not noticing the glares in the eyes of the pagan hostages in her very presence. "We must allow their barbarity in our midst because we are frightened of upsetting them?"

"My dear," said Colias with a smile. "It is well that you are a politician's wife and not a politician yourself, for you have no sense of diplomacy. Sometimes sacrifices must be made in order to keep the peace. Besides, there have been great improvements, it must be admitted. These pagan festivals used to be marked by days upon days of bloody fights to the death in the arena. Thankfully, Emperor Constantine outlawed such barbarity. That is something, at least."

"Instead, there will be bawdy plays and shows for the drunken mob," said Fulvia. "Less bloody but no less vulgar."

The three hostages remained silent, each of them thinking of the gods of their homelands: Modron, the Great Mother, Taran, Lord of Thunder, the horned Lord of Beasts and many more besides. If the likes of Fulvia had her way, they would be forbidden from worshipping them which would be an unthinkable outrage. It wasn't enough that the Romans stole their royal sons, they wanted to strip away every vestige that made the tribes of the north different from Romans.

But Vala had surprised Cunedag. Her vocal support for pagans had ruffled the feathers of her family and the assembled guests. She might be a spoilt brat, but it was clear to him that she had a mind of her own and the courage to speak it, even in front of Britannia's elite and that earned her a grudging respect from him.

Several days later, Cunedag and Morleo were brushing down their horses in the stables when Canaul entered and barked for the two slaves who were present to get out. Hostages didn't have any official authority over Colias's slaves, but everyone in the household treated Canaul with a respect due to his size and foul temper. Cunedag expected trouble. He and Morleo must have done something to raise his ire, and another fight was probably around the corner. Why else would he demand privacy?

"Are you two pups brave enough to become men for a night?" Canaul asked them in a low, conspiratorial voice.

"How do you mean?" Cunedag asked, guardedly.

"It's the festival of Quinquatria next week. It's a riot, I can tell you. The streets are packed. Whores, masked performers, musicians, soldiers getting drunk and causing trouble. There's wine and ale aplenty not to mention meat and cheese. We can fill our bellies to our hearts' content. I don't know about you two, but I'm sick of the meagre fare we're being given on account of the Christ's death day."

"Um, how exactly do you propose we carouse with pagans when we're hostages in a Christian household?" Morleo asked. "Ask Colias for the night off?"

"No, we sneak out, smart arse!" Canaul said.

"Just sneak out?" Cunedag said. "With armed guards patrolling the grounds?"

"Oh, don't you worry about them," said Canaul with a grin. "I've got their routes memorised. All we need to do is cross the courtyard to the armoury without being detected. There's a small door leading from the armoury to the street. I've been out loads of times, before you two got here."

"But the door is kept locked, surely?" said Cunedag.

"Aye, locked indeed. But I know where to get the key!"

Cunedag and Morleo gaped at him.

"When you've been in this household for a couple of years," he said, pleased to see that the younger boys were suitably impressed, "you pick things up here and there. So, are you interested?"

"I don't know," said Morleo. "If we're caught—"

"I should have known a Selgovae brat wouldn't have the balls!" said Canaul. "What of you, Votadini?"

"Aye, I'm in," said Cunedag. "If only to get some meat in my belly."

"That's the spirit."

"Count me in too," said Morleo, his voice a little uncertain but he clearly didn't want to be left behind when a good time was to be had.

Chapter 5

The evening of the tenth day before the kalends of April, the streets of Eboracum rang with the sounds of revelry which could be heard within the walls of the praeses' residence. There was a sombreness to the Christian household as of a disapproving parent who is somehow powerless to curb the mischief of its offspring and everybody did their best to ignore the racket.

After their meal of bread, stewed vegetables and water, the three boys retired to their cell and lay in their bunks, silently awaiting nightfall when the slaves would go to their quarters and the house would be silent. Cunedag found himself to be a bundle of barely restrained excitement. For the first time since he had left Din Eidyn nearly a month ago, he would do something of his own volition, go somewhere he had not been ordered to go. It wouldn't compare to true freedom, but it would be a taste and he was gasping for it.

Canaul had procured the key during the day and hidden it among the small collection of items he had to his name on the windowsill by his bunk. He remained reluctant to tell the other two where and how he had got it, clearly not trusting them enough to reveal his secrets. It seemed to take an age for the noises of the slaves at work in the household to recede and the darkness beyond the window deepen, signifying the lateness of the hour.

At last, Canaul whispered to them in the darkness.

"Right, you two. Get up and follow me, and for the love of Modron, don't make any noise!"

They slipped out of their bunks and got dressed, throwing on their hooded cloaks before following Canaul out of their cell and into the silent corridor. As they rounded the corner, they ducked out of sight as old Bucco the slave passed by on some late-night errand. Hurrying on, they descended to the courtyard and ducked down into the shadows of the colonnades, a silent signal from Canaul to keep low and stay put.

The night air was cool, and the sputtering wicks of the oil lamps reflected off the helmed head of a guard emerging from the other side of the courtyard. They waited in tense silence as the guard passed across the wide, open space and vanished into the shadows on the other side. At a nod from Canaul, they were off again, trying to minimise the sound of their sandals slapping on the tiles.

They opened the door to the armoury and slipped in, closing it softly behind them. Racks of weapons and shields glinted in the darkness. From a cord around his neck, Canaul produced the key and held it up triumphantly. Grinning, the other two boys hovered impatiently at his shoulder as he slid the key into the lock of the door leading to the street and turned it.

The hinges grated alarmingly as he pushed the door open just wide enough for them to slip out, one by one. He closed and locked the door behind them, and they turned to look up and down the street, the scent of freedom and excitement in their nostrils.

The revelry was happening a couple of streets over and they hurried towards it, emerging into a vibrant column of people banging drums and playing on pipes, wreaths of spring flowers on their heads and songs of celebration on their lips. Stalls sold food and drink while puppeteers and masked actors entertained throngs of people who laughed and jeered.

Canaul seized what was left of a jug of wine from beside a man who had drunk too much and lay dozing to one side and took a swig before passing it to his comrades. They drank thirstily, only recently having grown accustomed to wine and even then, in small amounts.

"Let's see about getting something to eat," said Canaul.

They wove through the crowd towards one of the stalls. None of them had any coin to their name but Canaul had already proved himself to be light fingered and he snatched a skewer of roasted lamb without being seen.

They hurried off down the street and ducked into an alley to eat their stolen meal, passing it between themselves while taking swigs of wine. The meat was juicy and well-seasoned and tasted like nectar to the three meat-starved boys.

"I've a mind we should take a look down at the shrine of Minerva," said Canaul as they licked the juices from their fingers and finished off the wine.

"What happens there?" Cunedag asked.

Canaul grinned. "That's where the women go to consult the priestesses who tell them their fortunes for the coming year. No men allowed. It's rumoured they all strip off and kneel before Minerva arse-naked! Let's go and see if it's true!"

Cunedag swallowed. He had seen naked women before – the women of the Votadini often bathed naked in the rivers and had little shame of their bodies – but the women of the south were much more prudish, always wrapping themselves up in their pallas and stolas and bathing separate to the men. Cunedag had noticed that some of them were really quite attractive, and their secretiveness only made him more curious about their bodies.

"How are we going to find out if the rumours are true if no men are allowed in?" Morleo said.

"Just follow me," said Canaul. "Have I led you boys wrong yet tonight?"

In awe of the older boy's knowledge about the goings on in every corner of Eboracum, the younger boys followed him through the crowds in the direction of the shrine of Minerva.

The shrine itself was cut into a rockface on the outskirts of the town with a Roman extension of bricks and columns supporting a tiled roof. Candles had been lit all around the entrance to the shrine, illuminating offerings of food, wine and flowers and many women were clustered around the doorway in hooded cloaks, seemingly waiting their turn to be admitted.

"Come on," said Canaul. "Up this way."

He led them down an alley which sloped up and around the rock into which the shrine had been cut. High up, a grating had been set into the stone presumably to ventilate the temple.

"Help me up," said Canaul.

The younger boys helped him scramble up and then, reaching down, he hauled them up so they could stand in a row, clinging to the grating which afforded a view of the shrine's smoky interior.

Incense smouldered in braziers and torchlight illuminated the golden statue of Minerva with helmet, shield and spear who towered above a small pool. Robed priestesses stood on ceremony while a young woman knelt before the pool, one of the priestesses whispering into her ear. After a while, the young woman got up, bowed to both the priestesses and the statue, before leaving the shrine.

A little disappointed that the proceedings had been a decidedly clothed affair, the three boys hung onto the grating as the next devotee entered. She approached the pool and knelt, lowering her hood.

"Modron's tits!" Canaul exclaimed. "Look who it is!"

The jaws of the three boys hung open as they gazed down on Vala, daughter of Decius Colias, their foster father, kneeling before a pagan goddess. Cunedag couldn't understand what was going on, but he was glad Canaul's claim that devotees appeared before Minerva in the nude had turned out to be nonsense for he had no wish to see Vala naked. It wasn't that she was unattractive (quite the opposite, in fact) but he didn't want her shamed like that, insufferable brat though she was at times.

They watched as Vala consulted the priestess, their words not reaching as high as the grating, before she got up and, with the usual gestures of respect, departed the shrine.

"What, by all the souls in Annun is she playing at?" Canaul said as they slipped down from the grating.

"Is Colias's daughter secretly a pagan?" Morleo said.

"We've got her by the ears now!" said Canaul. "She'll do anything to stop her father knowing that she visited a pagan shrine on Quinquatria! She won't be so snooty while we hold this over her!"

"We can hardly do that," said Cunedag, "for to tell Colias would be to incriminate ourselves."

"Cunedag's right," said Morleo. "Our knowledge of her business here tonight is useless as blackmail."

"But will she think of that?" Canaul said with a sinister grin. "I just want to see the look on her face when she finds out we know about her dirty little secret!"

There was some sort of commotion on the street the shrine faced, and it was decidedly less jovial than the celebrations. There were angry shouts and cries of alarm as the music died down.

"What's up now?" Cunedag asked.

They hurried down the alley and onto the street where a full-blown panic was in progress. People were surging past them in a state of alarm while further down the street, at the doors of the shrine, a brawl seemed to be taking place. Another group of people, not dressed in the bright colours and spring garlands of the pagans, were hurling stones at the merrymakers and ripe curses prickled the air.

"It's the Christians!" said Canaul. "They're causing a disturbance."

'Disturbance' was a mild word for it. Stones sailed through the air, striking the doors to the temple and thudding into the pagans, leaving them reeling with split skin and bloodied faces. The fallen were trampled as many sought to flee while others hurled themselves into the fray, picking up loose cobbles and throwing them back at the Christians.

"Vala!" said Cunedag. "She'll be in the midst of the worst of it!"

Even Canaul gave a reluctant sigh as they realised that they had to wade in there and get their foster sister to safety. She might be a rude and conceited pain in the arse, but they couldn't leave her to the fury of the mob.

Canaul, being the largest of the three, pushed his way through the crowd, fighting against the tide in the direction of the shrine. It was hard going but the three of them forced their way through.

The shrine had been stormed, the offerings around its doors smashed and kicked about and the priestesses had fled. They found Vala and her handmaid cowering behind an overturned cart. The surprise in Vala's eyes at seeing the three hostages from her father's household matched the look they had all shared moments before when they saw her lower her hood in Minerva's shrine.

"What are you three doing here?" she demanded, the fear still present in her voice.

"We could ask you the same, but I don't think now is the time," said Cunedag. "Follow us, we'll get you out of this mess!"

"Pagan scum!" somebody yelled as the two women emerged from hiding.

Somebody threw a stone which narrowly missed Cunedag's head, and a portion of the mob converged on the five escapees from the governor's residence, spitting and hurling insults.

"Get back, you bastards!" Canaul yelled, swinging his fist into the face of one of the Christians.

That only incited their rage further and the mob pushed in on them, hitting, kicking and foaming at the mouth with insults. The three boys held their ground admirably, but it was no good, there were simply too many of them.

"Come on!" Cunedag yelled, turning and seizing Vala by the wrist. "We'll take the backstreets!"

With the handmaid clutching Vala's other wrist, they succeeded in hauling the girl down a side street to the deserted alleys beyond the main thoroughfare. Canaul and Morleo followed close behind with the mob hot on their heels.

"Canaul!" Cunedag yelled. "You know the town best. Get us back home!"

"This way!" Canaul yelled, tearing off down the dim alley ahead of them.

They followed him as closely as they could, jumping over piles of refuse and scrambling over detritus. The mob had mostly given up now, the narrow alleys too crowded for them. Canaul turned this way and that, leading them closer to the governor's residence.

"I think …" Cunedag panted, his hands on his knees, "we made it!"

"The house is one street over," said Canaul. "But first, let's have some answers, your ladyship!"

"Yeah, what are you?" Morleo asked her. "Some sort of secret pagan?"

"I … I don't know what I am," said Vala, her eyes tearing up now that the danger seemed to be passed. "I try to be a good Christian the way my father raised me, but I just have so many doubts, so many questions that only the old faiths can answer. Brenna here has been my handmaid all my life and she is a pagan. If my father knew that she occasionally snuck me out of the house to speak with the priests and priestesses of the old gods, she would be horribly punished. Say you won't mention that you saw us in the town tonight?"

"It will remain our secret," said Cunedag. "If you'll extend us the same courtesy? We aren't exactly supposed to be out and about either."

"Don't worry about me talking," said Vala, "If my father found out about this I would be punished just as severely as you three."

"I doubt that," Morleo grumbled.

"Then nobody here will utter a word of what happened tonight," said Canaul.

"Agreed," said Vala.

"Is it always like this?" Cunedag asked, glancing back at the chaos they had escaped from. "Christians causing a ruckus?"

"It has got worse in the last few years," said Brenna. "The Christians have grown in confidence, year by year, ever since their faith became the official religion of the empire. But they have never stormed a temple or attacked its followers before, at least not in Eboracum. Truly, I fear for the followers of other religions in the days to come."

"Well, I for one fear for ourselves if we don't get back inside the house before we are missed," said Morleo.

"Brenna can sneak me back in," said Vala. "She and one of the guards have an understanding. But I don't know about you three. That might raise more than an eyebrow. However did you get out, anyway?"

"Never mind that," said Canaul. "We can get ourselves back in."

"Very well. Then Brenna and I shall take our leave. Oh, I suppose I should thank you for what you did for us tonight."

"I suppose you should," said Canaul.

"Well, there it is. Thank you."

"You're welcome," said Cunedag and they watched the two women scurry off down the darkened street, their hoods up and cloaks wrapped tightly around them.

So, from that night on, Vala's relationship with the three boys was less acrimonious than it had been before. They were not *friends* exactly, but Cunedag felt like their night's adventure had formed a bond not only between the three hostages, but between them and the governor's daughter. Then, as the years passed, no longer did they feel like captor and captives but something closer to family.

Part II

398 A.D.

"After this, Britain is left deprived of all her soldiery and armed bands, of her cruel governors, and of the flower of her youth, who went with Maximus, but never again returned; and utterly ignorant as she was of the art of war, groaned in amazement for many years under the cruelty of two foreign nations—the Scots from the north-west, and the Picts from the north." – Gildas, On the Ruin and Conquest of Britain

Chapter 6

The hooves of Cunedag's black Iberian stallion clattered on the cobbles of Eboracum as he rounded the corner of the praeses' residence. He bellowed his name and rank and the iron gates were flung open to admit him. He cantered into the familiar courtyard and swung himself down from the saddle as a slave came to take the reins.

He smelled the old smells of his days in Colias's household: the mint and rosemary of the herb gardens, the garlic and fresh bread of the kitchens and the lavender of the window boxes. He had been gone too long. Since he had been stationed with the Ala Second Asturum at Cilurnum on the Wall, he had been home only twice as far as he could recall.

Home? It was strange to admit, but Eboracum had begun to feel like home in the eight years since he had been taken from Din Eidyn. Despite his hatred of his early days in this house under the tutelage of old Catallus, once his military training began at the age of fourteen, he had missed it all as terribly as he had missed his childhood in the north.

But he had soon warmed to military life attached to an auxiliary cavalry unit garrisoned at the Wall. There was a sense of brotherhood and camaraderie he had never experienced before. It helped that Morleo was in the same unit for the two had grown as close as real brothers. Their quarters were a long row of barrack blocks with each cell housing three men and their horses. Living and sleeping with their mounts forged a close bond between the men and their horses, not to mention the warmth provided by the animals during cold winter months.

Cunedag had named his horse Bran after the ancient hero of the Britons. His skill in the saddle and eventual acceptance of Roman discipline had seen him rise fast in the cavalry wing.

He had only been promoted a few months previously to an officer in command of a turma, one of twelve which made up the ala. Thirty riders now saluted him and Morleo was his *duplicarius*, his second in command.

He found Vala in the triclinium, berating the slaves for not following her packing orders to the letter. It had only been a year since he had seen her last, but she seemed to have grown a little, despite already being an adult. Adolescence had refined her, the plumpness of a pampered childhood melting into the fine curves of an attractive young woman, although still one possessed of a wicked tongue.

"I'm glad to see that you are so keen to leave on time," Cunedag said. "My orders are to get you to Camboglanna before *dies Veneris*."

"If these fools don't do as I say, then it will be harvesttime before we set out."

He smiled. "It's good to see you, Vala."

"I wish I could say the same. But this journey is sure to be a tiresome chore. I don't know why Father insists that Mother and I travel to some dreadful frontier fort just to keep him company. I'm sure you men find it all very homely but for the fairer sex, a fort is a ghastly place. Oh, I suppose I should congratulate you on your promotion to decurion."

"Thank you," Cunedag replied with a nod. "Morleo is keen to see you too. I left him across the river with the rest of the turma. We leave as soon as you are ready."

"Is that you, Cunedag?" said a voice from the other room.

"Yes, Domina Fulvia," said Cunedag as his foster mother swept into the room.

"My word, don't you look handsome in your decurion's uniform?" she said. "Don't you think so, Vala?"

Vala shrugged noncommittally and continued ordering the slaves to pack her things properly.

"To think you were so recently barbarian boys brought into Rome's embrace," Fulvia continued. "It seems like only yesterday. And Morleo and Canaul?"

"Morleo awaits us at the fort, you will see him tomorrow, Domina," said Cunedag. "Canaul is posted at Vindolanda with the Cohors Forth Gallorum. We haven't seen much of him these past years, though I heard he was made a prefect."

"How proud I am of all three of you," said Fulvia. "But you must be famished, come, join us for dinner while the slaves finish packing."

Cunedag spent the night in his old cell with the memories of his youth floating around him in the darkness like lost spirits.

They set out the following morning after breakfast, Vala and her mother sitting in the carpentium along with Vala's faithful slave, Brenna, as it creaked across the bridge to the fort where Morleo had the third turma of thirty riders ready and waiting.

"Don't you find it strange that we were sent for this task?" Morleo said to Cunedag as they rode at the head of the column, the road stretching ahead of them over moor and through valleys. "Escorting civilians is more like a job for *equites cohortales*, not *alares*."

"Domine Colias thought that his wife and daughter would feel safer if there were some familiar faces in the soldiers escorting them."

"Then why not send Canaul and his men from Vindolanda? They're simple cavalrymen attached to a cohort."

"Would you send Canaul if the goal was to make anybody feel comfortable?" Cunedag asked him.

They both laughed.

It took a day and a half to reach Cataractonium where they stopped for the night and lodged the women at the mansio before seeing to the horses and men. Cunedag and Morleo dined with the women and found their meal interrupted by the arrival of several horses in the yard outside.

"More visitors?" Morleo said around a mouthful of lentils. "Cataractonium is getting crowded tonight."

The visitors were admitted and entered the dining hall, removing their helmets. They were cavalrymen, although with armour of a poorer quality than those of Cunedag's men. Their leader, however, wore the uniform of a prefect and Cunedag and Morleo rose to salute him, just as they recognised his face.

"Canaul!" Fulvia exclaimed.

"Ave, Domina!" said Canaul with a grin. "Cunedag. Morleo. At ease, brothers."

"What are you doing here, Canaul?" said Cunedag as the three young men clasped each other's arms in greeting. "I thought you were stationed at Vindolanda."

"I am," Canaul replied, he and his two comrades sitting down at the table and helping themselves to lentils and bread. "I received word from Domine Colias to ride down to Cataractonium to meet you with a turma. Quite the reunion, eh? Vala, you are well, I trust?"

"As well as can be expected, surrounded by military brutes," Vala replied. "You will be lodging here tonight, I assume? This mansio is bursting at the seams with soldiers."

"All for your protection, my dear," said Canaul. "My own men were forced to camp outside the fort's walls as Cunedag's boys have taken over the barracks."

"Sixty riders to escort two women to the frontier?" said Morleo. "Domine Colias is a little overzealous, don't you think?"

"The roads north are infested with bandits," said Canaul, shovelling food into his mouth while pouring a generous measure of wine. "Can't be too careful."

"Even so, it all seems rather excessive."

Canaul shrugged. "Who are we to question orders? Especially when they come from our dear foster father."

They all grinned despite themselves, and a merry evening was had with much wine drunk before the women retired to bed, leaving the men to swap military stories.

They left Cataractonium early the next day, Canaul's riders taking the lead with Cunedag and his men bringing up the rear. This caused some consternation among Cunedag's men. It was an age-old rivalry. They were *equites alares*, a cavalry unit to the bone, natural horsemen who were the best the Roman military had to offer. Canaul's men were *equites cohortales*, meaning that they were the cavalry detachment of an infantry cohort which, to the mind of the more accomplished *equites alares*, made them little better than infantry on horseback.

They followed the road north-west from Cataractonium as it cut through the hills that formed the backbone of northern Britannia, their peaks still dusted with snow. Their destination of the Wall and the fort of Camboglanna lay nearly three days' ride away. The first night, they camped not far from the road, the men forming a perimeter around the carpentium, allowing the women to get out, stretch their legs and eat a meagre meal, huddled by the warmth of a campfire.

Cunedag sat with the women, shoulder to shoulder with Vala, sharing the warmth of the flames and of their own bodies. He noticed that she was shivering, despite her blanket and he unfastened his cloak and draped it over her shoulders. She smiled her thanks at him.

"Eight years have passed since you came to us," she said as they watched the flickering flames of the fire. "Your time as a hostage is almost up. You are twenty now, are you not?"

"Aye, that I am," said Cunedag. "A man now, no longer a boy."

"Then you will be discharged from the army at the end of the season? Father always said that he could organise an early discharge considering the terms of your service. Will you return to your homeland?"

"I honestly don't know," he replied. "The terms of your father's arrangement with mine state that I can be released once I am twenty. I would like to go home, see my family whom I have not seen in eight years, but … I'm just not sure that it is home anymore."

"You feel Roman?"

"Perhaps that's it." He gave her a small smile. "Your father has done his work well. I know that I would miss the company of my men as much as I missed my family in those early days. It all seems so very long ago. My other option is to sign on for the remainder of my twenty-five years like Canaul has done. No backing out then."

"Well, I for one would rather you stuck around for twenty-five years," said Vala.

Cunedag looked at her in surprise. "Why?"

She shrugged. "I've got used to having barbarian foster brothers. Useful brutes if one is in need of protection." She gave him a playful smile.

Cunedag said nothing, not wanting to spoil the moment. It was the closest thing to a nice word he remembered Vala ever giving him.

It was as they were descending the hills into a wooded glen around midday the following day that disaster struck. A hail of arrows hummed out of the trees to the right of the column, striking several of Cunedag's men and one or two even embedding themselves in the wooden walls of the carpentium.

"Ambush!" Cunedag yelled, drawing his spatha, the long blade of a Roman cavalryman.

Sheilds were raised and the riders encircled the carpentium, ready for the next volley. It never came.

"What the hell is going on?" Canaul yelled as he rode down the column towards them.

"Bandits, most likely," said Cunedag as he scanned the bushes and trees for any sign of movement. "They gave us a dose but didn't follow through on it. Bloody odd, if you ask me."

"Too scared to take on two turmae," said Canaul.

"Then why bother attacking us at all?"

"Just causing a nuisance, most likely. Take your men into those trees and teach the buggers a lesson. I want blood for their impudence! We'll guard the carpentium."

Cunedag glanced at Canaul, surprised by his order. He thought to question it but then decided better of it. Canaul was his superior after all.

"All right, form up, men!" Cunedag bellowed. "Follow me!"

He led his thirty men away from the column and past the treeline, spreading them thin and moving in a north-westerly direction, following the road that ran parallel, with the aim of flushing out the attackers.

More arrows whistled through the foliage, but his men were ready and the forest resounded with the thudding of arrow tips hitting wooden shields.

"There!" Cunedag yelled, pointing his spatha at a rustling thicket as somebody scampered off.

Two of his men charged ahead, spears lowered, but the man had made his escape. The trees grew thick here and the light was dim. Finding their quarry was hard and there was little room to manoeuvre their horses. It was a cavalry unit's nightmare fighting infantry in such conditions.

The attackers were spotted every now and then, often in small clusters who would loose a few arrows at them and then flee. Every time Cunedag's men closed in on a group of the bastards, they would vanish into the deepest foliage where the horses couldn't follow.

"We're being led away from the column," said Cunedag. "Something about this isn't right."

"It's like they're trying to separate us," said Morleo.

"Aye, I don't like it," said Cunedag. "Come on, fall back!"

They turned their horses around and moved back to the rest of the column, leaving their attackers to celebrate their small victory.

By the time they reached the road, they could tell something was horribly wrong. The carpentium stood alone, its doors open and a single torn curtain fluttering from its rail. Inside, the body of Brenna lay on her side, her throat cut. Of Vala and Fulvia, there was no sign. There was also no sign of Canaul and his men.

"Modron curse us for fools!" Cunedag roared. "How did I not see this coming?"

"I don't understand," said Morleo. "What is Canaul playing at?"

"He's snatched Vala and Fulvia! Right from under our noses! I knew there was something odd about his appearance at Cataractonium!"

"So did I, but I don't understand his motive. And how does he think to get away with it?"

"There is more at work here than what it seems," said Cunedag. "We must be mindful. Canaul has betrayed everything we have grown up to serve. Who knows how deep his treachery runs?"

"You don't think he'll hurt the women, do you?"

They glanced at the body of poor Brenna. "I don't think so," Cunedag replied. "He dispatched Vala's slave so he would have one less prisoner. That means he has a purpose for the women. But what we know about all this is far outweighed by what we don't know."

"What shall we do?"

"We must ride north, as fast as possible. Perhaps we can overtake Canaul on the road, though I suspect he will have cut across country to throw us off his trail."

"Where could he possibly take them? Colias will raise the entire province to find his wife and daughter. Nowhere will be safe."

"The gods alone know," said Cunedag and he kicked Bran into a gallop to the head of the column.

The Wall lay a day and a half's ride away but Cunedag's turma made it in less than a day, almost killing their horses who were gasping and foaming as the walls of Camboglanna came into view. They had seen no trace of Canaul's men on the road and it was as Cunedag had feared. They had simply melted into the hills of northern Britannia with their captives.

"I will notify Colias of the bad news," Cunedag said to Morleo as they stabled their exhausted horses.

"Let me come with you," said Morleo. "I share the blame and am part of the family too, as it were."

"Very well," Cunedag said, pleased to have his friend at his side for what was undoubtedly going to be an unpleasant meeting.

As they walked along the via principalis towards the fort's headquarters, they knew that suspicion would immediately fall upon them. Could barbarians ever be trusted, even ones that had been fostered by a Roman family and trained as Roman soldiers? They had always been treated with scepticism and prejudice, and that would only sharpen with the kidnapping of the praeses' wife and daughter.

It had happened before. Arminius, the Germanic equite who had turned on Rome and wiped out three of its legions in the Teutoburg Forest had been a horror story for Romans for the past three-hundred years. And now, with Gothic auxiliaries turning on their masters whenever the wind blew in a different direction, it was a wonder Rome still recruited barbarians at all. They had no choice, of course, the empire being as overextended as it was, but resentment could be felt from many quarters.

Colias was predictably horrified at the kidnapping of his wife and daughter and told his two foster sons, in no uncertain terms, what he thought of their ability to protect what was most dear to him, which had been their very mission.

"And how could Canaul betray me like this?" Colias raged. "You're sure he gave no indication of his motive for this outrage?"

"None, Domine," said Cunedag. "Save occasional grumblings against Rome and its ways."

"Odd for a prefect in the Roman military, don't you think?" Colias said, his eyes narrowing at him.

"But perhaps not so odd for one who was taken from his home as a child," Cunedag replied. "With all due respect."

"I trust you two own no similar sentiments?"

"Not at all, Domine," they both chorused.

"Good. Because when I get my hands on that treasonous swine, I will make such an example of him that all Britannia will tremble at the fate of those who betray Rome!"

He walked over to a small table upon which stood a clay jug of wine. He poured himself a cup with trembling hands, his anger quickly giving ground to immense sorrow. "Now, my boys," he said, his voice strained with emotion. "I will go immediately to the Dux Britanniarum and ask for his help. But first, tell me how you would best suggest getting my Fulvia and Vala back."

"Send a message to every milecastle along the Wall," said Cunedag quickly, having pondered this very question on their frantic ride north. "Have them stop every band of travellers seeking to cross. Let no wagon through without checking it for two hidden women."

"You think he will try to smuggle them north?"

"It's possible. He can't keep them below the Wall. Not once the Dux Britanniarum rouses every soldier in the province to scour the hills and villages. The only place he could keep them out of your reach is by taking them north, to his tribe. I believe he may be going home."

"To hold them ransom perhaps?" said Colias. "But that would be suicidal. The Novantae know that we would send an army to crush them."

"True. There has to be more to this than a simple kidnapping. I don't know what, but I fear that it is just a piece of a much bigger puzzle."

Chapter 7

The temple to the three mothers was a small, shingled building just below the fort of Camboglanna, a little distance from the road and shrouded by bushes as if it was hiding from the world. Within, the votive candles flickered and the burning incense curled up to the smoke-stained rafters. Cunedag and Morleo knelt at the altar which depicted three women in robes and headdresses. These were the *matrones*; the Roman interpretation of Modron, the ancient mother goddess of the Britons who always revealed herself as one of three facets.

Openly worshipping pagan deities had been outlawed by the emperor some years previously, but while the masses flocked to the basilicas and churches to worship Christ, many soldiers still paid their devotions to Mithras, Mars, Jupiter and all the others in small shrines tucked away from the hustle and bustle of town or fort life. The new religion might have swept the Roman Empire but, for those who regularly risked their lives in its defence, the old tried and tested faiths died hard.

Cunedag and Morleo prayed to Modron for guidance in the search for Vala and Fulvia, asking Her to keep them safe. Although many of the men under his command were Christian, Cunedag still found himself drawn to the gods of his people who had been worshipped in Albion since before the Romans had come some four-hundred years ago. And, with so much riding on him recovering the women of Colias's household, he promised to sacrifice the plumpest pig he could get his hands on to Modron if she would only help them in their task.

Messengers had been sent along the Wall in both directions. Every milecastle, gate and fort was notified to be on the lookout for anybody trying to smuggle two women out of the province. Below the Wall, the Dux Britanniarum, an aging veteran by the name of Titus Gemellus, had sent out every patrol he could spare to scour the hills. Days went by, and no news was heard.

Cunedag and his turma spent the next week travelling the military road that stretched along the Wall from coast to coast, checking that the praeses' orders were being carried out and that every band of travellers crossing the Wall had been searched. Word reached them from Vindolanda that Canaul's turma had vanished while on patrol over a week ago and were considered deserters. There had been concerns that Canaul had been murdered by his own men but, once word of his treachery reached the cohort's prefect, two and two were put together and it became apparent that Canaul had been plotting his crime for months.

"He populated his turma with men handpicked for their loyalty to him," Cunedag said to Morleo as they stood on the Wall, one bright afternoon, eating bowls of wheat porridge and raisins. "Most were Britons of Valentia; our own people, Romanised just as we are."

"But even so, how could he convince so many of them to turn?" said Morleo. "What's he offering for their loyalty? Is it just that they want to return to their homes? I miss home too, but I'm not willing to risk execution or the shame of my family to get there."

Cunedag said nothing but looked north towards the hills of Valentia. "You forget, Morleo," he said at last. "We are royalty. Canaul's men are not. They can simply melt into their homelands and nobody will ever find them. Their families will not be shamed by their desertion."

"And Canaul? He's a prince too. What does he gain by bringing Rome's wrath upon the Novantae?"

"I gave up wondering what goes on in Canaul's head long ago."

They rode all the way to the end of the Wall where it faced the Northern Sea at the port town of Segedunum and then made their way back again, checking each and every fort once more for any sign of the fugitives. It was at the fort of Banna, not seven miles from where they had set out, that they heard some troubling news. As he had done at every other fort, Cunedag questioned the customs optio about who and what had passed through the gates.

"Only a merchant interested in purchasing Caledonian hounds from some northern tribe," said the optio, "A wagon of Gaulish wine and a couple of Christian missionaries."

"And you checked everybody thoroughly?" Cunedag asked. "No women among them?"

"I should be so lucky!" the officer said with a grin. "There ain't much call for women up here. Even the whores steer clear. They don't like the weather or the living quarters."

"And the cargos?" Cunedag pressed. "You checked those, I trust."

"Well, like I said, the only cargo that's passed through this gate was a wagonload of wine. There were a few men with it to guard against bandits. Not nearly enough, if you ask me—"

"You looked inside the barrels?"

The officer looked stumped. "Looked inside 'em? But that would mean breaking them open and spoiling the wine. They wouldn't have thanked me for that."

"Tell me, officer," said Cunedag, a deepening sense of dread welling up in his gut. "How often do you see wine transported in barrels? Are amphorae not usually employed?"

"That was a bit odd, come to think of it," said the officer. "But the barrels came from some arse-end province in Gaul. Gods know how they do things over there."

"These men who accompanied the wagon," said Cunedag. "How many did you say there were?"

"About ten. Like I said, not nearly enough to protect a cargo like that from the first band of rovers they come across."

"Gauls?"

The officer shook his head. "Britons. At least some of them. I did hear a few northern dialects from a few of them when they were talking together."

"Northern like mine?"

"That's it, Sir. It's natural they would have a few locals from the tribes north of the Wall to guide them, maybe talk those bandits out of cutting their throats."

Cunedag swore. "When did they pass through?"

"Two days ago," said the befuddled officer. "I kept a lookout for two women, like you asked, Sir—"

"They were in the barrels, you idiot!"

Cunedag hurried to the stables where his men were seeing to their horses and told Morleo the bad news.

"Send a rider to Camboglanna," he said. "Inform Colias that his wife and daughter have crossed into Valentia and we are on their trail."

"Shouldn't we wait for orders to pursue?" Morleo said. "An expedition north of the Wall requires a special sanction—"

"There's no time! Canaul has two days on us. If we don't catch up to them before they reach the lands of the Novantae, we'll never get Vala and Fulvia back!"

The rider was sent galloping westwards along the military road while Cunedag and his men mounted up and prepared to set out. There was some arguing with the fort prefect concerning their lack of orders to cross the Wall but Cunedag explained what his foster father, the praeses of Britannia Secunda, would think of the man who had allowed his wife and daughter to be taken across the Wall on his watch and had then tried to stop a rescue party from setting out after them. The pale-faced prefect agreed that, under the circumstances, some protocols could be set to one side.

They rode north, as hard as they could until night fell and then they rode some more. When the horses seemed like they were nearing their breaking point, Cunedag allowed them to rest. He posted sentries as his men seemed on edge, glancing at the shadowed hills that surrounded them. It was rare for a Roman unit to spend the night north of the Wall and rarer still for as little as thirty men to camp in the wilderness.

The muttering of prayers to various gods sounded throughout the camp and a small group of Christians prayed to the Heavenly Father to protect them. They were led by Elffin, a native-born Briton and the draconarius of the turma who was responsible for carrying the unit's draco standard.

"It never ceases to amaze me that followers of a religion that prohibits war choose to join the army," Cunedag overheard Marcus saying. Marcus was a Carthaginian who came from a long line of soldiers who had served the empire. He worshipped the gods of his ancestors like Ba'al Ḥamon as well as paying lip-service to the Roman gods when the occasion demanded it. "Didn't the Nazarene say, 'he who lives by the sword shall die by the sword'?"

"It's likely we'll all die by the sword," said Elffin as he finished his devotions and got off his knees to join the others by the fire. He was a typically glum fellow but stoic in his own way. "Especially if we spend many more nights beyond the

Wall. And, as to the teachings of our Lord Jesus, I'll thank you to leave their interpretation to us, pagan."

"And a draconarius at that!" Marcus continued, winking at his comrades. "How does a Christian reconcile that with his god's prohibition on idolatry?"

The draco was the military standard of the turma, its bronze head fashioned in the likeness of a dragon. When the wind passed through its mouth, it moaned mournfully and the long, fabric tail would stream behind it. Like the eagle of the legions, the draco had a religious significance for the soldiers who fought under it and, in days gone by, sacrifices were made in its honour.

"I fight for Rome and whatever standard they put into my hand," Elffin replied. "Rome is the light, as is Christ. They are one, for I serve one master unlike you, Marcus. How many gods do you pray to? It's a wonder you have time to fit them all in."

"Look around you, Elffin," said Marcus. "Do you think the light of one god is enough to keep these shadows at bay?"

"Lack of faith, that's your trouble. You can't hedge your bets where God is concerned."

Marcus grinned and even Elffin returned a small smile. The friction between the two soldiers was constant but comfortably familiar to them all. Even the teasing of comrades strengthened the spirit when they were behind enemy lines and surrounded by shadows.

"What I can't understand," said Morleo as they ate hardtack and dried meat by the light of the fire, "is what happened to the rest of Canaul's men. You say only ten men accompanied the wagon. We might be tearing off on a wild goose chase."

"It was them," said Cunedag, his eyes reflecting the blazing embers of the fire. "I just know it."

"Then why did he leave twenty-odd deserters south of the Wall? It won't take too much effort to find and punish them."

"He knew he couldn't get them past the Wall without raising suspicion," said Cunedag. "So, he left them in the south. But for what reason, I don't know."

They rode on as soon as it was light and swung west, deep into the lands of the Novantae. If Canaul was still transporting the women on the wagon, then they had a chance of catching them before they reached the Novantae royal seat at the foot of the rugged hills to the north. If they had dispensed with the wagon and taken the women on horseback, then they were as good as lost.

They rode westwards for all of the next day until the peat smoke of a settlement could be seen upon the banks of a river. It was a small fishing village but Cunedag was hopeful that its inhabitants could tell them if Canaul had passed through this region and if he had a wagon with him.

The villagers scattered in terror as they rode into the village which had no defences but a pathetic wattle palisade and gate which they struggled and failed to close in time. The horses clustered in the main clearing and Cunedag bellowed for the village headman to show himself. The village elders crept out of their roundhouses and approached the horsemen timidly. Roman soldiers were a rare sight beyond the Wall and practically unheard of this far west.

"Have any other riders passed by this settlement in the past few days?" Cunedag asked the headman. "Or men with a wagon, perhaps?"

The headman shook his head vigorously. Too vigorously. *He's lying*, Cunedag thought. He got off his horse and approached the man, drawing his spatha with deliberate slowness. This village had no warriors. He and his men could butcher them all if they wanted. He would never give such an order, but these simple fishing folk didn't know that. He turned to Morleo and gave the order for the roundhouses to be searched.

The villagers cried out in alarm as his men began ransacking the place. The headman looked at the ground, avoiding Cunedag's eyes.

"Two Roman women were kidnapped by Novantae traitors," Cunedag said to him. "We believe they passed this way. If you do not wish the full might of Rome to fall on this village and every Novantae village like it, then you will help me recover these women."

There was a sudden shouting from inside the stables and the clang of steel. Cunedag's men rushed to aid their comrades but, before they could enter the stables, two ponies bolted from them, a man upon each with a woman draped across his saddle horn, bound hand and foot.

"Stop them!" Cunedag yelled as he ran for his own horse and swung himself up into the saddle. The two fugitives were circling the enclosure and heading for the gate. Cunedag could see that the lead rider was Canaul, stripped of his Roman armour and wearing a saffron tunica and breeches with a billowing cloak.

They were out of the gate by the time Cunedag's men had saddled up, but Cunedag knew that they had them. Two native ponies bearing a rider and a passenger each hadn't a chance of outrunning Roman cavalry.

They galloped across the reedy ground, following the river north towards the hills. They gained on their quarry quickly and soon rode them down, surrounding the two terrified ponies and holding the fugitives at spearpoint.

Canaul had drawn his sword and looked ready to go down fighting while his companion looked less eager and had not even drawn his weapon. The muffled screams and curses of their gagged captives burned the air but were ignored by all.

"It's over, Canaul," said Cunedag. "End of the road."

"To think that it was my own foster brothers who came out here after me!" the Novantae prince sneered. "Still on Colias's leash, the pair of you!"

They hauled the traitors down from their horses and bound their hands while Vala and Fulvia were gently lifted down and released of their bonds. Fulvia wept with relief, but Vala hurled herself at the bound Canaul, raining slaps and kicks upon him while cursing him and explaining just what her father would do to him now the shoe was on the other foot.

It was an amusing sight to see Canaul receive his medicine from their foster sister but, eventually, Cunedag had to drag her off him and try to calm her down.

"Have they harmed you?" he asked her, finding that he was ready to repay any cruelty Vala had suffered in kind.

"None but keeping us in various states of captivity and discomfort for days on end!" Vala said. "The worst of it was being sealed up in stinking wine barrels and jolted across the country. Fortunately, they let us out once we were beyond the Wall, to carry us bound in a cart like criminals! And they murdered Brenna! Sweet, innocent Brenna who has been my companion since childhood! I could scratch out their very eyes!"

"Why did you do it, Canaul?" Morleo demanded, every bit as indignant as Cunedag was.

"For reasons a Romanised pup like you would never understand," said Canaul. "You were ever too comfortable below the Wall. Cunedag on the other hand, has surprised me. What happened to you, Votadini? What happened to the rage in the boy who was brought as a hostage to Eboracum? Has the company of Morleo turned you soft? Turned you against your own people?"

"So, you always were a traitor," said Cunedag, ignoring the uncomfortable feelings Canaul's words raised in his gut. "All along you despised Rome and plotted your escape. But why have you waited until now? And why this mad scheme to kidnap the two women Colias would raise the entire province to reclaim?"

At this, a grin stretched across Canaul's face which, for reasons he didn't quite understand, sent a chill through Cunedag's soul. "You think you've won?" Canaul said. "You've only delayed the inevitable."

Cunedag didn't waste more time on Canaul's cryptic threats and the turma rode back to the fishing village. They would replenish their rations and refresh their horses for the night at the villagers' expense and then, on the morrow, begin their journey back to the Wall.

The remainder of Canaul's men were found hiding in the stables, looking like they wished they had the numbers to mount a defence that wouldn't amount to suicide. The return of Cunedag and his men humbled them into submission, and they joined their leader in a roundhouse, bound hand and foot, with a heavy guard posted outside.

Elffin and Marcus found the wagon with its empty barrels in the stables and Cunedag thanked the Great Mother that Canaul had been confident enough in his escape to use it to cart his prisoners westwards or they would never had caught up with them.

"What will you do with Canaul?" Vala said to him when they were alone and darkness had fallen.

"I should execute him," Cunedag replied. "Make an example of him and his men."

"But you won't because he's your foster brother. Or is it for another reason?"

"Such as?"

"You are both from these lands north of the Wall. It is clear that Canaul's heart yearns to be with his people."

"And you think mine does, or at least is sympathetic enough to spare him his fate? Does my being here count for naught? Does my pursuit of Canaul in the name of Rome not tell you where my allegiance lies? Canaul will return to the south with us and face your father's justice."

"Sorry," she said, truly the first time Cunedag had heard her utter the word. "I suppose I shouldn't question your loyalty after what you have done. "Thank you. For coming out here after my mother and I."

Cunedag gave her a grin. "Are you jesting? Do you know what your father would have done to me if I had failed?"

A small smile played across her features and, not for the first time, Cunedag thought she was very pretty when she wasn't being such hard work. Her pale-blue stola was muddied and torn and her usually impeccable hair was a tangled rat's nest. But the sharp defiance that burned in her appealed to Cunedag and he almost pitied Canaul for the hard words she must have lashed him with him every step of the way north.

Chapter 8

It was as dawn was breaking over the hills that the alarm was given by one of Cunedag's sentries that riders were approaching from the north.

"Damn!" he said as he strapped on his helm and joined his men at the wattle palisade. "I had hoped to get away this morning before all the Novantae learned of our foray into their territory."

"I don't think those are Novantae," said Morleo, shielding his eyes against the morning sun. "Some of them, perhaps, but others have a dress unlike my peoples' neighbours."

"Well, who are they then?" Cunedag asked.

"I don't know, but they're kitted out for war. I count forty-two. Those are bad odds."

Cavalry were not well-suited to defending settlements on foot and the fishing village offered scant use as a military position in any case, so Cunedag gave the order to mount up and ride for the trees where he hoped they could lure the enemy in and destroy them using Roman tactics. They couldn't outrun the newcomers, not with two women and half a score of prisoners to carry. They had to either bargain or fight their way out and Canaul might still be useful to them in that respect, if these men were friends of his.

The strangers rode straight for the treeline and halted, just out of bowshot. Their leaders, of which there seemed to be two, came forward.

"My brother," said Canaul from where he sat, his arms still bound behind him. "We were supposed to meet with him today before riding to my father's seat with our hostages. He will butcher you all for spoiling his plans."

"Hold your tongue!" Cunedag barked at him. "Morleo, follow me. Let's see how willing Canaul's brother is to parley."

They rode out of the trees and approached the two riders. The one in the Novantae tribal colours, whom Cunedag took to be Canaul's brother, was approaching his middle years, tall and proud with the same arrogant smirk Cunedag had grown accustomed to. The other man was of a similar age but dressed in cruder clothing of skins and furs with the gold torc of a chieftain around his neck.

"If you have harmed my brother …" the Novantae prince began, "you will die screaming beneath my blade this day."

"If you wish to see your brother in one piece," Cunedag replied, "then you will put a rein on your loose threats."

"Who are you?" the man in the skins and furs snarled. "I know Roman scum when I see them, but I would like to know the name of the man who's head I will send back to the Wall." He spoke British with the unmistakable accent of the men of Erin and at once, Cunedag knew who these men who rode with the Novantae were.

"I am Cunedag mab Etern of the Votadini," he said to the both of them. "Foster brother to Canaul." He gave Canaul's brother a grin. "Practically family."

The Novantae prince threw back his head and laughed. "A Votadini hostage still doing Rome's dirty work. I'm sure my brother had his reasons in not involving you in his plan and they speak much about your character. Tell me, Cunedag of the Votadini. When did you last return home?" Cunedag was silent and the Novantae prince grinned. "You may find it less friendly to Rome than when you left."

"Enough of the veiled threats," said Cunedag. "We have your brother and nine of his fellow traitors. If you wish to see them alive again, you will accept them in payment for our safe passage out of your lands with the two Roman women."

"You think I give a rat's turd about my brother who somehow bungled a simple kidnapping?" the prince snarled. "I want those two women and if you don't hand them over, then I will butcher your entire company. How's that for terms?"

"No deal," said Cunedag.

"Then prepare to die!" the man from Erin said.

Without any further words, Cunedag and Morleo wheeled their horses around and galloped back to the treeline.

"That man," said Cunedag as they rode. "He's—"

"Attacotti, I know," said Morleo.

Attacotti. Gaelic raiders from Erin who had settled in the lands around the western end of the Antonine Wall, smashing the Damnonii tribe into submission and absorbing them into their new kingdom which they ruled from the old Damnonii tribal seat at Alt Clut.

"How is it that the Novantae ride with Attacotti warriors?" Morleo wondered. "There has ever been bad blood between Britons and Gaels."

"I don't know but I'm quickly getting the feeling that we have not kept as close an eye on our homelands as we should have."

"I'm inclined to agree with you. Something odd is brewing north of the Wall."

"Aye, and the kidnapping of Vala and Fulvia is just a part of it. We know now that Canaul wasn't acting on his own. His father must have sanctioned the kidnapping."

"What the hell are the Novantae playing at?"

"Questions for later. Right now, we have to get the women to safety."

As soon as they were back under the cover of the trees, Cunedag ordered two of his men to escort the women east.

"Stay within the forest," he told them. "Don't try to cross open ground. We don't know if there are any more Novantae patrols about."

"What about you?" Vala asked him as she was helped up onto a horse.

"I'm going to deal with Canaul's brother and his new friends," Cunedag said, grimly. "We will catch up with you once this is done."

"I wouldn't wait for him if I were you," Canaul called to the women from where he sat with the other prisoners. "My brother is twice the warrior Cunedag is."

"Silence!" Cunedag snapped.

"Although he has a point," said Morleo. "They outnumber us. How do you plan to beat them?"

"We head north, through the trees," said Cunedag. "The ground rises there, and we need every advantage."

"And the prisoners?"

Cunedag glanced at Canaul. "He has outlived his usefulness. His brother doesn't care enough to save him. We leave them here."

Canaul ground his teeth in rage as Cunedag and his men abandoned them and headed through the trees.

It was slow moving, pushing through the woodland as the ground rose into the hills. A scout rode up to Cunedag and reported that the enemy had retrieved Canaul and his companions and given them horses, increasing the odds against them by ten. They were now following them across open ground, gradually catching up to them.

"Soon they will flank us," Morleo warned.

"Aye," said Cunedag. "It's time for us to make our stand. We circle them and attack their rear. That should confuse them enough to give us the advantage, small though it may be."

They burst from the trees at the top of the slope, Cunedag at their head, shields unslung, and spears pointed ahead as the wind rushed through capes and horsehair plumes, howling through the draco Elffin carried aloft.

The enemy saw them and attempted to form a defensive formation, but the slope and their more powerful horses gave the Romans a terrifying speed and they had soon passed the column of Novantae riders which rode ahead of their Attacotti allies.

With a signal from his spear, Cunedag turned his turma and drove them into the side of the Attacotti warriors. Spearheads slammed against shields, punctured mail and flesh and the cacophony of battle erupted across the rugged landscape.

Cunedag skewered an Attacotti warrior beneath the chin and the weight of the dying man tumbling from his saddle wrenched his spear from his grip. Quickly drawing his spatha, he hacked the head off an outthrust spear and drove his blade into the guts of the man who had attacked him, feeling the hot spurt of blood washing over his knuckles.

He had killed before. Patrols north of the Wall often encountered bandits or small groups of troublemakers but this was his first engagement against an actual warband. He had been trained for this moment all his life and, as he caught a spear thrust on the boss of his shield before hacking open the throat of another assailant, he knew that he had been born for it too. Killing men was easy. It was dealing with the living that was hard. Leave that to the politicians. War was his path through life.

The Novantae up ahead had turned and were riding to aid their allies while what was left of the Attacotti floundered amid the slaughter, many of their riders butchered by Cunedag's men.

Canaul's brother led his riders in a fan formation which swept its arms around the battle like an octopus, each rider a tentacle seeking a way in. The hot, steamy press of panicked horses and flailing men and the stink of blood and ruptured bowels was thick and overpowering. Cunedag roared encouragement to his men as they fought on, every enemy warrior slain, a great triumph in evening the odds. He saw the Attacotti chieftain up ahead and forced Bran on through the tangle of battling warriors. If he could just cut the head off the snake …

The Gaelic chieftain saw him coming and the two men locked eyes long before they locked swords, each pushing aside his comrades to get at the other. Their horses slammed together, rearing and squealing as the two leaders cut at each other with their swords. Iron clanged and slithered off iron, many of the blows landing on the round bosses of their shields. Both men wore helms and mail coats meaning that the fight was set to be long and exhausting.

The Novantae were well and truly embedded in the fight now and Cunedag could hear their cries all around him as his own men pressed against them. If he slew this Attacotti bastard, then he might be cut down by Canaul's brother and his men, but such was war. All that mattered was taking as many of the enemy with you as possible.

The Attacotti chieftain tried to work his sword beneath Cunedag's shield and Cunedag slammed its steel rim down on his forearm, hearing the bone crack. The Attacotti yelped and his sword tumbled from his grip; a deadly piece of misfortune for him. Unarmed, he desperately reached for a dagger at his side with which to defend himself. Cunedag gave him no such chance, using his brief moment of opportunity to thrust his sword into the man's throat.

The chieftain gasped and clutched the reddened blade with both hands. Cunedag ripped it free, severing a couple of fingers as his did so, wheeled his mount around and booted him from his saddle.

The remaining Attacotti howled and cursed to see their leader fall. The Novantae looked deeply troubled, no more so than Canaul's brother who was somewhere to their rear, far enough from the kernel of the fighting to be safe. Cunedag's men cheered at their victory and the fight seemed to leave their enemy like a receding tide. It took only a few more fallen Novantae for Canaul's brother to bellow the call for retreat.

Cunedag raised his bloodied sword into the air in triumph as the Novantae turned and left the fray, galloping back towards the village, the dead left behind far outnumbering the living. As far as Cunedag could tell, he had lost five men and seven horses and this was in addition to the two men who had been feathered by arrows in the ambush weeks previously. It pained him greatly for he knew each and every one of the thirty men under his command. Their absence would be sorely felt by them all.

The journey back to the Wall would be slow and dangerous but they had won themselves a little time, paid for in blood. They rode east and picked up the women before heading back to the border between Novantae and Selgovae lands.

The journey was uneventful but took longer than Cunedag would have liked. Vala and her mother, to their credit, did not complain, although the conditions of their journey were far from comfortable. Cunedag supposed that after what they had been through, anything was a relief. They were being returned to civilisation and, for their part, seemed content enough.

They made for Camboglanna as the men on the Wall told them that the praeses was still there. Their arrival was greeted with jubilation on the part of Colias as he met his returned women with open arms and much gratitude for their rescuers whom he sent to the bath house with a promise of a hearty meal to follow. Cunedag sent his men off but requested a private audience with the praeses as he had important news to share.

"And you are sure they were Attacotti?" Colias asked once Cunedag had explained what had happened.

"They were Gaels, that much is sure," said Cunedag. "Morleo recognised them as Attacotti and he should know. His people have suffered Attacotti raids more than my own have."

"It is deeply troubling that the Novantae have allied themselves with them," said Colias. "Peace beyond the Wall has always rested on the trust that the tribes remain in a state of conflict with one another."

Cunedag said nothing. He knew Rome's tactics well enough.

"What concerns me more are the comments Canaul's brother made regarding your own people. Could it be that your father has turned against me?"

"I have not seen the man since I was twelve," said Cunedag. "But he did grow to manhood below the Wall, the same as I."

"Yes. We must take courage in that, though your father did not take to Rome's ways as well as you have, my boy, it must be admitted. He and I rarely saw eye to eye. I would like to know for sure. How do you feel about returning to your home?"

Cunedag blinked, thrown off guard by the question. "Home, Domine?"

"To see which way the wind blows in the lands of the Votadini. I must know, Cunedag. If the tribes of the north are plotting together, we might have a rebellion on our hands the size of the Great Conspiracy our grandfathers faced. I will send Morleo with you so that he might do the same in the household of his own father."

He poured them both some more wine and approached Cunedag with his cup in his hand, other arm reaching around his shoulder in great familiarity. "Be my eyes and ears, Cunedag," he said. "And if your father has somehow been swayed by the Novantae, try to make him see reason. But do not outstay your welcome. Return to me for I may have need of loyal soldiers if my worst fears have any truth to them."

Cunedag felt overwhelmed by conflicting emotions. The thought of returning home to see his family and the places that were so lost to him that they existed only in dreams was a heady prospect. But he would be returning home not as a Votadini prince but as an agent of Rome. Colias was asking him to spy on his own people, his own father.

He felt a deep resentment for his situation. None of this was of his own making. Years of training with the Roman army made him feel as much Roman as Votadini and he knew that he had no choice. There never had been any choice.

"Yes, Domine," he said. "I will go."

Chapter 9

Six days later, Cunedag and Morleo reached the Aber Teu that flowed past the ruined walls of Rome's deserted frontier fort of Trimontium. They had wasted no time in setting out and took with them a small contingent of five riders from the turma including Elffin and Marcus. They had abandoned their armour and weapons for plain, rough spun clothes in the British style and rode native northern ponies, leaving their cavalry stallions with their distinctive Roman brands at the Wall. The road north was treacherous at the best of times but these days, the lives of Roman soldiers may well be forfeit.

They spent the night at Din Eil with Morleo's family who were ecstatic to have him returned to them and threw a feast in honour of his return, temporary though it may be. Cunedag wondered if he would receive so warm a welcome once he reached Din Eidyn. The Selgovae knew nothing of the Novantae's alliance with the Attacotti, save that their neighbouring tribe had grown more quarrelsome of late.

"There have been raids along our western borders," King Tasulus said. "Small groups of Novantae stealing our cattle and grain. I have sent out punitive expeditions, but they never give me a response strong enough to be a declaration of war. But the Attacotti … we have heard evil rumours from those people, though we have seen none of them."

"What rumours?" Cunedag asked.

"They have a druid who pours poison into the ears of their chieftains. A twisted old lunatic from Erin who still practises the darkest of sorceries that the druids of Albion gave up generations ago."

"What is this druid's name?"

"That, I do not know, though it is said that the Attacotti themselves fear him as much as their victims do."

"Victims?"

"Aye, human sacrifice, boy."

There was a murmuring of nervous voices around the roundhouse at this. Human sacrifice had been practiced by the Britons in days gone by but had long since been outlawed by Rome and even the northern tribes had stopped doing it these days. This druid of the Attacotti sounded like a bloody relic of the past.

"I wonder if the princeling you slew was the son of one of their chieftains," Morleo said to Cunedag.

"More than likely," he replied in a resigned tone. "Another reason for them to hate Rome, though if they are following the orders of a deranged druid, then they have little need of any more encouragement."

Cunedag took his leave of Morleo and his family the following day and set out with the remainder of his escort, crossing the Aber Teu and entering the lands of the Votadini. It was a strange feeling, almost dreamlike, as he rode across the moors and through the wooded glens of his childhood. He passed close to the spot where he had slain the boar and saved his brother's life mere weeks before he had been taken away from his family. So much had happened since then that he could scarcely believe these were his memories. They felt like things that had happened to somebody else.

Din Eidyn was as he remembered it, smaller perhaps, but still a formidable fortification against the rugged hills. His men, who were used to Roman towns and small British settlements were suitably impressed.

"Arses of the gods, that's a fine place to call home!" Marcus said. "I'd hate to be the one trying to attack those fortifications!"

"It's the strongest hillfort north of the Wall," said Cunedag with a curious sense of newfound pride. "Only Din Peldur to the east rivals it. Both are under Votadini control."

"Then we'd better hope the tribe of your birth are still Rome's allies," said Elffin.

Cunedag said nothing, knowing his draconarius was right. If his people had been coerced into standing against Rome, then the war would be long and bloody.

They made their way up the main approach and in through the gatehouse without much fuss, most people thinking them no different to the scores of traders, travellers and wanderers who came daily to the royal seat of the Votadini. It was once they had stabled their horses and requested permission to ascend to the upper enclosure where the Great Roundhouse stood that the commotion started.

"And what business have you with King Etern?" asked the guard at the gate.

"Private business with my father, the king," said Cunedag. "For I am Cunedag mab Etern, royal prince of the Votadini and decurion in the Ala Second Asturum."

The guard's jaw dropped, and a ripple of excitement spread around the enclosure. Cunedag ignored the unbelieving jeers and fixed his stare on the guard, daring him to deny him entrance.

The guard turned and sent a fellow warrior up the hill to fetch Queen Ceindrech and Cunedag felt his stomach turn into a hard knot. For the first time in eight years, he was going to see his mother.

She approached the gate in a swirl of green fabric, her hair greyer than he remembered but her face exactly the same. Her dark-brown eyes looked him over, her expression suggesting that she didn't dare believe it was true.

"Can it really be you?" she asked.

"Yes, Mother," he replied. "I have come home."

"Great Modron be praised! You *are* my son, I can see it in your eyes! How big you are!"

They embraced and the crowd burst into polite applause, those who had jeered clapping all the more enthusiastically.

"You have returned to us at the most opportune time," his mother said. "Your father is sick and may not see out the year."

Cunedag swallowed. The king, sick? What might that mean for the Votadini during such tumultuous times?

"But come," she said. "Come and feel the warmth of the hearth you once knew."

Cunedag and his men were taken up to the Great Roundhouse where the queen quickly had the slaves bring them broth and bread. The roundhouse began to fill with curious types, keen to catch a glimpse of their long-lost prince. Cunedag's little brother Murcho was there, now a youth of seventeen and a warrior who had nothing but awe for his estranged big brother whom he barely remembered.

"And where is Alpia?" Cunedag asked his mother.

"Your sister was married to one of your father's highest nobles," she replied. "Tegid mab Calgo who rules Din Peldur."

"Aye, I remember him. A good match, I am sure, though I would have liked to have seen her."

"She has grown into a beauty of a woman," said his mother. "And just as wise as she is fearsome."

"She always was a canny one. I expect Tegid has his hands full with her as his wife."

His mother smiled fondly. "Quite. In fact, it's a little unclear who rules Din Peldur these days, Tegid or Alpia."

As they were sopping up the remains of their meal, a tall figure in brightly coloured tunic and cloak entered from one of the side rooms. It was Brude. Cunedag glanced up at his older brother, noticing how he had matured. He wasn't much taller but had filled out a little, leaving the reedy adolescent behind in favour of a moustached, athletic man in his early twenties.

"Brother," said Cunedag, rising, his men following his lead to pay their respects to the crown prince.

"Cunedag, it really is you, then," said Brude, ignoring his brother's offered arm. "I heard the commotion from Father's bedchamber. He's sick, you understand."

"May I see him?"

"Later perhaps." Brude looked Cunedag up and down, unimpressed with his brother's common attire. "No Roman clothes?" he asked. "No armour? We heard that you held a position of some command."

"Aye, a decurion," said Cunedag. "These men are five of the thirty riders I have under me. We thought it best not to travel north as Roman soldiers."

"You come as wolves dressed as sheep, you mean."

"Brude, I am still Votadini. And most of these men are Britons who have taken service with Rome, the same as I."

"Then they can hardly be called 'true' Britons, can they?" Brude snapped. "And, as you have not been home in the past eight years, I would hardly call you 'Votadini'."

"Why the insults, brother? I could hardly help being taken from my home as a child."

"Yet you are now a man grown and you still serve Rome. It's not hard to see where your true loyalties lie."

"My loyalty is to the treaty we have with Rome," said Cunedag testily. "To the agreement our father and grandfather honoured. Such a thing is not easily cast aside without shame."

"Canaul of the Novantae wouldn't agree."

Cunedag felt a chill down his spine. "What do you know of Canaul's treachery?"

"Only that he had the nerve to do what you apparently cannot. To unshackle himself from the Roman yoke and return to his people a free man."

"Canaul tried to take two high-born Roman women hostage," said Cunedag. "As part of some misguided plan of his father's which also involves an alliance with the Attacotti. Tell me, brother, that the Votadini have not also fallen in league with madness."

"What you call madness others might call courage," said Brude. "And do not think to lecture me when you are no more than a Roman dog on a leash!"

"Boys, do not fight!" said their mother, rising to calm their tempers just as she had done when they had been children. "Cunedag is not back for more than a moment and already you are at each other's throats as if the past eight years never happened!"

Brude left the roundhouse then, his face seething. An embarrassed silence hung in the air. Murcho looked at his feet, his face forlorn at the fighting of his older brothers.

"You must forgive Brude," said their mother. "He is under great pressure at the moment. With your father so ill, it has fallen to him to make most of the decisions for the tribe. He is too young to be king and these are difficult times for all the north. The other tribes may try to exploit our weakness."

"What is wrong with Father?" Cunedag said. "What ails him so that he cannot rule as he has always done?"

His mother's expression darkened and Murcho continued looking at his feet. "It is perhaps best that you see him now," she said. "So that you may understand."

She led him to his father's chamber where a guard was posted and undid the latch on the wattle door. As soon as Cunedag entered, he was hit by the stench of sickness and human filth.

King Etern lay on his pallet of furs and looked a shadow of the man Cunedag remembered. Gone was the proud warrior who inspired awe and respect from all around him, replaced by a feeble man still in his forties but looking like he was at death's door. His greying hair was splayed around his head and one side of his face drooped alarmingly. A slave sat nearby with a bowl and a cloth, whose job was apparently to mop up the saliva that continually dribbled from the downturned corner of his mouth.

"It happened two months ago," said Cunedag's mother. "He was fine one day and then, while he was examining his horses in the stables, he fell as if struck down by the gods."

"What's wrong with his face?" Cunedag asked in a hushed tone.

"Paralysed. Like one half of his body. He can't walk. His mind is addled too. Can't feed himself or empty his bowels without help. I'm at my wits' end!"

Her voice trembled as she tried to hold back the tears and Cunedag placed a comforting arm on her shoulder. "Can he hear us?"

"I believe so," she replied. "But he can't speak. He mumbles and wails quite a bit, but it is as if he's been robbed of his speech like the Cauldron-Born of legend."

"What does Gonar say, if that wise old owl still lives?"

"Oh, Gonar lives. He says that it is the will of the gods. But how can your father have angered the gods so? What crime deserves the punishment of living death?"

"Who else knows about this?"

"The whole tribe knows that the king is sick, but they know nothing of the severity. We could not conceal his absence, so everybody just thinks that he is unwell and that Brude is stepping in for him in the meantime. But this can't go on forever! Your father is unlikely to improve yet Brude cannot succeed him while he still lives. Oh, what have we done to deserve this predicament!"

They left the king's chamber, Cunedag having no wish to reacquaint himself with his father when he was in such a state. He ordered the roundhouse cleared and he, his mother and

Murcho sat down by the hearth to discuss what had to be done.

"Your brother is doing the best he can to rule in your father's stead," their mother said. "But he is too impetuous. Too easily affronted. I fear he will be goaded into doing something rash. He already sees himself as king and listens to me less and less with every day."

"Have there been any envoys from the other tribes?" Cunedag asked. "Do they sense our weakness?"

"I fear so. Not long after your father was struck down, the Novantae sent riders. Brude received them in private. What they discussed, I have no idea and he won't tell me."

"An offer of some sort of alliance, no doubt," said Murcho.

Their mother shook her head. "The Novantae have never exactly been friends to the Votadini but there has been peace between us for many years now. Why offer a formal alliance now?"

"Murcho is right," said Cunedag, glancing at his younger brother. "Things are happening in these lands that require the strengthening of bonds. Only I'm willing to wager the Novantae offered more than a renewal of friendship. I have recently engaged them in battle and slew a good number of their warriors after they tried to kidnap two women of the Roman governor's household. We pursued them deep into Novantae lands and rescued the women but learned that the Novantae are now allied with the Attacotti."

"The Attacotti!" Murcho exclaimed. "Those bastards ally themselves with nobody. They hate all Britons and think only of expanding their own kingdom with that evil druid of theirs egging them on."

"They think to expand their lands below the Wall, to my mind," said Cunedag. His mother and brother stared at him, wide-eyed. "I have reason to believe that a conspiracy is brewing in the north which could lead to a war the like of which we have not known in our lifetimes. It could be the seed of a full-scale rebellion against Rome."

"The Novantae wouldn't attack the Wall, surely?" said his mother. "Even with Attacotti allies."

"No, they wouldn't," Cunedag agreed. "Which is why they have tried to recruit the Votadini to their cause. They will probably approach the Selgovae too, though their king had received no such offer when I passed through Din Eil the other day. But have no doubt, war is coming, and we need to make sure the Votadini are on the right side."

"And what side would that be, brother?" asked Brude from the doorway. He entered the main chamber, his face like stone but his eyes blazing at Cunedag.

"The side of sanity," said Cunedag. "What did the Novantae offer you? A piece of the ruins once they have driven Rome from the shores of Albion? It can't happen, Brude. An impossible dream that refuses to die in the north."

"Well, we know where you stand, of course," said Brude. He looked around at the empty room. "I see you have taken it upon yourself to clear the roundhouse so you can poison the minds of my family in private. You always did struggle to remember that you are the younger brother."

"You're not king yet, Brude," said Cunedag through gritted teeth.

"But I will be soon, and you had best remember your place, *little brother*," came the snarled reply. "And you've made it abundantly clear that your place is below the Wall. Why did you return? Was it to spy on me and report back to your Roman masters?"

Cunedag said nothing, his silence confirming his brother's suspicions. Brude grinned. "Well, you might as well run back south and tell them that the north is rising. An early warning won't save them. Events have been put in motion that cannot be stopped. No longer will we be the client kings of a corrupt and dying empire. Soon, the sword will be in the other hand, and they will seek *our* favour."

"Is that what the envoys from the Novatane told you?" Cunedag said. "Fine words but you can't win, Brude. And with Father sick, you don't have the authority to lead us to war."

"Us?" Brude sneered. "There is no *us*, Cunedag. You have traded your Votadini heritage for Roman long ago. You have no say in this family, and you have no say in this tribe."

"Perhaps not," Cunedag admitted. "But others do. While Father lives, you are not king, and the clan chieftains will not let you lead them into disaster."

"The clan chieftains are sick of Rome's heavy hand," said Brude. "They do not share your enthusiasm for our overlords."

"Perhaps they share my enthusiasm for survival."

"Enough of this!" said their mother. "Your father lies sick in the next room, and he must listen to the pair of you squabble like children! Cunedag has the right of it, Brude. Your father is still king and all this talk of joining some glorious rebellion against Rome is for naught."

"We'll see, Mother," said Brude. "It's only a matter of time before the truth comes out. How do you think the nobles will react when it becomes known that Father is no longer fit to rule?"

Chapter 10

Brude's words haunted Cunedag over the next few days, and he feared that his brother would do something rash to hasten his way to the throne. He was ashamed to admit to himself that what occupied his mind most in those days was Vala. The thought of his own people marching against her and his adopted family was almost unbearable for him. Oh, they would never get past the Wall and, even if they did, plenty of Roman soldiers stood between the Wall and Eboracum, but the conflict between the tribe of his birth and the Romans mirrored the conflict within himself.

He had been on the verge of returning south to bring Colias word of the growing rebellion in the north, but it appeared that Brude was wasting no time either. He called a council of all the Votadini clan chieftains to discuss the king's health and his potential succession.

"Hadn't we better ride south before the council meets?" Elffin asked Cunedag as they stood atop the palisade and watched the clan chieftains of the Votadini ride through the gates of Din Eidyn. "If they decide to support your brother's ascension to the throne, then it might get dangerous for us here."

"They won't do that while my father yet lives," said Cunedag. "And I want to know how the nobles feel about Brude's desire to join this fated rebellion. Perhaps I can even persuade a few to see the folly in such a plan. I don't like wasting time here, but Colias would rather have as much information as I can give him, even if it comes a little late."

So, they waited while the chieftains from all corners of the Votadini lands trickled into Din Eidyn. Cunedag watched them come with their entourages, these old subjects of his father, many of whom he had known briefly in his youth. They greeted him with far more decorum than his brother had done, even if a few seemed wary of his connections in the south. One couple who were particularly happy to see him were Tegid and his wife, Alpia who arrived with their seven-year-old son, Tancorix.

"Brother!" Alpia cried upon being introduced to him, the same look of incredulity in her eyes that he had seen in his mother's. "Can it really be you?"

"Aye," said Cunedag with a grin. "It's me. And I barely recognised you, Alpia. Mother told no lie when she said you had blossomed."

His sister was equal to him in height and had the straight, black hair of their family, braided down the back. She wore a tartan tunica over woollen breeches for ease of riding, confirming Cunedag's suspicions that even being a clan chieftain's wife had not curbed her rugged spirit.

"I am glad to see you have returned home, lad," said Tegid, a tall, swarthy man with a long moustache. "As your father did, so too have you survived the debauchery of Rome and returned to us a man."

"Temporarily, I fear," said Cunedag. "I still hold a position in the Roman military and must return south after the council."

"Then you are something of an envoy?" said Alpia. "No doubt to bring news to the Romans of the goings on in the north?"

"Something like that," Cunedag admitted.

The smile faded on the face of his sister and Tegid regarded him curiously, but nothing further was said.

When the last of the nobles had arrived, the council was held without delay in the main enclosure of the fort beneath the night sky where torches illuminated dozens of nobles from the Votadini's warrior class. There were young men and old and some women, all dressed in their finest cloaks and gold ornamentation. Torcs and arm rings glinted in the night as did their keen eyes by the firelight, eager to learn the reason for this gathering.

Brude addressed them and immediately confirmed the rumours surrounding the king's condition. It was as Cunedag had feared. He was going to use their father's illness to claim that he was unfit to rule and ask the tribe to vote on his early succession. But would the nobles agree to it?

"We all know that the world is changing," Brude went on. "Rome is slowly losing its grip on the fringes of its empire. Now is the time to have decisive leadership, not a sick old man who can't even stand."

There were grumbles at the perceived disrespect for the king from the lips of his own son, but most of the assembled watched the young prince intently.

"Some of you are aware of the growing sentiment among the other tribes that the time has come to throw off the shackles Rome forced upon our ancestors," Brude continued. "Their once great empire has split into two. As we speak, the Goths, once Rome's allies, now rebel against their former masters while the Romans squabble among themselves over grain in North Africa. I tell you all, now is the time for us to bite through the leash that binds us to their fading power."

Cunedag wondered how his brother was so well acquainted with the troubles Rome faced in the distant parts of its empire. The average Briton this far north had never heard of the Goths or Africa for that matter. It was Canaul's doing, he supposed. He had brought something other than his Roman training back home with him. He had brought news of Rome's vulnerabilities.

But not all of the nobles were convinced by Brude's words. Tegid in particular, voiced his scepticism.

"Rome may have its woes," he said. "But they are still powerful enough to crush us if they had a mind. Have you forgotten the Wall and its garrisons? And even if we take it, Rome will bring every legion it can spare to punish us for our trespass."

"It was so very nearly achieved once before," said another noble. "Few here remember King Gartnait who united the northern tribes in the Great Conspiracy, but we all know how he nearly brought Rome to its knees."

"Aye, *nearly*," said Tegid. "And what happened to King Gartnait?" There was a rumbling agreement among the faction who were opposed to attacking Rome. "Butchered by Roman troops and his confederacy smashed," Tegid finished.

"Rome's power has dwindled since those days," said Brude. "Since Maximus left this island with most of its legions, the number of troops here are a fraction of what they once were. The failures of the past do not determine the future."

Cunedag couldn't keep quiet any longer. He rose from his seat and demanded to be heard. There were some confused faces and much muttering concerning his identity and Brude refused to make any introduction for him, but he would not be silenced. He was the king's son, damn it, and a prince of these people despite his absence during the past eight years and he would have his say.

"I am Cunedag," he bellowed over the hubbub. "Son of King Etern." There were cries of realisation at this and some mutterings about his Roman ties, but he ignored them. "You all know that I was fostered to a Roman family at the age of twelve. I make no apologies for Rome, but I must warn you against pursuing this folly. Not one of you has been below the

Wall. I have and I know the might of the Roman army. There are nine-thousand frontier troops stationed along the Wall alone. Then there is the mobile field army which numbers an additional five thousand. And these are disciplined, professional soldiers. Rome has ruled this island for four-hundred years. They won't let a confederation of tribesmen attack them without ruthless retaliation."

"They have never ruled the entire island," said one noble. "Even their turf wall north of our lands lasted a mere twenty years until we forced them back south. Our ancestors were not so easily ruled by Rome. Have you no pride, boy? Or has your fostering below the Wall turned your mind to Rome's favour? You are well-named 'Good Hound' it is said!"

There was a ripple of mirth at this. Cunedag's name did indeed mean 'good hound' and the idea that he was now a loyal hound of Rome amused many of the nobles who lent their voices to this assessment, and there were cries that they shouldn't have to listen to one who may have been sent here deliberately to dissuade them from rebellion.

"Peace, everyone!" Brude called once the clamour of voices rose to an intolerable level. "My brother has had his say, and we can all see where his loyalty lies. For those of you who are concerned about Rome's might and our chances against them, perhaps my special guests here tonight will bolster your courage."

He turned to a pair of men near to him who had sat in silence throughout. They were richly attired like every other noble present, but Cunedag didn't recognise them and had noted that they had spoken to nobody since their arrival at Din Eidyn.

"Allow me to introduce Prince Calgac of the Caledonii and Prince Uradech of the Epidii," said Brude. There was an intake of breath at this. The Caledonii and the Epidii were tribes to the far north, beyond the Antonine Wall. They only ventured south to raid and when they did, they painted themselves blue in the old fashion. These were the true Picts.

Brude beamed at the effect his guests had on the assembled nobles. "The Caledonii and the Epidii have allied themselves with the Novantae and the Attacotti. You see? This rebellion is far larger than you all thought. All the unconquered tribes of the north are rising up against the southern oppressors! We would be fools to sit on our haunches while others win our freedom for us, nay, cowards even!"

"But one thing remains," said Tegid, standing to be heard over the excited chatter. "Only King Etern can decide that we go to war. And he is not here."

"But the king can't speak for himself!" cried one of the pro-rebellion nobles. "Brude leads the tribe in his stead!"

"But does he have the authority to lead us to war?" Tegid asked.

"In all things!"

Brude, who watched this exchange in quiet satisfaction, spoke up. "It is true that in a matter so serious as war, a prince standing in for his father lacks the proper authority. Would that I were king, I would marshal our warriors immediately and pledge ourselves to this heroic confederation."

"Then Brude must be our king!" came the cries from the pro-war faction. "We must vote! All in favour of Brude to succeed his father as king of the Votadini!"

The vote happened almost as a formality. Tegid and a few others voted against the motion, but Brude won by a large margin. The nobles roared their approval and carried him around on a shield as a pretext to the official ceremony which would take a few days to organise.

Cunedag glanced around at his people as they celebrated their own destruction. It was over. There was nothing he could do for them now. Brude had won their hearts with vain promises of liberty. He had played on their honour, using their pride as a weapon and threatening them with shame if they did not act. All he could think to do now was to flee south and warn Colias of what was coming.

As Din Eidyn was swept up in the post-council celebrations, Cunedag went to his men and told them quietly that it was time to fetch their horses and leave.

"Not before time, either!" said Marcus. "I don't like the smell in the air. We'll find our arses in hot water if we stick around here much longer."

They made their way to the stables and saddled up while the fortress revelled in singing and drinking. They had no time to gather provisions and would have to find food on the road south. It was going to be a hard, hungry ride for Cunedag didn't want to waste a moment in reaching Colias and warning him of the northern conspiracy. But, before they had finished tightening the straps around their horses' middles, several armed warriors entered the stables. Brude was with them.

"Running off to your master already?" the newly appointed king of the Votadini said.

"I believe we've outstayed our welcome," said Cunedag, eyeing the hands of the warriors as they tensed near the hilts of their weapons.

"I'd say you were right," said Brude. "But I'm afraid I can't let you go after all. Not now you know so much about the rebellion and its plans."

"I mean you no misfortune, Brude," said Cunedag. "But you've made it clear that my place isn't here. I must return home."

"Oh, Cunedag," said Brude. "You *are* home. And home is where you will stay. Take their weapons."

This last was addressed to his warriors who stepped forward to disarm Cunedag and his men who could only stand helpless.

"Take them south of the fortress and dispatch them," Brude instructed his men. "I won't have their blood spilled in the home of our mother."

"Brude, I am your brother!" Cunedag yelled as his hands were bound behind him with rope. "Don't do this!"

"You *were* my brother," said Brude as he turned to leave the stable. "But if you truly considered yourself kin, then you would support me in my fight against Rome."

Cunedag swore as he and his men were manhandled out of the stables and led to the main gate. Nobody seemed to notice that they were being taken away and even the guards at the gate watched in dumb acceptance as they were led through it and down the main approach. Cunedag wondered if Brude had briefed them on his treacherous plan.

They weren't taken far. Their captors were passing a mead skin around and were keen to get back to the festivities. A small, moonlit glade not much more than a league from the fortress rock seemed to serve. There were seven guards for the six prisoners. Even unarmed and bound, Cunedag knew that Brude had sorely underestimated them, and a smile spread across his face.

"Elffin," he said to his comrade in Latin, which he knew the guards wouldn't understand. "When I drop down, knock the guard to your left on his arse. Marcus, you do the same to the guard on your right. The rest of you, free yourselves while they attend to us. Then we overpower them as one, got it?"

"Shut your hole, Roman scum!" bellowed the lead guard.

Cunedag replied by dropping suddenly to one knee. As the man at his side looked down at him in confusion, his men, well-trained to following his orders to the letter, acted immediately. Two guards went sprawling and, before they hit the dirt, Cunedag scooped his bound wrists beneath his legs and brought them up in front of him.

The guards knocked Elffin and Marcus to the ground and began beating and kicking them, keen to teach them a lesson before they killed them. They didn't notice the three remaining prisoners doing as Cunedag had done and wriggling their bound hands into a position of more use to them.

Cunedag sprang to his feet and looped his bound hands over the head of one of the guards while his men followed suit, hauling their captors to the ground. The remaining guards looked about in confusion at the quick Roman discipline which had so suddenly turned the tables on them.

Within seconds, Cunedag and his men had cut their bonds on the unsheathed blades of the men they grappled with and both Cunedag and one other had wrestled blades from them. Cunedag thrust the tip of his short British sword down into the throat of the man he had overpowered and then rounded on the leader of the group who gaped at him in fear, his own blade wavering in a trembling hand.

The guard made an admirable attempt, but surprise and mead got the better of him and, after a couple of parries, Cunedag worked his blade in behind his defence and gutted him, ripping his sword through his entrails and sending him to the ground with a kick.

The other guards suffered similar fates as, one by one, they were overpowered by Cunedag's men who freed themselves and turned their captors' weapons upon them. It was over in moments and Cunedag couldn't have been prouder of his men.

"Take what we need from them," he said, kicking the body of the lead guard, trying to swallow down the awful feeling at having killed several of his own people. "More's the pity they did not bring horses for we shall need them to reach the Wall. We make for Din Eil as soon as we are ready. We might be able to borrow some horses from Morleo's folk there."

"Din Eil?" Elffin said. "That's at least a day, even on horseback."

"Aye, and we're walking so let's move out," Cunedag commanded. "I just hope we receive a better reception among the Selgovae than we did among my own people."

They stripped the dead guards of weapons and leather but found no food on them. Their minds on the long, empty trek ahead of them, they took off at a jog, following their leader as he cut through the woods in a southerly direction.

Chapter 11

They jogged until the sun came up and could jog no more. The sweat making their tunicas cling to their backs, they gasped for air and looked around at the barren hills.

"How long before your brother discovers our escape and unleashes hell, Sir?" asked Marcus.

"He'll know his men never returned by now," Cunedag replied, "and has probably discovered their corpses too. I would think a detachment will be leaving Din Eidyn about now to apprehend us. Let's hope the bastards have one hell of a hangover."

"We'd better get under the cover of those trees there," said Elffin.

"My thinking exactly," said Cunedag. "We need a breather in any case, though the gods know we can't spare much time."

They hurried for the trees and sat for a brief time with their backs against the trunks, breathing the cool piny air and massaging their aching limbs.

"My throat's parched," said Elffin.

"Aye, too bad we didn't bring that mead skin with us," said Marcus.

"There's a tributary of the Aber Teu that flows down from the hills not far from here," said Cunedag. "And it's better if we move under the cover of the trees in any case. My brother's men will be following the road. Come on, time's up. Let's push on."

With barely stifled groans, his five men roused themselves and they hurried off through the wooded portion of the vale, following his lead.

Before long, they arrived at a thin stream that bubbled over the rocks as it wound its way through the woods. Gasping with relief, they knelt at its banks and scooped up handfuls of water which was still icy cold with spring melt.

Cunedag froze as his ears picked up noises that were not natural to the forest and the trickling stream. He could hear dogs howling. Men calling to one another. The tramp of horses.

"Quiet, all of you!" he hissed.

They each looked to one another as the noises approached.

"Tanit's tits, they came upon us fast!" hissed Marcus.

"We follow the river south," said Cunedag softly. "Once we reach the Aber Teu, we will be in Selgovae lands."

"But will your brother's men halt at the border?" Elffin asked.

"Most likely not," Cunedag admitted. "But if we can make it to men loyal to Morleo's father, then we might be safe."

"If they haven't succumbed to the same madness as the rest of the north," Marcus grumbled.

Keeping their heads low and trying to make as little noise as they could, they hurried along the riverbank. The rushing water widened as it wound its way south and the sounds of the hunt behind kept pace with them.

"Following our scent, no doubt," said Cunedag. "Let us cross the river and follow the east bank instead."

They waded through the water, holding their weapons above their heads to keep them dry, each of them wincing as the frigid river rose around their middles. Once they reached the other side, Cunedag led them in a jog to bring some warmth back to their legs.

The bank grew rocky and made for hard going the closer they got to the Aber Teu. They scrambled up over curling roots and hacked at stubborn bushes with their swords, knowing that they were losing precious ground. Sure enough, before the tributary reached its destination, Marcus spotted movement on the other side of the river.

"They've spotted us!" he said as an arrow sailed across the water and clattered against the stony east bank.

Cunedag swore as he saw mounted Votadini tribesmen through the foliage on the other side. The dogs were going berserk and straining at their leads, keen for blood.

"Keep moving!" he shouted.

More arrows whickered through the air, narrowly missing their marks. The dogs had been released; large Caledonian hounds, who splashed into the water and swam to the other shore.

"Watch it!" Cunedag yelled.

Most of the dogs attempted to climb the rocky bank, their claws scrabbling against wet rock. One of them was smart enough to go around where the bank dipped down a little and came upon their rear. Marcus yelped as it attacked him, clamping its jaws on his calf, its wicked-sharp teeth sinking down to the bone.

Marcus hammered at its snarling face with the pommel of his sword before turning its point on the dog and ramming the blade into its neck. The hound howled but did not release its prey.

Cunedag could see that Marcus needed help but two of the other dogs had succeeded in scrambling up the rocks and were nearly upon them. As one slavering face poked up above the rocks, Cunedag slammed his fist into its jaws, knocking it back down into the water. Two of his men, armed with a sword and a knife, dispatched the other which had made it up over the rocks a little further along. The rocks soon ran red down to the waterline with its blood.

Cunedag slithered down the embankment to aid Marcus and, between the two of them, they were able to kill the hound and prise its reddened jaws from Marcus's leg. The three remaining dogs were now wise to the shortcut their fallen companion had found and were swimming against the current to reach it. Soon they would be upon them and Cunedag didn't fancy their chances. There was only one possible escape to his mind, desperate though it was.

"Into the river!" he called to his men. "We let the current take us south!"

His men briefly glanced at the icy water rushing below them, but their hesitation was only for a moment. With loud splashes, they hit the water and hugged their knees as the current pulled them downstream.

Cunedag helped Marcus stand on his one good leg. The other was bleeding profusely, his breeches red below the knee. As the dogs clambered out of the water further down the bank, Cunedag grasped Marcus around the middle and, as one, they rolled off the rocks and hit the water.

Cunedag gasped as the coldness of the river hit him. It wasn't deep and his heels dragged against the stony bottom as he still held onto Marcus. The warriors on the opposite bank shouted and raged to see their prey floating away from them and followed them along the riverbank, shooting occasional arrows at them. Cunedag knew they would have to increase their speed if they were to put any distance between them.

"Drag yourself along," he said to Marcus. "Use your good leg to push. We have to catch up to the others."

He was concerned by the paleness of his comrade's face and could tell that he had lost a lot of blood. The wound would need binding, but the coldness of the water should stem the blood loss at least a little.

"Push, Marcus!" he said. "Push!"

They struggled through the water, drifting a few feet and then shoving themselves further as they were swept around bends through mild rapids. The shouts of their pursuers receded into the distance as they struggled to push through the dense greenery, hindered by the trees and bushes.

When he judged that they had lost their pursuers, and when he could no longer feel his arms or legs due to the cold, Cunedag ordered his men out of the river. They clambered ashore, their teeth chattering and their bodies trembling. Marcus was in a bad way and Elffin bound his injured leg with strips torn from his tunica, his shaking hands making the job a difficult task.

"We must press on," said Cunedag. "For the sake of our own bodies at least. If we sit around here too long, we'll freeze and night is fast approaching."

With weary abandon, the group of survivors stamped their feet, rubbed their arms and blew on their fingers as they desperately tried to get some warmth back into their extremities. Cunedag was beyond proud of his men. He had handpicked these five members of his turma for he knew their loyalty and perseverance knew no bounds. They had been on the move without food for nearly a full day and still obeyed his orders without question.

They took turns supporting Marcus who hobbled along as best he could. Night had fallen by the time the river joined the Aber Teu and, although they had warmed up a little, their clothes still clung to them and were bitterly cold at the slightest breeze. They moved along the north bank of the Teu and crossed the bridge at the ruined fort of Trimontium.

This was where Cunedag had spent the night of his first journey south at the age of twelve, seemingly a lifetime ago. There was no time to kindle a fire and scavenge for food this time and he found himself missing even the company of the ill-tempered Beliatus.

Skirting the ruins, they finally began their ascent to Din Eil, still unsure how they would be received. Whatever the Selgovae's position, Cunedag couldn't press his men on any further. They were freezing, starving and exhausted. Even a prison cell would ensure food and rest and that was all that occupied the minds of the six weary fugitives as they hailed the sentry at the gate.

They were admitted without immediately being pounced on, so Cunedag took that as a good sign. King Tasulus was at table in the Great Roundhouse and the fugitives could have wept with relief at being admitted to its warm interior where the smell of roasting meat drove their senses wild.

King Tasulus even seemed pleased to see the men who had so recently accompanied his son to Din Eil and provided immediate medical attention for Marcus while the others were invited to eat and drink and tell their tale to his assembled household. They listened with deep concern as Cunedag told them everything that had occurred in the lands of their northern neighbours.

"This is deeply troubling news you bring to us, Cunedag mab Etern," said King Tasulus. "Although not altogether unexpected."

"Then you too have been approached by the Novantae?" Cunedag asked, eager to learn where King Tasulus stood.

The king nodded gravely. "They arrived not two days after you left. I made it clear to them what I thought of any foolish notions of rising against Rome and they slunk back to their homeland cursing me for an old fool. Since then, their incursions into our territories have grown bolder. No longer is it the work of common cattle thieves. Now it is warbands who raid my lands, seeing me as much their enemy as Rome. My son rode for Eboracum as soon as the Novantae envoys departed to bring word to your shared foster-father of their plans."

"I am glad he did," Cunedag said. "For they are now forewarned but the conspiracy is graver than what Morleo knows, I fear. As we speak, my brother is mustering the

Votadini for war, joined by his new allies from the north. I must ride for the Wall at once. Have you horses you can spare?"

"Of course, my boy," said Tasulus. "But you are half dead with exhaustion! Rest here for the night. Eat well and sleep, at least for a few hours. I will have horses prepared for you at daybreak, the fastest I can spare."

"My thanks, my lord."

They ate heartily but drank sparingly, knowing they had a long ride ahead of them. Before they bedded down in one of the roundhouses, Cunedag told Marcus that he was remaining with the Selgovae. "You're not up to the ride. I want you to stay here until you are recovered, then ride south and rejoin us at the Wall."

"Damn that wolf from Hades!" Marcus cursed. "I'd rather be with you. I feel somewhat out of my element here."

"Think yourself lucky, you ungrateful swine," said Elffin. "You get to sleep and fill your belly to your heart's content while we must push on."

"Just don't drink too much of King Tasalus's mead," Cunedag cautioned. "I don't want you shaming me or the ala."

"And keep your hands off the Selgovae women," Elffin added. "Remember that ugly episode with that Carvetii woman at Brocavum?"

"That wasn't my fault," said Marcus. "How was I supposed to know she was married?"

"Would it have made a difference if you had?" said Elffin with a half-serious grin.

At the crack of dawn, as promised, King Tasulus had five horses saddled and laden with provisions. After a hasty breakfast of oat porridge, they mounted up and prepared to set out.

"I can't thank you enough for your help and hospitality, my lord," Cunedag said to Tasulus. "I will strongly commend you in my report once I reach the border. You have shown the courage that my own people could not, but I fear that the Selgovae now stand alone."

King Tasulus shook his head. "No, lad," he said. "We stand with Rome."

CHAPTER 12

They made the Wall in less than two days, nearly breaking the fine horses King Tasulus had given them, reaching the fort of Onnum in a lather of exhaustion. Cunedag immediately went to the prefect of the Ala First Sabiniana to deliver his warning that the northern tribes were rising.

Prefect Metellus, whom Cunedag knew as a lackwit thoroughly undeserving of the position privilege had granted him, had little time for the sensationalist babblings of a scruffy decurion who wasn't even in uniform. Cunedag was forced to explain at length why he was so shabbily dressed and exactly what he had been doing north of the Wall before he could get his message across, and he got the feeling that the prefect was eyeing him up as some sort of mad deserter.

Officious little prick, Cunedag thought as he was finally granted permission to relay his news which, predictably was met with incredulity. This was an administrator in the final stage of his *tres militiae* and no doubt had his mind set on returning to Rome and beginning a career in politics. Facing a full-scale rebellion was not something he had envisioned or wanted in his final year.

"Word must be sent along the Wall, Sir," Cunedag insisted. "The Dux Britanniarum must be notified. I don't know when the attack is coming but it will be soon."

"I am not required to take orders from a decurion," said Metellus scathingly.

"But they must be warned, Sir!"

"Don't raise your voice to me, decurion! I will decide what must be done regarding your … *story*. After I have verified it, of course."

"Did my duplicarius not pass through here with a similar story?" Cunedag asked. "A man named Morleo of the Selgovae."

"I can't say the name is familiar to me."

Cunedag was confused. Had Morleo crossed the border at a different gate? Why then had this fool of a prefect not been notified of what was going on? Morleo would have ensured the message was relayed along the Wall. Unless he encountered a similar pompous arse as this one. "He rode south several days ahead of me with news of Novantae raids on Selgovae lands, Sir," he explained.

"These northern tribes are always at each other's throats," Metellus replied. "Why should a few cattle raids north of the border concern us?"

"Because it is part of a much larger conspiracy, Sir! The Novantae recently abducted the wife and daughter of Praeses Colias. I was part of the force sent north to recapture them."

Metellus raised his eyebrows at this and Cunedag knew he had finally made an impression. "You are the praeses' foster son. I *have* heard of you." He rubbed his chin in thought. "Very well. It may be prudent to warn the other forts to be wary of an attack. I will dispatch riders to see that it is done."

"And the Dux, Sir?"

"I will inform him personally. I had intended to ride to Eboracum next week anyway. You may accompany me and present your news to him by my side."

"Next week?" Cunedag gaped. "The Dux must be notified immediately, Sir."

"I'm not having you running off telling everybody south of the Wall your wild stories about a second barbarian conspiracy. You're likely to have the whole province in a flap. I'm still not convinced this isn't all some great exaggeration. Even if the northern savages are plotting something, we are safe enough behind our wall, I assure you."

Cunedag could see that it was useless. This inexperienced aristocrat had enjoyed a career in peacetime. He didn't remember the last barbarian conspiracy and saw it as something along the lines of a fairytale to frighten young Roman recruits. That such soft incompetents should be allowed to run Rome's military!

He swallowed his rage and politely took his leave of Prefect Metellus before riding back to his men who were resting at the nearby milecastle. He found the optio in charge there to be much more receptive to his warning and had some choice words to say about Prefect Metellus.

"He's an arse-headed bureaucrat, if you'll pardon me saying so, Sir," said the optio. "Has about as much military sense as that donkey over there. It doesn't surprise me that he didn't take you seriously, Sir. It's alright for him, he won't be on the front line if the bastard Picts do attack. It's us that'll have to get our swords bloody if what you say is true and I don't fancy our chances much. Not if all the northern tribes descend upon us as one."

"I'm afraid it may come to that," said Cunedag. "Which is why the Dux must be warned, regardless of Metellus's orders. Do you have a horse I can take?"

The optio grinned. "I think we can manage that, Sir."

"Just say I stole it if you are questioned."

"As you say, Sir."

Cunedag's men would remain at the milecastle in the hope that their presence would mask his flight. He gave them orders to return to the Second Asturum at Cilurnum in three days' time where he would meet them once he had relayed his message to the Dux.

"Metellus will be after your skin for disobeying orders," Elffin said.

"Then he can ask the praeses for it!" said Cunedag as he swung himself up into the saddle and headed for the southern gate.

Three days later, Titus Gemellus, the Dux Britanniarum, poured wine into two cups and passed one to Cunedag who accepted it gratefully. He considered himself fortunate to have been granted an immediate audience with the Dux who held the chief military command in northern Britannia and was in charge of the limitanei troops who guarded its northern frontier. Cunedag had only seen him at a distance before, on parade grounds. Gemellus was a man approaching the winter years of his life but the iron hardness of a lifetime of Roman military discipline showed in his bearing.

"I must thank you for agreeing to receive me at such short notice, Sir," said Cunedag once they had toasted the emperor and taken a gulp of wine each. "I tried to reach you through Prefect Metellus of the First Sabiniana but he didn't take me seriously."

"Metellus is an incompetent buffoon," said Gemellus. "I suffer him because I must. His father is a man of some standing in Rome but were it up to me I wouldn't let him scrub the latrines of an auxiliary cavalry fort, let alone command an ala. As soon as I knew that you were Colias's foster son, I had you sent straight to me for I recently received your foster brother who also brought me troubling news from the north."

"Morleo, Sir?" Cunedag asked, brightening with the knowledge that his duplicarius had got through after all.

"The same. He told me that the Novantae are causing trouble, most likely connected with the attempted kidnapping of Colias's wife and daughter."

"Yes, Sir, but the Novantae aren't acting alone." He proceeded to tell the Dux all that had occurred in the lands of the Votadini and the conspiracy against Rome. Gemellus listened intently without interruption. He was an aging warhorse with more grey hair than black, but his tactical mind was still razor sharp.

"The involvement of the Caledonii and the Epidii is troubling," he said once Cunedag was finished. "They have long been enemies of the lowland tribes. It suggests a level of cooperation not seen since Gartnait united the north against us twenty years ago."

Cunedag was briefly surprised that Gemellus knew the name of the Pict who had formed a confederation during the Great Conspiracy but then realised that he had probably been a soldier even back then and had helped put down the revolt personally.

"I have also received troubling reports from the south," Gemellus continued. "The Saxons are being a nuisance again. Those forts along the south-eastern shore do little good when much of the trouble comes from within. My counterpart, the Comes of the Saxon Shore, has long employed Saxon auxiliaries, but they rebel at the slightest provocation while their countrymen sneak up the waterways in their boats, raiding and burning."

"Do you believe they are in league with this northern confederation as in the Great Conspiracy, Sir?"

"It's possible. And it's not just Saxons anymore. Franks, Angles, Jutes – tribes I'll wager you've never even heard of – crawl out of their godforsaken fens in Germania to plague our shores. Rome is weaker than ever, and our island is under attack on all sides. I must write to the magister militum and request reinforcement from the continent."

"Flavius Stilicho, Sir?" Cunedag asked for he had heard of Rome's highest military commander who had won the Battle of the Frigidus against the usurper Eugenius four years previously. Stilicho was the guardian of the fourteen-year-old Emperor Honorius and had recently married his daughter, Maria to him, further strengthening his ties to the purple.

Gemellus nodded. "He is currently in North Africa dealing with that traitor Gildo, but reports suggest that the whole business will be resolved soon. I believe he will be able to spare us a legion or two if Britannia is to be saved.

"What do we do until then, Sir?" Cunedag asked.

Gemellus gave him a wry smile. "Hold the bloody Wall."

Cunedag returned to his command at Cilurnum and busied himself as Rome's northern frontier prepared itself for attack. Spring turned to early summer and there were still no signs of movement from the north. The Dux intensified patrols, but all returned without harassment. Marcus returned to the unit, his leg healed, keen to rejoin his comrades and anxious of missing out on the battle to come. He brought news that raids on the Selgovae borders had ceased. It was as if their enemies were biding their time, waiting for the right moment to strike.

Eventually, before the Kalends of June, word was carried along the Wall of a large warband approaching its middle section.

The decurions of the Second Asturum assembled in the principia for a briefing by the prefect of the ala, a fair but stern man called Candidius whom Cunedag and his colleagues held in high esteem.

"They seem to be heading for Vercovicium," Candidius said. "The strongest part of the Wall."

"A natural move, Sir," said Cunedag. "The traitor Canaul was prefect of the Fourth Gallorum. He knows both

Vercovicium and Vindolanda inside and out and I'm willing to bet he's part of the warband."

"Then I sincerely hope you are provided with the opportunity to bring your foster brother to task," Candidius said.

"What are their numbers, Sir?" one of the other decurions asked.

"We don't know, but it's a good bet we're looking at something in the thousands."

There was an audible groan at this.

"The First Tungrorum hold Vercovicium against insurmountable odds and time is running out for them," Candidius continued. "The Fourth Gallorum will be coming up from Vindolanda plus the First Batavorum from Brocolitia. Other than that, we're their only hope so we must ride immediately."

"What of Onnum, Sir?" asked Cunedag, thinking of the pompous Prefect Metellus who hadn't believed his warning of a northern conspiracy. He'd take great pleasure in seeing how that arrogant fool coped when faced with a horde of howling tribesmen as they swarmed the Wall.

"The First Sabiniana is staying put for now," said Candidius. "In case the bastards try to swarm the Wall to the east. As it stands, two cavalry units and two infantry cohorts should be enough to see them off."

Cilurnum projected north of the Wall and the entire ala rode out of its western gate, following the Wall as the ground rose and fell in dramatic dips. This was the most uneven stretch of the Wall which crested a great rocky sill and if they weren't careful, they ran the risk of tiring out their horses before they even reached Vercovicium.

As they passed Brocolitia, they overtook the First Batavorum which was an infantry cohort, marching at a run on the other side of the Wall. They couldn't see them but could hear their cheers of encouragement while soldiers atop the Wall saluted the passing cavalry.

A cavalry charge always lifted spirits. There was something about the sight of four-hundred and eighty riders following their draco standards as the wind roared through their bronze mouths, red tails streaming out behind, that roused even the most jaded of hearts.

For Cunedag's part, he couldn't ignore the thrill of the moment. It was rare that the entire ala rode out together and this was the first time it had ridden into battle during his time in its ranks. But he knew that he might be riding against his own countrymen. Had the Votadini marched south with the other tribes to attack the Wall? Would he see his own brother in their ranks? Would he be forced to kill men he recognised?

As the Wall took a sharp turn south-west, the ala rounded the bend and could see the barbarian horde on the grassy plain. The air rang with their war chants and the bellowing of carnyxes while the black shafts of arrows and javelins streaked the air.

Candidus had not been wrong in his estimation of their numbers. There had to be over five-thousand tribesmen clustered around different standards denoting the various tribes of this hellish confederation. Cunedag squinted and tried to spot the dragon standard of the Votadini but was unable to.

The main focus of activity was on the fort's north gate. The mounted squadrons of the Fourth Gallorum had already arrived from Vindolanda and were harrying the enemy on its right flank.

"Looks like the brave riders of the Fourth Gallorum need a hand!" Candidius bellowed to the nervous laughter of the ala.

"Form up!" he yelled, the aeneatores blasting signals from their curved cavalry horns.

Cunedag led his men to the right wing, forming his turma into three decuriae. The horns blared the signal to charge, and they were off, hooves churning up clods of earth and grass, the wind rushing past them, stealing away the pant and gasp of the horses.

They came upon a detachment of the enemy who were assaulting the small gate to the east of the fort which guarded a small stream bubbling through a stone culvert. They had already rammed the gate open and put the soldiers to flight, but the onrush of Roman cavalry sent them fleeing back to the main body of their warband. The turmae on the left flank scored first blood, reddening their swords in the backs of the tribesmen as they fled.

Once the gate was won, the ala reformed and charged the main warband which was assailing the fort walls with ladders and long, hooked pikes with which they dragged screaming soldiers down from the stonework to break their bones on the ground where they were finished off with knives and swords.

The ala slammed into the left flank of the barbarians, ten turmae arranged in two rows, four riders deep, extending over four-hundred feet to curl around the tribesmen like an enveloping arm. The tribesmen tried to mount a defence but were too slow and undisciplined. Spears slammed into shields and skewered the necks and torsos of those less prepared. Men were shoved this way and that by the powerful flanks of cavalry horses, kicked by hooves, knocked to the ground and stamped to death.

"Hold the line!" Cunedag yelled to his men, his eyes on the wavering front line as it seeped into the mass of enemies. "Push but stay in formation!"

His spear tip lodged in the neck of one enemy who fell, wrenching it from his grasp. He let it go and drew his spatha, thirty inches of cold steel which he ripped through the enemies on both sides of him, hacking through spear shafts and slamming down on upraised bucklers as the panicked enemy tried to defend themselves.

They were painted in the traditional blue woad; swirling patterns enhancing muscle structure, depicting tribal markings and images of animals to lend ferocity and protection in battle. These couldn't all be Caledonii and Epidii, Cunedag thought, and he realised with grim understanding that even their lowland allies had painted themselves in the old way. It was as if his own people had gone back four-hundred years. This alliance with the tribes north of the Antonine Wall had dragged them back to their barbaric past. They were all Picts now; the dreaded painted people.

Stop it! he told himself. *Stop pretending you are one of them! You are a Roman, today of all days! These are not your people! These are the enemy, and it is your job to kill them!*

He swung his spatha down on an unprotected head and split the skull like a melon. The man screamed and went down under the hooves of the rider next to him. Sweat soaked the tunic beneath Cunedag's armour, and he could feel Bran wheezing beneath him as they pressed on, hacking, slashing, kicking and stamping.

The barbarians were retreating but, with no proper formations as in the Roman army, it was a slow and chaotic process as they scrambled over each other to get away. The Second Asturum, joined with the Fourth Gallorum, pushed them away from the smashed gates and they fled in a north-westerly direction to where their supply wagons stood on a green ridge against the pale sky.

Many of the tribesmen who had made their way into the fort were now cut off and were caught between two forces; the fort's defenders and the left wing of the Second Asturum who made short work of them, forcing themselves in through the arches and pressing them against the spears and swords of the infantry.

The first bout was over, and the enemy had been routed. For now.

CHAPTER 13

Candidius regrouped the ala and set men to smashing the ladders the enemy had abandoned and dispatching the wounded men and horses. The gates were hastily repaired with whatever timbers could be salvaged and the air rang with the sawing and hammering of men at frantic labour as they tried to ignore the screams of the wounded and dying as they were carried to the surgeons.

"We've lost seven men and six horses from our turma," Morleo reported to Cunedag as a wine skin was passed around.

Cunedag grimaced as the stinging wine hit the back of his parched throat. He hated to lose men, especially after having previously lost seven due to Canaul's kidnapping attempt. Those positions had only recently been replaced by green recruits, two of whom had fallen that day. But it could have been worse. A *lot* worse.

The First Batavorum finally arrived in a muck sweat from their march and seemed glad that they didn't have to throw themselves into a battle immediately. They were sent up to the walls to replace the defenders who had died in the initial attack. Cunedag didn't envy the infantry at times like these. The walls had to be cleared of the dead and sluiced clean of the blood which ran down the stonework like the meat juices from a gigantic set of teeth as it feasted on human flesh.

How many men has this wall devoured in its two-hundred years? He wondered. *How many lives have watered this stonework?*

Candidius called his decurions into the fort to report to him. One of them had been slain in the battle, necessitating a hasty promotion from the ranks. The turmae on the left flank, closest to the Wall, had suffered the worst of it but their losses had been slight considering the odds they had faced.

"We did well, men, but can't afford to rest on our laurels," Candidius told them. "Those bastard Picts aren't going anywhere for the time being and are no doubt planning a second assault as we speak."

"Do we attack them first, Sir?" Cunedag asked, hoping that Candidius wasn't going to order a charge.

"No, though they're most likely hoping we will. There's enough of them to make a mess of us and they hold the high ground. We wait here and meet them as they come to us. I want the ala arranged in one row in front of the northern gate, two riders deep. That way the Wall can give us cover."

They left the fort and mounted their horses while the soldiers atop the Wall restocked their supplies of arrows and javelins. Then, they waited. As the hours passed, the barbarians made enough of a nuisance of themselves to keep the Romans on their toes but never mustered a full attack. Scouts and messengers rode the length of the Wall for several miles to the east and west and reported that a small detachment of the enemy had broken off to mount an assault on the milecastle to the west. The Fourth Gallorum rode to see them off, reinforced by three turmae from the Second Asturum. All the while, small bands of Pictish cavalry charged at the Roman defenders, hurling javelins before wheeling back, reluctant to engage.

"Anybody else get the feeling we're being toyed with?" Cunedag said to Morleo.

"It's almost as if they want to keep our attention," his duplicarius replied.

"Which means they're probably attacking some other point on the Wall."

"Could they spare the men? How many more of them could there be?"

Cunedag looked out at the painted horde. "I don't know," he said. "I'd like to think that this is all they could muster for this foolhardy exercise but if the Votadini, Novantae, Attacotti, Caledonii and Epidii all contributed their warriors then we're facing but a fraction of the enemy."

It was a sobering thought, and he immediately regretted voicing it within earshot of his men. They needed their morale boosted, not dragged down to the mud that was still visibly reddened by the blood of their fallen comrades.

Candidius rode over to him, his tattered and torn cloak billowing behind him. "I've a mind we're being kept here on purpose," he said.

"Our thoughts exactly, Sir," said Cunedag.

"As we while away the day here staring at those smug bastards on the hill, more of them might be assaulting the Wall at other points. I want you to ride east, Cunedag. You will take the third, seventh and eighth turmae and reinforce any position that needs it. Send a messenger to me immediately if you spot the enemy."

"Sir?" Cunedag asked, scarcely able to believe the command he was being given.

"Yes, decurion, I'm giving you command of three turmae, now ride!"

"Yes, Sir!" Cunedag answered, snapping off a salute.

"Looks like rescuing the praeses' wife and daughter really does do wonders for a career," said Morleo. "You'll be the next Praefectus Alae at this rate, *Sir*!"

"A blessing or a curse?" Cunedag heard Elffin mumble. "Three turmae against unknown odds? We'll see how that works out."

"I don't know," said Marcus. "We may be landing on our feet here. Those bastards on the hill will see us leaving and the reduction in the fort's defence might persuade them to attack. Even with three turmae gone, the rest of the boys can handle them. I only hope there are enough of the enemy to the east to give us a good time!"

Cunedag ordered his men to hold their tongues as he gave the decurions of the seventh and eight turmae their orders.

They rode two abreast back towards Brocolitia and found the small garrison left in charge in a state of panic. Men were in the process of lighting the signal tower atop the principia.

"Smoke from the east!" a terrified young soldier bellowed. "Cilurnum calls for aid and we have none to send it!"

Cunedag dismounted and ran to the top of one of the gate towers. He froze as he saw a distant plume of smoke marring the horizon to the east. But it was far too much smoke to be from its signal tower.

He half ran, half stumbled down the stairs to where his men were waiting. "Cilurnum is burning!" he cried as he swung himself up into the saddle.

His men regarded him with disbelieving horror. Attacks on the Wall were one thing, but Cilurnum was their home and if it was burning, then the fight had not gone well.

They galloped the rest of the way, their horses gasping for air by the time they came within sight of the fort. Sure enough, several of the buildings were ablaze and dead bodies littered the ground outside the gates which had been smashed and then repaired, much in the way the gates to Vercovicium had been.

They rode within range of its walls and several arrows and insults were sent their way by the victorious conquerors who clamoured atop its walls to jeer at the fort's former residents. Cunedag detected a Gaelic flavour in their voices. "Attacotti," he hissed, the name more repugnant to him than those of any rebellious tribe.

After making a pass, he led his men back beyond the west gate where they drew up, out of range.

"Those bastards must have taken the fort not long after we departed," he told his men.

"They were probably waiting for us to ride out," said Elffin.

"Then it was all a ruse," said Marcus. "The attack on Vercovicium was meant to draw us away from Cilurnum. But why take a cavalry fort and then just hold it? Why haven't they marched south, pillaging and burning? They surely know that we'd be back and, by the looks of it, they only have fifty or so men. They can't possibly hold the fort once reinforcements arrive."

Cunedag frowned as he tried to think as a tribesman would. Marcus was right; taking a fort they could never hold made no sense.

"Unless …" he said. "Unless they are just holding the door."

"Come again, Sir?" asked Marcus.

"They are waiting for a much larger force," Cunedag explained. "There is currently a gap in the Wall's defences, meaning that a much larger warband can enter Britannia Secunda. And Cilurnum guards the Aber Tina."

Understanding dawned on his men as the strategic importance of holding Cilurnum, even just for a little while, was realised. The Wall crossed the Aber Tina to the east of Cilurnum, supported on four sturdy arches with a guard tower on each bank. With a friendly force holding the fort, the enemy could slip between the arches in boats and travel downriver, striking deep into Britannia Secunda.

Although the signal fires would soon be blazing the length of the Wall, Cunedag sent a rider back to Vercovicium to alert Candidius of the situation and a second rider east to ask Metellus to muster the First Sabiniana. "It will take time for reinforcements to arrive," he told his men. "Too much time. A barbarian warband might be marching upon us as we speak. Men, we need to take back Cilurnum!"

"We're cavalry, Sir!" Marcus protested. "We have no siege equipment."

"We don't need to besiege them," said Cunedag. "We most likely outnumber them so all we need to do is get inside the fort. I need thirty men for the task. The rest will keep the enemy's attention north while we climb the walls, sneak in and unbar the gates. They seem to be in a jovial mood so I think we can assume they've helped themselves to the wine stores, meaning that they will be careless."

The men stared at him, unwilling to protest but he could see the uncertainty in their eyes. They were tired and frightened and he was asking them to attack an enemy on foot who had barricaded itself behind walls. More than that; he was asking them to attack the Wall, the very same Wall they had spent a good portion of their lives defending.

"Rome's northern frontier stands open!" he barked, trying to summon the spirit of loyalty in them. "Our home has been overrun by savages! Now, I don't know about you boys, but I'm not going to let a bunch of greasy Gaels lord it over our barracks and our stables, eating our stores and drinking our wine! Cilurnum is ours and, by all the gods, I'm going to take it back! Now, who's with me?"

"I, Sir!" Marcus yelled.

"And I!" said Elffin.

A dozen or so volunteered, each one bolstering the courage of their fellows. Cunedag ordered several more who remained uncertain, handpicking a team of thirty, mostly drawn from his own turma for he needed men he could trust and who trusted him.

"We make another pass at the northern gate," he told them. "My team will break off and head down to the river. The rest of you, swing around and pass them again. That should keep them busy. We're going to be passing within arrow range so be careful. Ride hard and fast and stop for nothing. I want no heroics or dead men, understood?"

"Yes, Sir!" came the chorused reply.

They set off, kicking their horses into a gallop as they passed under the fort's walls. The Attacotti swarmed the ramparts and sent a hail of arrows and slingstones their way, but Cunedag and his men were too fast and the enemy either too drunk or disorganised to hit any of them. They settled for roaring insults at what they assumed to be an impotent cavalry unit making a futile gesture before their defences. They had to know that reinforcements had been sent for and didn't seem to care which told Cunedag that their own force was probably not far off.

They reached the bank of the Aber Tina which the great stone bridge spanned, its legs mossy and ivy strewn. Cunedag and his thirty men dismounted beneath the bridge and hobbled their horses, letting them drink from the river while the rest of the unit wheeled around to make another pass.

"It looks like the enemy are falling for it," said Cunedag. "That's good. We need as much time as possible to scale the walls."

"Speaking of which, Sir," said Elffin, glancing up at the bridge looking for any sign of Attacotti sentries. "At which point do you plan on scaling it?"

"We'll come upon its south-eastern corner and bring what we can from the old bath house to aid us."

The old bath house was an isolated structure beyond the fort's walls which had fallen into disuse after a newer set of baths had been built adjoining the praetorium. Like the abandoned vicus which clustered around the fort's southern walls, it was little more than a ruin, its timbers and broken masonry overgrown and forgotten.

Taking their oval shields with them and armed with nothing more than their spathas and daggers, they set off along the riverbank. The bodies of several Attacotti warriors were strewn across the ground, one half-submerged in the water, an arrow jutting from his back.

"Looks like they had the same idea we did," said Marcus as they jogged on, his voice muffled by the cover of his shield. "Let's hope we have better luck than they did."

As they emerged from the shadow of the bridge, they had technically entered Britannia Secunda and Cunedag briefly considered how tenuous the border was. Entering the empire was as simple as walking under a bridge. It was a testament to the fact that Rome's borders were held not by stone and mortar but by men such as he and his comrades. Men who would give their lives in its defence.

They reached the derelict bathhouse and succeeded in finding a selection of timbers that would serve as something to climb on in order to reach the tops of the walls. He hurried his men along, knowing that the others would be galloping past the northern gate by now and the enemy must surely notice that there were fewer of them. If they didn't get inside the fort quickly, the Attacotti might start looking in their direction.

They carried their timbers to the feet of the eastern wall, not far from its southern corner and hastily constructed a platform four feet high. Cunedag had two of his men stand atop the platform, holding their shields above their heads. Then, in pairs, the rest of them scrambled up.

He and Elffin went first, their shields slung over their backs. By standing on the shields of the men below them, they were just able to grasp the parapet and haul themselves up and over it.

They immediately unslung their shields and drew their spathas, one facing north, the other south as the next pair of soldiers scrambled up. From the walls, they could get a better view of the destruction. Two barrack blocks and a stable were blazing merrily in the south-western quarter of the fort which had been abandoned. The smoke rose thick there and every so often the crack of an overheated roof tile popped loudly.

The Attacotti, drunken, victorious fools that they were, clustered on the northern wall, no doubt enjoying the show Cunedag's riders where giving. He grinned as more and more of his men clambered onto the wall. There were no sentries, but they would have to get to ground level quickly so as not to be spotted on the walls.

They moved south to the corner tower, entered it and hurried down the stairs to ground level. The bodies of the fort's defenders were strewn in between the buildings, many having been knocked down from the walls or tossed down there by their killers. It was a grim sight and Cunedag's men said nothing as they quickly followed him westwards between the barrack blocks.

Anger boiled in Cunedag's breast, and he knew his men shared it. Every person they had known who had not ridden out with them had been butchered and it wasn't just the soldiers. He spotted old Publius the baker among the dead, along with his dog, both skewered by a spear. The pretty slave girl from the praetorium lay in the mud, her throat cut and her tunica up around her middle. Even the young lad who carried water had not been spared, the back of his head split open by a heavy blade.

"Bastards ..." he heard Marcus utter under his breath, despite the need for silence. "Utter bastards."

"Hush, Marcus," Cunedag said to him. "We'll avenge them. We'll paint the walls with the blood of their killers."

Chapter 14

They neared the blazing barracks and stables and were forced to ascend the wall once more to avoid the searing heat. They would come upon the western gatehouse from the south and let the rest of the men in who by now must have completed their pass and were mustering somewhere out of range to the west.

The heat of the burning buildings scorched them as they hurried along the wall and the acrid smoke burned in their lungs, but it at least shielded them from being seen from the north. They followed the wall along, through its guard towers and entered the western gatehouse.

Finally, somebody spotted them. A lone sentry stood atop the wall between the two towers, gazing at the cavalry who were reforming to the west. The clash of hobnails on stone made him turn around, gripping his spear in surprise.

Cunedag was too fast for him. He battered the sentry's spear aside with his shield and thrust with his spatha, sliding the blade in between his ribs, sheathing it in the man's guts.

From the rampart, Cunedag could see two more sentries at ground level near the gate. They were playing with dice on the cobbles, their spears propped against a nearby workshop.

"Take three men and finish those two off," he said to Marcus. "Before they can raise the alarm."

The soldiers hurried down as silently as they could but, as they emerged at the base of the tower, one of the sentries spotted them and, with a cry, grabbed his spear. His comrade, alerted by his movement, tried to turn around but wasn't fast enough and cried out as Marcus gutted him with his spatha. The first sentry was quickly overcome and hacked down, his blood raining on the cobbles where his dice still lay.

"Right, men!" Cunedag said. "I want a defensive line fifty feet from the gate, four men wide and three deep. The same to the north between the wall and the stables there."

Marcus and one other soldier grabbed the spears of the men they had just slain. Along with the one belonging to the sentry atop the rampart, that made three spears divided over a couple of small shield walls and not a javelin between them. Hardly a good Roman defence, thought Cunedag, but it would have to do until they got the gate open and let the rest of their comrades in.

As the two defensive lines hastily assembled themselves, he set the rest of the men to unbarring the gates. Once they were open, he borrowed one of the spears and sent Elffin out with a torn cloak attached to it with instructions to wave it like a madman so the rest of his soldiers could see it.

"We've got company, Sir!" he heard Marcus yell as soon as Elffin was gone.

"Shit!" Cunedag said as he turned to see a group of warriors converging on their position at the middle of the via principalis. He had hoped to be undetected for longer than this, but he supposed somebody had heard the slaying of the sentries. Soon they would have the whole Attacotti force descending upon them. They had to hold long enough for the rest of his men to reinforce them.

"Hold position!" he yelled. "Let them come to us!"

Several javelins were thrown and were embedded in the shields of Cunedag's men before the Attacotti rushed them. Bucklers slammed against oval cavalry shields, iron bosses scraping as swords and long knives tried to work their way in. Feet slid on the cobbles as each side tried to gain ground against the other.

One of Cunedag's men fell to a Gaelic blade, blood spurting from his opened neck to run down his shield. His body was quickly hauled away and a fresh man took his place in the shield wall. As more Attacotti warriors appeared from the northern part of the fortress to join the fray, Cunedag knew they couldn't hold out against such odds for long.

The streets heading east and north were jammed with warriors, his own men four soldiers wide, shield rims scraping the walls on either side as they tried to hold back the press of enemy warriors on both fronts. At last, to his great relief, he heard a cavalry horn bellowing to their rear. His men had arrived! They were saved, at least for the time being.

"Push!" Cunedag yelled, lending his weight to the rear of his men, shoving the man in front of him forward with his shield. "Give our boys some room!"

The cavalry dismounted at the gate and rushed into the fort to aid their comrades. The extra press of bodies as more and more men flooded in through the gate pushed the enemy back and boosted the morale of those in the shield wall no end. They took up a war cry; "Roma! Roma! Roma!" as those who had dared sack a Roman fort were forced away from the gate, leaving more room for the rest of Cunedag's soldiers to swarm in.

Eventually, realising that they were now the ones who were outnumbered, the Attacotti gave up the fight in the streets and headed back to the northern part of the fort, some darting between the barrack blocks while others headed for the towers to mount a defence atop the walls.

"Hold!" Cunedag roared to his men as they made to pursue. This couldn't turn into a disorganised rout, or he would lose more men than he had to. They would move in an organised fashion, from street to street, sweeping them clean of the enemy like vermin.

He divided his men back into what was left of his three turmae. None were at full strength anymore, but he took some satisfaction in knowing that he had more than enough men now to clear the fort of Attacotti warriors and reclaim it for Rome. What happened after that, he tried not to dwell on.

He sent one turma along the via principalis to the eastern end of the fort and led his own to the middle, just below the principia, leaving the remaining one by the western gate. The left and right turmae would move north, following the walls, clearing them of enemies while his own would search the principia. In this fashion, they would sweep the fort as one, pushing the enemy towards the northern gate where they would converge and slaughter them all.

The enemy were panicked. They knew they had lost the fort and had failed in their mission. Cunedag's men marched, shields overlapping, along the streets and walls, stabbing and hacking at any Attacotti who dared get too close. They moved like a machine, Roman military discipline at its most ruthless.

They found the principia empty but for the bodies of those who had died defending it, the signs of smashed barricades telling of a valiant last stand in the courtyard which had ended in butchery. The praetorium was likewise deserted, the bodies of Candidius's slaves strewn across the bloodstained mosaics. As they passed the barrack blocks, every contuburnium was checked for hiding warriors, but none were found. The Attacotti tribesman had all fled to the northern gate where they were mounting a futile defence from its towers and walls.

"We've got the bloody bastards pinned!" said Elffin as they marched up the via praetoria that led to the northern gate. "Nowhere to run!"

"It's time to finish them and avenge Cilurnum," said Cunedag as the tramp of hobnailed sandals could be heard to the left and right of them. At each end of the street, between the barrack blocks, he could see the other two turmae marching and up on the walls they marched two abreast, four or five deep. Cavalrymen were not used to marching on foot like legionaries, but they were performing admirably. They were coming upon the enemy from all sides and the steady stamp of approaching death must be wreaking havoc on their nerves, he considered with a grim smile.

"Advance!" he bellowed, and his men broke into a steady jog.

The Attacotti yelled in defiance, some shooting arrows and hurling the last of their javelins. A few sling stones bounced off shields, but it was a pitiful effort. There weren't much more than twenty of them left and they knew they were done for. The northern gate remained closed at their backs. The Attacotti had made the decision to stand their ground. There would be no running and they wouldn't get far on foot in any case. They howled their death cries and charged at the advancing Romans.

"Roma!" yelled the triumphant voices of Cunedag's men as they pushed the Attacotti against the gates, stabbing and slicing, hacking them down and stamping anything that writhed on the cobbles.

The fallen of Cilurnum were avenged in a bloodbath at its northern gate. The men on the walls stormed the gate towers, stabbing and hurling its defenders down to join their dead comrades. It was over. Cunedag's men roared their victory. Every last Attacotti tribesman had been slain and the fort was theirs. They were dog tired but had little time to relax. Cunedag wanted the fort in operational order as soon as possible for the gods alone knew how many more tribesmen might be descending upon them at any moment.

"If I have judged our enemy correctly," he said to his assembled officers, "then the river is our weakest point. After all, we snuck under the bridge and retook the fort. I don't want to give them the same opportunity, nor do I want any boats slipping past to attack some other poor bastards downriver. We are the front line, men, and we *will* hold it!"

"Man the bridge then, Sir?" said one of the other decurions. "But what if they attack the northern gate?"

"We must be prepared for any eventuality," Cunedag replied. "Dividing our forces is dangerous but I am confident we can reinforce any position as needed. I want plenty of ammunition up on that bridge to hurl down on them. Masonry, timbers, even prise up some of the cobblestones. Anything that will give a man a nasty headache. Whatever bows we can find are to be put into the hands of the best archers among us. They will take position on the northeast corner of the fort to cover both the bridge and the northern gate."

There was much to organise, and the men set to it with weary determination. The burning buildings were doused with water from the river and the horses were brought within the fort and hastily stabled. Everybody was hungry and thirsty, so food and wine were fetched from the stores and passed around to be consumed by grateful mouths. The severely wounded were taken into the hospital but those with only minor injuries were quickly patched up and set to work alongside their comrades. The dead were dragged out through the south gate and tossed into the ditch while the bodies of the fort's residents were respectfully laid in the courtyard of the principia to be buried or cremated according to their individual beliefs at a more opportune time.

They worked hard and within the hour they had the fort in some sort of semblance of its former self, battle-scarred and undermanned through it was. Spears and arrows had been collected and stockpiled on the walls within easy reach of the defenders. Baskets and pails of rocks and other projectiles were placed at regular intervals along the bridge.

Daylight was fading as Cunedag made a final inspection of the defences. It was as he was overseeing the scant force of archers on the northeast corner that a lookout in one of the gate towers cried the alarm.

"Lone horseman, Sir!" he called as he ran along the rampart from the tower. "Took one look at us and then disappeared over that rise."

"A scout," said Cunedag. "He'll have seen that it's no longer his own people who hold the fort. They'll be coming soon, boys! Prepare yourselves and remember your orders!"

There was a mumbled 'yes, Sir!' as he headed east along the rampart to carry the news to the men on the bridge personally. *Great Mother, where are our reinforcements?* He wondered. His riders would have reached Onnum and Vercovicium ages ago and *somebody* should be marching to their aid. He had hoped for cavalry which would reach them quicker, but even infantry units should be close by now.

Night had fallen before lookouts to the east and west reported enemies approaching. A warband was headed straight for the fort while several boats could be seen paddling downriver towards the bridge.

"Gods, they mean to attack us on two sides at once!" Cunedag muttered. It was the worst scenario he had imagined. He simply didn't have the men to hold the fort against a double-pronged attack. "Keep to your stations until told otherwise," he said to the men on the bridge. "Wait until those buggers are beneath you and then rain hellfire down on them."

They shouted their assent, trying to drown out their fear with enthusiasm. His men were dog tired, with red raw eyes and soot-smeared faces. How much more could they take?

Come on, Candidius, Cunedag thought. *Or Metellus, for that matter. Send us our salvation.*

Thousands of torches prickled the hills as the enemy warband approached the north gate. They were mostly mounted and Cunedag realised that they had hoped to pass through the fort unhindered to lend support to the warriors who were moving downriver in the boats as they struck into the lands below the Wall. He was glad to be a thorn in their side and foil their plan but how long they could keep it up, he didn't know.

"Save your arrows until they are close enough," he told his archers. "Gods know we don't have many of them."

He was pleased that the warband had not come prepared to take the fort and, in a curious twist of fortune, the attackers were now in a similar situation Cunedag and his men had been in mere hours ago; a cavalry force attacking a fort. They may get the same idea and try to pass under the bridge as Cunedag had done, but they would find his men ready for them if they did. He almost *wanted* them to try it.

The enemy horsemen wheeled around in an arc, sending a few slingstones and arrows up at the walls which fell pitifully short. Cunedag ordered a volley in response which struck a couple of riders who spilled from their saddles, wild hair flailing as they fell. Drawing up well out of range, they dismounted and attacked again on foot, running up to the walls with ropes in their hands.

The defenders marshalled on the north wall and Cunedag was tempted to call for the men on the bridge to reinforce the position, but the boats were not far off now, and he was forced to leave them where they were.

His archers sent as many arrows as they could into the mob of tribesmen as they clustered at the feet of the walls but had to lean out over the parapet to aim which made them vulnerable to enemy missiles.

"Morleo!" he cried to his duplicarius. "Send the archers to the bridge and bring twenty men to replace them. Bows can do no more good here."

Morleo saluted and Cunedag watched as his archers hurried along the walls towards the bridge. He'd rather give them the chance to feather the approaching boats with arrows in exchange for twenty extra men on the fort walls.

The first of the enemy tribesmen were reaching the parapet to meet the eager blades of the defenders. It was pure attrition. The enemy outnumbered them nearly ten to one. The first to scale the walls would undoubtedly die, but they had enough men to keep climbing until every last one of Cunedag's brave soldiers was dead. The only advantage the defenders had was that the enemy had not come prepared for a siege. They had no ladders or the ghastly long pikes their brethren had used at Vercovicium to pluck men from the walls. They did have ropes though, and they spread themselves out and scrambled up the wall like ants, looping coils of rope around crenelations with the expert hands of men accustomed to horse wrangling.

All Cunedag's men had to do was hold out for as long as they could. That was all Rome asked of them. They swung their spathas and stabbed with spears at anything that poked above the stonework, sending screaming men tumbling from the walls. They desperately cut through every rope they could but there were simply too many points along the wall to defend at once.

Cunedag hurled himself into the thick of it, shoulder to shoulder with his companions, hacking at necks and thrusting at abdomens. Lopped heads tumbled to earth, blood ran in rivulets across the rampart and still they kept coming.

The enemy losses were staggering as the dead piled up at the feet of the walls, filling the ditch and providing their living comrades something to tread on. But then, with a blasting of horns, they retreated.

"They're falling back!" Elffin cried. "We've done it!"

Cunedag squinted through the sweat that ran down from under his helm as the enemy pulled back into the darkness like ghosts. He did not share Elffin's enthusiasm. This retreat seemed too sudden, too rehearsed. Their losses were appalling, true, but they had retreated as one, without question.

He looked east at the moonlit river and saw the dark shapes moving silently down it.

The boats were coming.

CHAPTER 15

"Hold the position here," Cunedag said to Elffin. "In case they attack the fort again. I'm going to the bridge."

Braziers flickered in the night atop the bridge and Cunedag ordered the archers to wrap strips of cloth soaked in oil around the necks of their arrows before lighting them and sending them sailing through the air like falling stars to light up the approaching enemy. Blazing arrows sizzled as they landed in the water while one or two embedded themselves in the boats before being quickly doused. One man screamed as an arrow thudded into his shoulder and set his hair and tunic alight. His comrades heaved him over the side to thrash about in the water.

"Aim for the banks!" Cunedag commanded as the archers nocked a second volley. "Light them up!"

Fire arrows streaked in an arc from the bridge to land in the bushes and trees on either side of the river. Flames licked at the foliage and long grass, illuminating the boats and glinting off cold steel gripped in the hands of the men who had come to kill.

"Now, pick your targets!" Cunedag said, grinning as he saw the faces of the enemy, well-lit and well within range.

A volley of arrows thudded into the first few boats, riddling their occupants with feathered shafts. Small bucklers were held up to shield themselves, but one boat drifted wildly, every warrior it carried slain. The other boats picked up the pace, paddling harder for the legs of the stone bridge. Nearly out of arrows, the men atop the bridge discarded their bows in favour of other ammunition.

"Wait until they're nearly beneath us!" Cunedag cried. "Hold!"

Men gripped cobbles and chunks of masonry. Cunedag helped a soldier heave a massive cornerstone up onto the rampart and they both held it there, waiting for his signal.

Peering over the rampart, Cunedag could see the prows of the small hide-covered boats approaching the legs of the bridge. "Now!" he yelled.

As one, they dumped their load on the boats below. The cornerstone slipped out of Cunedag's grip and tumbled through the air to land in the middle of one of the boats, smashing it in two and dragging several warriors to the bottom of the river.

The night resounded with the heavy splashes of stone hitting water and human flesh amid the cries of men being pummelled into pulp. The water was a churning confusion of smashed boats and bodies, some dead, some living. The arches of the bridge became clogged with wreckage as the survivors tried to swim to the shore through the floating corpses of their brethren.

The soldiers atop the bridge cheered to see their enemy clambering to the shore, sodden, wounded and beaten.

"Sir, look!" yelled one of the men.

Cunedag glanced in the direction he was pointing and uttered a foul curse. The remainder of the warband that had attacked the fort had remounted their horses and were galloping around the north-eastern corner of the fort which was now undefended and were headed for the bridge.

"Archers!" he yelled.

"We've hardly any arrows left, Sir!" one of them yelled back.

Cunedag swore again and they watched impotently as the stream of horsemen galloped along the riverbank and began to pass under the bridge, two abreast, shields held overhead to protect themselves from the remainder of the missiles the men atop the bridge hurled down on them.

The survivors from the boats salvaged what weapons they could and joined their mounted comrades in a charge south, passing beneath the Wall and entering the ruined vicus. They had done it. The barbarians had entered Britannia Secunda and there wasn't a damned thing Cunedag or any of his men could do to stop them.

But, the Great Mother be praised, the barbarians had a bloodlust on them that demanded to be sated and they turned on the fort, swarming its southern gate.

"The mad bastards really want to kill us," said Morleo as Cunedag called for all the men on the bridge to move along the southern portion of the wall to meet the enemy.

"Aye, we've killed enough of them, and they're not disciplined enough to stick to their original mission," he replied.

"Still enough of them to keep us busy," Morleo replied.

Cunedag smiled grimly and said nothing. Morleo was good at keeping his spirits up under dire circumstances though his words were an understatement. The enemy would try to scale the walls again and his own men were exhausted and severely depleted. How much longer could they hold out?

He called for the men on the fort's northern walls to join them at the south gate and they prepared to mount a last-ditch defence. He estimated he had only sixty or so left and precious few weapons. This could be it. Their last stand.

The ropes came coiling out of the darkness like vipers to clutch at the crenelations. As before, the defenders hacked through what they could but, before long, the shaggy-headed tribesmen began to appear at the parapet, slavering for death like blood-mad wolves. Cunedag roared his defiance along with his men. If this was to be their last fight, then, by all the gods, they would make it a good one.

The sound of the horns rolling across the hills sounded like the trumpets of heralds come to usher them into the afterlife. It took a while before Cunedag realised that it was not just in his own head, but the others heard it too.

He levered the blade of his spatha out of a tribesman's skull and let him slide off the rampart which was now slippery with blood and turned his head. The enemy had heard it too and a sense of fear gripped them.

"They've come!" Cunedag said. "Reinforcements from the west!"

A great cheer went up from the remaining defenders atop the walls. Bloodied weapons were raised, and the barbarians seemed to shrink from the fort, sensing defeat. Gazing west, Cunedag could see the streaming dracos of a dozen turma galloping towards them, the standards of the Second Asturum and the Fourth Gallorum following close behind. They had come!

He sent men to open the west and south gates to allow the cavalry to pass through the fort and reach the enemy on the other side of the wall. The tribesmen might storm the south gate, but it would only be for a few moments before they were ridden down by Roman cavalry.

As it happened, few of the tribesmen tried it. The southern gate swung open but the enemy was dispersing, knowing that the battle was lost. Their own cavalry mounted their horses and took off towards the bridge, attempting to circumvent the fort, but Candidius, who rode at the head of the column, had anticipated that, and had sent two turmae to meet them as they passed back under the bridge. The rest of the cavalry passed through the fort in a long chain, two horses wide, hooves clattering against the cobbles.

The men on the walls cheered them on as they passed through the gatehouse beneath them and gave chase to the enemy who were fleeing towards the trees to the south. It was over. They were saved and Cilurnum remained in Roman hands.

Cunedag gave a great sigh of relief and wiped his bloodied spatha on the hem of his cloak before sheathing it and heading down to ground level. Candidius was near the gatehouse, instructing the last of his troops in the pursuit of the enemy.

"By Christ, we got here in the nick of time, didn't we?" he said as he saw Cunedag approach. "Glad to see you're still alive, Decurion. Though it looks like you've had a hot few hours."

"Damn near took us down to our last few men, Sir!" said Cunedag, saluting his superior. "I can't thank you enough for your timely arrival."

Candidius dismounted and approached him. "It is I who should be thanking you, Cunedag. Thanks to you, we still have our home. How you were able to take this fort with three turmae and then hold it against a second warband we knew nothing about is a tale I want to hear at length over much wine."

"The battle at Vercovicium, Sir?"

"Won. They had another few runs at us and then buggered off back north. Probably turning west with a mind to cross the Wall here. They'll have a nasty surprise!"

"Then the whole thing was a diversion," said Cunedag.

Candidius nodded. "Designed to draw us from Cilurnum and leave it vulnerable." He looked around at the ruins of their home, his face grave. "Were there any survivors? Of the ones we left behind, I mean?"

Cunedag shook his head. "No, Sir."

"I thank God that my wife and children are in Eboracum. Well, you boys gave them a bloody nose they won't forget. And they're not the only ones. But why did you not send to Onnum for reinforcements?"

"I did, Sir. They never came."

Candidius's face coloured at this. "Didn't come, by Christ! What the hell is that fool Metellus playing at? We'll get to the bottom of this soon enough, mark me. The dux is on his way north with the Sixth Victrix. He'll want a full investigation and if anything is found amiss, you can count on some heads rolling."

Under other circumstances, Cunedag might have taken great pleasure in the prospect of Metellus getting his just deserts, but he found that he was too tired to even raise a smile. Too many men had died. Too many lives wasted. And the enemy was still out there, still strong.

Part III

"Next spake Britain clothed in the skin of some Caledonian beast, her cheeks tattooed, and an azure cloak, rivalling the swell of ocean, sweeping to her feet: "Stilicho gave aid to me also when at the mercy of neighbouring tribes, what time the Scots roused all Hibernia against me and the sea foamed to the beat of hostile oars." – Claudian, *On the Consulship of Stilicho*

Chapter 16

Two weeks later, at the port of Segedunum on the eastern terminus of the Wall, Cunedag and Morleo strolled through the vicus towards the amphitheatre. They were both dressed in their parade ground finery, polished to a high sheen. In fact, the entire settlement and fort had been whipped into shape. Prostitutes and beggars had been chased to the outskirts, the refuse and animal dung swept away, and every soldier was on high alert with scrubbed mail, polished cuirasses and helms, re-dyed crests and re-painted shields.

Flavius Stilicho was coming.

At first it was thought that he'd merely send reinforcements. A few cohorts to bolster the Wall garrisons, maybe some naval vessels to fight the Saxons in the south. A legion if they were lucky. But when word reached Britannia that the great Stilicho, hero of the Battle of the Frigidus and guardian of the young emperor himself, was personally accompanying a massive force to fight Britannia's enemies, morale in the garrisons reached heights unseen in a generation.

Cunedag and Morleo had been tasked with taking the prisoners captured after the siege of Cilurnum to Segedunum to be sold at the market where boats would take them to Gaul or Hispania. Cunedag had requested the task personally as he knew that Colias and Vala would be there as part of the reception for Rome's *magister militum*.

Candidius had gladly granted his request. Nothing was to be denied the heroes of the Wall who were still the toast of the north. The dux himself had presented Cunedag with a harness of three bronze phalerae depicting a lion's head, a cavalryman and the image of Emperor Honorius during a ceremony in front of the whole ala during which the third, seventh and eighth turmae received laurel wreaths for their dracones, though there were few men left in each who had survived the battle.

The small metal discs clinked against Cunedag's mail shirt as they walked towards the market stalls that clustered around the walls of the amphitheatre. A deluge of rivalling voices and smells drifted up as they sold hot foods, spices, religious talismans and incense. The arena itself had once rung with the clash of arms and its sand had soaked up the blood of generations of gladiators but Christian opposition to the games in recent years had called a halt to the bloodshed and now the arena was largely used for theatre, animal shows, public executions and the slave market.

The prisoners were mostly Novantae with a sprinkling of Caledonii and Epidii and Cunedag had discovered, to his great annoyance, that there were a few Votadini among them too, confirming his fears that his own people had been part of the attack. One of them – a large man with a reddish shock of hair and part of an ear missing – had spat at him upon learning who he was. Cunedag had struck him across the face for his insolence and split a knuckle in doing so. The gash in his skin still pained him.

They entered the tiered seating area of the amphitheatre and found the praeses with his wife and daughter in what passed as the box or seat of honour. Vala waved to them, and they headed over, taking their seats with their adoptive family.

"I must say, you two are looking more and more Roman each time we see you," said Fulvia. "Don't you think so, Vala? Very dashing. I expect every woman north of Eboracum is clamouring for their favour."

"You're embarrassing them, Mother," Vala replied, but Cunedag was pleased to note by the rising colour in his foster sister's face, that she was the one who was embarrassed.

"I must congratulate you on the honours you received, my boy," said Colias, eyeing the polished phalerae on Cunedag's chest. "You have done me proud, the both of you."

"The honour was ours, Domine," said Cunedag.

"If only we had a hundred more men like you," Colias went on, "our northern border would be secure indefinitely. Still, let us see what Stilicho brings us."

"When is he due?"

"Tomorrow or the day after, the winds willing."

"Hopefully once all this vulgarity has had its day," Fulvia said, indicating the spectacle in the arena.

"Oh, I don't know," said Colias. "I think it's rather important that we show him that life goes on, even at the frontier. I think it shows a certain stoicism in the face of barbarian hostilities."

Down in the arena, a troupe of painted dwarves were putting on a play. Ever topical, they were depicting the final battle between Theodosius and the Pictish high king, Gartnait. The crowd roared and cheered at this comical rendition of Britannia's last great battle against the north perhaps to lighten concerns about the current one.

Once the diminutive Gartnait had been slain and the victorious Theodosius had raised his stubby arms in triumph to the applause of the crowd, the dwarves were chased away as soldiers trooped into the arena. It was time for the slave auction.

First came the domestic slaves. Colias and his family watched with indifference as young men and women and even children were hauled up to the auction block. Most were the property of households who, due to reduced circumstances, had to sell off some of their slaves. Others were criminals whom magistrates had condemned to slavery and were useful to buyers who owned mines and factories. Fates were determined to the sound of haggling and the faint jingle of coin.

The sale of the defeated tribesmen was saved for last, being something of a spectacle in itself to rival any other show. With no more gladiatorial combat to sate the bloodthirst of the plebs, getting a good glimpse at barbarians hauled about in chains and a chance to hurl abuse and refuse at them was the next best thing.

There was much booing and jeering as the Picts were dragged into the centre of the arena, manacled together and closely guarded by the soldiers. It wasn't unheard of for a proud barbarian warrior to make a break for it and risk death on the spot than face the humiliation of the auction block.

Cunedag watched the big Votadini warrior and rubbed his split knuckle. To see a man who, under other circumstances, would have been somebody he would have fought to the death beside, sold as a slave was a hard thing. He forced himself to remember that this man had attacked Rome. Had attacked the Wall and the men Cunedag called brothers. It was only right that he feel Rome's justice. But deep down, Cunedag knew that it had been his own brother who was the cause of this man's fall and his hatred for Brude burned all the brighter for it.

Some quarry owner outbid his rivals and the Votadini warrior and three others were unchained from their comrades and dragged away. The quarry owner was a Gaul and they would be taken across the sea, never to tread the heather of their homelands again. The Gaul had several burly guards with him to keep their master's new property inline and a lash fell heavily across the Votadini's broad shoulders as he snarled curses and tugged on his chains. Cunedag swallowed and put the image of the man from his mind.

After the slave auction, Cunedag sent Morleo back to the fort on a hastily invented errand and then accompanied Vala on a stroll through the market. He had been looking forward to seeing her more than he could credit it, and some time alone with her made his heart soar for reasons he couldn't fathom.

"I am pleased you did not come to harm in the battle," she said.

"Thank you. It was my first real battle, and I was lucky to come through unscathed. So many of my men did not."

"Was there no sign of Canaul in the fighting?"

"None. Nor of my brother. I suspect the leadership of the enemy confederation are far to the north and the warband we faced was merely the first assault. It may only have been a fraction of what we might have to face later this summer."

"Your brother is now king of the Votadini, is he not?"

"Yes. Though our father still lives, his mind is diminished. The tribe voted for Brude's early succession."

"I have not seen you since you visited your homeland," she said.

"No, it has been rather a busy time. I am glad of the reprieve now, however. Mainly because I had a chance to see you."

She smiled and he felt himself blushing of all things. Damn it, what was wrong with him?

"If your brother is killed in the fighting this summer, would that make you the next king of the Votadini?" she asked.

"I suppose it would. I have a younger brother, but I am the next in line."

"If that happens, would you seek an honourable discharge and return home to claim your crown? I'm sure Father could arrange it if that's what you really want."

Cunedag sighed. The thought of returning north to his family had been with him his entire life below the Wall like a constant, if rather quarrelsome bunkmate. Part of him had always wanted to but he knew then that he would never see the men under his command again; Elffin, Marcus and all the others whom he had come to love almost as brothers. Then, there was Vala. The thought of never seeing her again was more than he could bear, not that he'd ever admit that to her. "I honestly don't know," he said at last. "The future is in the lap of the gods."

"Still a pagan, Cunedag?" she asked, giving him a playful nudge in the ribs.

"Are you?"

She laughed. "I do my duty as the daughter of a Christian governor."

"That's not an answer."

"No, I suppose it isn't. But you didn't answer me either. Listen, Cunedag, I know you hear the call of your homeland and your people, and you have every right to return to them once this awfulness is over. I just hope you know that Rome needs you. *I* need you. Life would be so very dull without a pagan foster brother."

"Then I will serve both for as long as they need me. Rome and you."

She laughed again and they headed over to a stall to buy something to eat.

Cunedag and Morleo spent the night in Segedunum and, on the flood tide the next day, Stilicho's fleet of transports was spotted approaching port. They met Colias down on the waterfront along with Titus Gemellus who stood with his personal guard, their red cloaks vibrant against the drab colours of the docks and their blue shields emblazoned with the Chi Rho brighter than the sky.

The ships carried a vexillatio of eastern cavalrymen wearing conical helmets and knee-length scale armour. They carried flat, composite bows of the type favoured by the Huns and other eastern barbarians while their white shields bore a draco and pearl design. But, what impressed Cunedag most of all were their horses. Easily fifteen hands in height, they were a fine, eastern breed and were armoured much like their riders with scale coats. They even used stirrups; a curious eastern practice which had not caught on in the empire.

"Who are they?" Cunedag asked Colias as troop after troop of these strange riders disembarked from the transports and rode ashore.

"Taifals," the praeses replied. "A Sarmatian people of the Lower Danube. They were once stationed at Banovallum but, like most of our military, were taken to Gaul by Magnus Maximus to support his ill-advised claim to the purple. Stilicho is returning them to us, praise God!"

The entire town watched in awe as the hooves of the Sarmatian horses clattered on the stone wharves, eyes wide at the mighty cavalrymen marching in a long column that followed the Wall from the transports to the fort while the rest of the military expedition disembarked.

Flavius Stilicho himself was a man approaching forty, strong and hale with only the barest touch of frost to his dark hair. His father had been a Vandal and Stilicho had inherited the blue eyes of his people which were a sharp contrast against his dark face, still tanned from the African sun.

"Ave, Flavius Stilicho, Magister Militum!" said Colias, saluting Rome's highest military general, and father-in-law of the emperor. "Welcome to Britannia Secunda. I am Paulinus Colias, praeses of the province. This is Titus Gemellus, Dux Britanniarum and defender of the northern frontier."

The dux saluted his military superior. "My congratulations on your victory in North Africa, Sir," he said.

"An unpleasant business, Romans fighting Romans," Stilicho replied. "Still, it is done, and the breadbasket of the empire has been returned to the west. Alas, there is always another war to fight. Come, I have no desire to waste time gossiping on the wharves. Take me to the fort so we can begin our task of setting Britannia to rights."

Cunedag suppressed a smile at the faces of those assembled who no doubt found the magister militum a tad abrasive. For his part, he took a liking to the man. He was a soldier to the bone and not one for frivolities or niceties. He might be just what Britannia needed.

Chapter 17

The following week, Cunedag was back at Cilurnum, ahead of Stilicho's inspection tour of the Wall. While the burned-down stables and barrack block were still being rebuilt, much of the time was spent getting the garrison ready to greet the magister militum and endure the severest of inspections.

Stilicho arrived with a cuneus of around two hundred Sarmatian cavalrymen who would serve as a flying wedge in battles, sweeping around to flank an enemy. They immediately pitched their hide tents in the pastures below the fort. While Candidius gave Stilicho a tour of the fort, Gemellus approached Cunedag.

"Good to see you again, Decurion," said the Dux. "The rebuilding looks to be coming along well."

"For all the good an extra barracks block and a stable are without men and horses to fill them, Sir," Cunedag replied. "We've tried to recruit locally but most people have fled south, not liking their chances much. We could do with some of those Sarmatian mounts, not to mention their riders."

"Cocky bastards, but they get the job done. Stilicho has given them back Banovallum and I think they like the idea of returning to their unit's old fort. Some of them are even old enough to have served under Theodosius and Maximus. These lads are for Bremetenacum," he said, nodding in the direction of the drifting smoke from the cook fires of the cuneus encamped to the south. "Stilicho wants it rebuilt and operational as soon as possible."

"Are we to march north, Sir?"

"Not under Stilicho's command," the dux replied. "He won't be here for long. His duties in Rome can't wait. He's going to reinstate the post of Comes Britanniarum to run things in his absence."

Cunedag raised his eyebrows. The Comes had been the highest military rank on the island and had command of Britannia's field army as well as the limitanae troops commanded by the Dux Britanniarum and the Comes of the Saxon Shore. It was a command previously used only on an ad hoc basis when absolutely necessary and with good reason. Placing the military might of an entire diocese under the command of one man was always a dangerous policy and the previous Comes had been Magnus Maximus whose own troops had proclaimed him emperor.

"Any idea who might get the job?" Cunedag asked.

Candidius shrugged. "I'm too old and Quinctilius on the Saxon Shore is too ineffectual. Ambrosius Aurelianus is my best guess. He's Britannia's rising star."

Cunedag had heard the name. "Does he not have some connection to the royal house of Amorica?"

"Yes, he is the nephew of King Aldroen of Amorica and came over here with his father some years back before entering the military. He's young but has shown great promise."

The kingdom of Amorica was something of an oddity. As a region of Gaul which jutted out into the sea, it had been settled by Cynan, a soldier in the army of Magnus Maximus, who had been able to retain control of it after Maximus's execution. Cynan founded a British-speaking dynasty which continued to this day, ruled by his successors, provided that he supplied troops for Rome's wars in the east.

As evening approached, Cunedag and the other decurions were summoned to the praetorium for wine with their guests. Once the emperor had been toasted, small talk broke out in little clusters and Cunedag found himself approached by Stilicho, Candidius and Gemellus.

"Is this the fellow?" Stilicho asked, looking Cunedag up and down.

"It is, Sir," said Gemellus. "The man who saved Cilurnum."

"I am told you are a Pict by birth," Stilicho said, his keen blue eyes boring into Cunedag's as if trying to find any evidence of a traitor within. "It seems to have presented no obstacle to your service to Rome."

"I do not consider myself a Pict, Sir," said Cunedag, meeting the magister militum's stare. "In fact, no Pict does. It is a Roman term and a generalisation at that."

"Votadini, then," said Stilicho with a humouring smile. "But Pict or no, the enemy is the enemy under any name."

"I hope that my efforts to defend the Wall and my recapture of Cilurnum from the enemy are sufficient enough to convince Rome of my loyalty, Sir."

A small smile spread across Stilicho's face. "Come now, Decurion, I make no insult to you. You have served Rome well and your conduct is well deserving of merit. But what I want to know now, Cunedag of the Votadini, is exactly how far your loyalty to Rome goes. Does it, for instance, overrule any remaining loyalty to the people of your birth?"

Cunedag cleared his throat. "Sir, among the prisoners that were captured as they fled from the walls of this fort, was a Votadini tribesman. I personally escorted him to Segedunum and saw him sold as a slave a week ago. His presence in the warband indicates that my own people have abandoned their treaty with Rome and are now our enemies. That makes them *my* enemies. And I am sure that the ashes of many Votadini warriors drift on the wind from their funeral pyres, their shades sent to the afterlife on my orders."

"Easy words to speak when one is on this side of the Wall," Stilicho said, turning to Gemellus with a smile. "But would your resolve be so strong were you in the company of your countrymen? Would you still favour Rome when confronted by your own family?"

"Seeing as my own brother now leads the Votadini to war against Rome," said Cunedag. "I can assure you that familial ties have no bearing on my loyalty."

"Exactly what I wanted to hear, Decurion," said Stilicho. "Gemellus, I believe we have found our man."

"I did say so, Sir," Gemellus replied.

"Sorry, Sir," said Cunedag. "Man for what?"

"May we discuss this in private?" asked Stilicho.

"This way, gentlemen," Candidius said and Cunedag found himself following the three men to a small room adjacent to the cross hall. It was Candidius's study, with racks of scrolls and a wide table upon which a map of Britannia was spread, its corners weighted down with oil lamps.

Gemellus closed the door and Stilicho walked around the table, so the map of Britannia was between him and Cunedag. He set his wine cup down and gestured to the part of the map which depicted the tribes of the Selgovae, Novantae, Damnonii and Votadini. "The wilds of the north," he said. "Your homeland."

"Yes, Sir," said Cunedag. "Although, I must point out, that your map is out of date."

"Oh?" asked Stilicho, seemingly amused. "How so?"

"The Damnonii no longer exist, or rather, only as a subjugated people. The Attacotti have taken these lands here," he placed a finger on the map, "on either side of the western end of the Antonine Wall."

"Ah, the infamous Attacotti from Hibernia, I believe?"

"Correct, Sir. The building of the Antonine Wall split the lands of the Damnonii in two and made them weaker. Of all the tribes assailed by Gaelic raiders, the Damnonii were the most vulnerable and the only one who fell to them. Now these hounds of Hibernia have joined the confederation of tribes who stand against us."

"I must commend you, Gemellus," Stilicho said to the dux. "This decurion is most useful." He turned back to Cunedag. "It was Gemellus who informed me of exactly who you are and your use to us."

"Sir?"

"You are a royal prince of the Votadini."

"Yes, Sir."

"And it is now your older brother who is king of that tribe."

"Yes, Sir."

"It might be you instead of him."

Cunedag blinked. He could see how he might be useful to Rome as king of the Votadini. A client king. *A hound of Rome*. But it was impossible. "My brother would have to die first," he said.

"Or be deposed," said Stilicho. "Is he a popular ruler?"

"He is a *new* ruler," said Cunedag. "Our father lies sick, struck dumb by some malady. My brother was voted regent in his stead."

"But do the people revere him?" Stilicho asked. "Do they agree with his war on Rome?"

Cunedag considered his words carefully. "There are some who don't, but nobody wants an invalid king. The confederation of tribes includes the Caledonii and the Epidii and is strong. They have convinced the Votadini that they can win. Most have been fooled into thinking that Rome is weak and that the time has come to throw off their shackles."

"It would be advantageous to re-educate them," said Stilicho. "Gemellus and I believe you are the man for the job."

A gnawing fear swelled in Cunedag's gut. As soon as he had been taken aside by these highest of military men, he had known that he was being recruited for some dangerous and probably impossible task. "Sir?"

"Rome wants to support your claim to the crown of the Votadini," Stilicho explained.

"Sir, I have no claim. I am the younger brother—"

Stilicho waved his hand impatiently. "War between brothers is nothing new. I have recently come from Africa where I successfully helped one brother defeat another to the advantage of Rome. Gildo had the proper claim to his father's crown, but he was a tyrant. With my aid, his brother Masceldelus overthrew him, and North Africa was brought back into the fold of the Western Empire. A striking parallel to the situation we face here, don't you think?"

Cunedag nodded and said nothing of the rumour that had reached his ears of Stilicho's jealousy of Masceldelus which had led him to have the Berber general drowned while crossing a bridge shortly after his victory. Being a good soldier was one thing, it seemed, but one must never steal the thunder of a man like Stilicho. Cunedag made a note to remember that.

"Are there any nobles within the tribe who might be inclined to support you over your brother?" Gemellus asked.

Cunedag tried to think of the best path ahead. They were asking him to instigate a civil war among his people. It was a classic Roman tactic; defeat the enemy by dividing them. And yet, perhaps it was the only way to save his people from ruin. This war Brude had dragged them into could not be won and eventually there would be punitive action against the tribes who had dared defy the empire. He had no desire to be a part of that action which would see villages burnt and people yoked into slavery.

His mind dwelled on the big Votadini tribesman who had been sold at Segedunum. A civil war and a change of leadership might save other Votadini warriors from similar fates. If the tribe could be steered away from the path of madness Brude had set them on, many lives could be spared.

"I have a sister," he said, "who is married to one of the most powerful noblemen in the tribe. He alone spoke against my brother."

"Does he still have his lands or has your brother stripped them from him?" Stilicho asked.

"He rules Din Peldur, a day's ride from the Votadini royal seat of Din Eidyn," Cunedag answered. "It is a large and highly fortified site known as 'the fortress of the spears' in the British tongue. My brother would not have been able to take it from him, I am confident of that."

"Good," said Stilicho. "This is good. A powerbase for a burgeoning rebellion. Do you believe this brother-in-law of yours would follow you?"

"I honestly don't know," said Cunedag.

"We must find out. You are to leave as soon as possible. You will take three turmae from the Second Asturum. The third, seventh and eighth, I believe. The very men who followed you in your stunning recapture of this fort. I am told they hold you in great esteem."

"Sir, are you suggesting I ride north to fight my brother with only three turmae?" Cunedag asked, a cold sweat starting on the back of his neck.

"No, Decurion, I am suggesting that three turmae accompany you to this Din Peldur where you will try to recruit the support of your brother-in-law. If you succeed, you are to rally as many other supporters to your cause as you can. I will send a chest of hacksilver to you with which you are to buy the support of the nobles who remain harder to convince. We *will* have the Votadini back as our allies, Decurion. And you *will* be their next king."

"As far as we know, the Selgovae remain our allies," said Gemellus. "At least, they took no part in the attack on the Wall."

"King Tasulus is friendly to Rome," said Cunedag. "He wants no part in the confederation."

"Yet, he has allowed thousands of hostile tribesmen to pass through his territories to attack us," said Stilicho.

"He may not have had much choice," Cunedag replied.

"This is true," said Gemellus. "The Selgovae may prove to be useful allies if given the chance."

"Then we shall send a second delegation to the Selgovae and remind them of where their loyalties are," said Stilicho.

"King Tasulus is the father of my duplicarius," said Cunedag. "His royal seat lies near to the border of the Votadini lands. We will pass very close to it on our journey north."

"Good," said Stilicho. "Two birds with one stone. Speak with this Tasulus. Perhaps a visit from his son in the company of Roman soldiers will bolster his courage. I want him to muster his warriors and provide aid to us when necessary. In return, we will do what we can to protect his lands from further incursions from his northern neighbours. Now, good Candidius, call for more wine. We must toast the success of our plan!"

Chapter 18

Four days later, the column of Roman cavalry approached the Aber Teu and the ruins of Trimontium. They had made good progress due to not moving with a collection of baggage wains but carrying supplies on mules. Speed was everything and not just because Stilicho wanted to secure his allies as quickly as possible. The lands north of the Wall were treacherous now and Cunedag didn't know if there was still a hostile warband lurking nearby or if they had retreated further west.

The three turmae had been replenished by transfers from the rest of the ala and they rode at full strength; three groups of thirty riders. As they rode north, there were signs everywhere of the enemy's passing. Looted settlements, the remains of camps scattered with the bones of stolen livestock while starving villagers could be seen trying to eke out a living from whatever was left of their crops. King Tasulus was none too pleased about Roman cavalry tramping through his territories so soon after another warband had all but stripped his lands bare.

"Not only must I suffer a damnable warband of Novantae and Attacotti trampling crops and looting villages," he grumbled, "but now I must suffer an incursion of Romans? It is good to see you, Morleo, and you Cunedag, but I do wish you'd left the cavalry escort below the Wall. My people will consider this a direct violation of our treaty with Rome."

"Peace, my lord," said Cunedag. "Those men encamped down there are part of Rome's way of honouring the treaty."

"Rome has a funny way of dealing with their friends," the Selgovae king replied. "I suppose I must feed them?"

"It would be appreciated. And more will be coming. We ride north to deal with my brother. Before long, a Roman army will be marching through your lands to smash the enemy confederation. That would certainly be in your interest, no?"

"Aye, after what they've done to my lands, I'd like to see them all driven into the sea."

"Then show your support of Rome, Father," said Morleo. "Muster your warriors and fight for your lands."

"My son," Tasulus said. "We do not have the luxury of a wall separating our lands. Long have we suffered raids from the Novantae. Now, their gall is increased a hundredfold by their new alliances. The only way I have avoided being besieged in my own fort is by taking no side in this conflict. Those scum may use my roads and eat my crops, but they do not burn me alive inside my own lys."

"Courage, Tasulus," said Cunedag. "Have you lost all faith in your southern neighbour? What is a loose band of roving tribesmen compared to the might of Rome?"

"I do not doubt the might of Rome," Tasulus said. "Only its punctuality. If I muster my warriors and start shaking my spears, then who's to say Rome will be there to defend me when the next warband passing through my lands turns its attentions on Din Eil?"

"The next warband will most likely have its attention fixed north," said Cunedag. "On the lands of the Votadini. Meanwhile, a Roman army will be marching from the south. Together we can defeat them, Tasulus. But we can't do it without your help. The Votadini won't be able to stand against the confederation alone."

"Father, you have ruled your people well," said Morleo. "They love you and you have ensured many years of peace. This war was not of your making but now is the time to be strong and stand your ground. For too long have the Novantae ridden roughshod over you. It is time you stood with your allies and joined the fight."

Tasulus sighed. "You sound just like your brothers, my son. I had not expected my youngest to chastise me for my indecision. The impetuousness of youth! Perhaps I am too old. I fear too much to lose what I have spent my lifetime building."

"Just ready your warriors," Cunedag said. "You will not stand alone."

King Tasulus nodded. "Very well. May the Great Mother save us. I will join the fight. I wish you luck in the north, my boys. Whatever happens, you will find the Selgovae ready to fight by your side."

The following morning, they crossed into Votadini territory and continued north, cutting west around the northern slopes of the hills towards Din Peldur. The great bulge of the fortress stood stark against the grey sky, peat smoke drifting from a hundred cookfires and workshops. The earth and timber ramparts encircled a large settlement with cattle pens enough to feed a huge warband. Cunedag just hoped that his brother-in-law still felt as strongly about not attacking the Wall as he had done on their previous meeting.

They camped on the flat pastures below the great hillfort and a mounted band of warriors was sent down to ascertain their business. Romans this far north would be a cause for concern, but a ninety-man cavalry force was too small to offer much of a threat to Din Peldur. Once it was known that Cunedag, prince of the Votadini was with them, the warriors seemed to relax, although cast suspicious eyes at the encamped Romans.

Tegid mab Calgo was ecstatic to see Cunedag brought before him.

"You live!" he exclaimed, embracing his brother-in-law in a mighty hug. "By all the gods, you live! We had almost given up hope. Your brother was keen to have it said that you had paid the ultimate price for standing against him, but it was clear to any fool that his bluster was to cover the fact that you had slipped through his fingers. I was worried you had died in the heather of some wound and ended up as wolf food, but your sister never gave up hope."

Alpia rose from her seat and embraced her brother. "Thank Modron," she said as she squeezed him tighter. "If only I could get word to Mother that you live."

"Have you no contact with her?" Cunedag asked.

"Brude has banished Tegid and I from Din Eidyn," she replied. "After Tegid refused to lend his warriors to his warband. I was not even permitted to attend Father's funeral."

"Our father is dead?"

"You did not know? I apologise, Brother, of course you had no way of knowing. But yes, our king and father is dead and Brude rules the Votadini with impunity."

"And Murcho?"

"He is at Din Eidyn, under Brude's control, though I don't know how much his heart is in it. I would like to have brought him here, but there was no way I could get him away from Brude."

"You both managed to hold out against him," Cunedag said, looking from his sister to Tegid.

"Only because we are untouchable here," Tegid replied. "But now you have come with Roman cavalry. What are your intentions?"

"To take the crown of the Votadini from Brude," Cunedag answered. "By realigning the tribe with Rome, we hope to cripple the confederation and be poised to attack them from the north-east while Rome's forces march from the south come harvest."

"It could work," said Tegid, rubbing his chin. "But you won't defeat your brother with a paltry Roman cavalry, even with the aid of my warriors."

"Then you *will* aid me?" Cunedag asked hopefully.

"Aye, I'm with you," said Tegid. "But I hope you have something else up your sleeve. Is there any hope of more men from the Wall?"

"No, three turmae are all they could spare me. Are there any Votadini nobles we can turn to our cause?" Cunedag asked.

"Some of the coastal chieftains, perhaps," said Tegid. "They have little interest in fighting Rome. But that doesn't mean they'll help defend it either."

"Perhaps they will for silver," said Cunedag.

"Do you have any?"

"Not with me, no. But my superiors are sending a chest of hacksilver to me once I have established a base. It should be enough to recruit some of the coastal chieftains."

"Bring it here by all means and I will safeguard it," said Tegid. "I do not need to be bought. All I want is to see your brother deposed and a little sanity restored to the tribe. If that means paying our own people as mercenaries, then so be it."

"I won't forget this, Tegid," said Cunedag. "Once I am king, I will see that you are properly rewarded for your loyalty not just to me but to our people."

Tegid gave him a wry grin. "Let's see if we can survive the season first."

"What are your intentions beyond winning the crown?" Alpia asked him, her eyes narrowed. "If you become our next king, will you leave your position in the Roman military?"

"I can't very well be a king and a cavalry commander," said Cunedag. "So, yes, I would leave the army if I were to rule the Votadini."

"And Rome? What are their plans regarding us?"

"How do you mean?"

"You are using Roman soldiers to fight your war. Surely, they want more out of this arrangement than simply ensuring peace north of the Wall?"

"By gaining the Votadini as allies, they will be dealing a severe blow to the confederation of enemy tribes," said Cunedag, not sure what his sister's wiley mind was chewing over.

"Allies, yes," she said. "But are you sure they don't want something more than that? Already we have ninety Roman cavalrymen on our doorstep, and you say more Romans will be here by harvesttime."

"What your sister is wondering," said Tegid, "is how can we be sure the Romans will leave Votadini lands once the war is won? With one of their cavalry commanders on our throne, it may seem like our lands will be under the jurisdiction of the Roman military."

"I swear to you, that I will not rule the Votadini as a client king of the Romans," said Cunedag. "No more than our father did. Rome wants allies in the north, but they don't have the manpower to extend themselves north of the Wall. Once the war is over, they will return south to guard their frontiers. We will be left in peace so long as we honour our treaty with them."

"I believe you, Cunedag," said Tegid. "Let's just hope we can persuade the other clans to believe you too."

Cunedag nodded his thanks, but Alpia said nothing, and he detected a coolness in her eyes as she gazed at him.

The cavalrymen were lodged within the walls of Din Peldur and Cunedag took one turma to the coast to gauge the feelings of the coastal clans. It was certain that Brude would know of his presence at Din Peldur by now, and of Tegid's support of him. How he was going to transport a wagon of silver north without it falling into the enemy's hands, was something he spent many a night contemplating.

The coastal clans were mostly simple fishing villages nestled among the rocks, overlooking grassy dunes which swept down to seaweed-strewn beaches. Their chieftains were dressed in seal skins with ornaments of coral and shell. They were a proud people but had few warriors. Still, if he could rally enough clans to his cause, he might raise a decent force to supplement his cavalry and Tegid's warband.

Amid the racks of drying fish and smoking huts, Cunedag did his best to appeal to their sense of honour. Few saw any danger in the actions of their distant king and his war with Rome. They would continue to live as they had always lived, fishing and giving thanks to Manawydan, lord of the waves.

"When my brother's alliance with the western tribes fails and their plot against Rome is beaten back," he warned them, "Rome will march north to punish those who rebelled. Villages will be burned, crops razed, and livestock and slaves taken. Do you think they will stop to ask if your village was part of the conspiracy? All will be punished if the Votadini stand against Rome."

That seemed to give them pause for thought but he could tell they weren't fully convinced. The promise of silver helped make up a few minds and Morleo recorded the agreements of payment for warriors on a wax tablet.

"How exactly are we going to get a chest of silver to these lands without it being robbed by Brude's followers?" Morleo asked Cunedag one night while they were camped in the hills to the west of the coastal clans.

"Getting it through the lands of the Selgovae should prove no problem," said Cunedag as he used his knife to slice off a sliver of the mutton leg that was roasting over the fire.

"It's once the wain has crossed the Aber Teu that I fear for its safety."

"I can arrange a Selgovae escort through my father," Morleo replied.

"That would be a help, but I've been thinking about this a lot, and it doesn't make much sense to me to send the silver up the Roman road towards Din Peldur when most of it will be used to pay off the coastal clans. Why not have it sent directly to the east coast?"

"By boat?"

"Aye. We'll need to be there to receive it, but it seems to me to be the safest route."

"There is the danger of Saxon and Gaulish pirates."

Cunedag shrugged. "No more than bandits or my brother's raiding parties on the road."

When they returned to Din Peldur, Cunedag put his idea to Tegid.

"It's risky," Tegid said. "Those waters are infested with pirates."

"The cargo would have to be disguised as something mundane," said Cunedag. "Something that would make pirates feel it isn't worth the bother."

"Even so, those sea wolves will steal anything," Tegid replied. "And how would you disguise the armed escort? You not thinking of sending a treasure trove out with only a few sailors to guard it?"

"No, it would have to have an escort," Cunedag agreed. "But a small one. As you say, any large contingent of men would arouse suspicion."

"Risky," said Tegid, shaking his head. "Very risky."

He was right, but Cunedag still found the idea preferable to sending the silver by road. A boat could reach its destination in a fraction of the time and would be more inconspicuous than a wain trundling up the Roman road.

A few days later, Cunedag and Morleo headed south with a ten-man escort along the coast to Segedunum to make arrangements for the shipment of silver. They had to wait around for a couple of days for the dux's man to come up from Eboracum to make the arrangements on his behalf.

He was a grey-haired old Greek called Philokal with a clerical air to him and seemed to pride himself on being difficult. He wanted to know exactly what the silver was going to be used for, how many warriors it would buy and the names of the chieftains Cunedag had made arrangements with. Cunedag left the explanations to Morleo who calmly tried to make the cleric see that it was impossible to account for all that the silver would be used for. Much of it would be kept in reserve for greasing palms, buying grain and loyalty over the course of the season. And they needed as much as they could get.

The clerk seemed to view them as a couple of barbarian chancers who were abusing their responsibilities in order to pocket some silver at Rome's expense. Cunedag lost his temper.

"Listen, you copper-counting little shit stain!" he said, seizing the man by his tunica and dragging his face close to his. "I have been sent north to win a tribe's loyalty to Rome by Stilicho himself. I was promised a chest of silver to help me in my efforts. What do you think the Magister Militum would think of a scruffy little Greek who stood in the way of him winning his war?"

Philokal paled and made his apologies. Cunedag released him and, soon enough, the arrangements were made for a large amount of silver to be brought to Segedunum in sacks much in the way salt was transported. Salt was a popular commodity but not especially valuable in small quantities. Cunedag hoped that would be enough to persuade pirates to favour other cargoes and let a small salt trader slip by unmolested. All he needed was a trustworthy vessel and crew.

He found one down at the docks and arranged transport for the silver to be taken north to a settlement he had picked on the east coast. He left behind five men to oversee the transfer of cargo and ensured that they were dressed in common sailor's attire with their knives concealed about their persons as their only weapons. The captain was bemused by the request to take on five extra crewmen, exclaiming that he had more than enough hands onboard, but a few extra denarii in his hand and the promise of further reward upon safe delivery of the shipment, persuaded him not to ask too many questions.

Cunedag, Morleo and the remainder of their escort rode back north and waited at Din Peldur until the time came to return to the coastal chieftains to receive the shipment. The year had turned now, and summer was on the wane. Soon it would be harvesttime and the campaigning season would draw to a close. There was still no word from below the Wall on when the Roman army would be marching north, but Cunedag knew he had to ensure he had a strong enough power base before they did.

When they reached the coastal settlement, the ship had not arrived and, after waiting another day, it was clear that there was some delay. Cunedag began to grow nervous. All his hopes on winning the crown were carried in the hold of that small trader, disguised as sacks of salt. After three days had passed, he and Morleo rode south to see if they could spot the vessel from the dunes.

Not far north of the Selgovae boarder, near a Selgovae hill fort named Din Guaire, they saw the utter calamity of their plans keeled over on the mud in a small cove, the departed tide having left its mast angled towards the sun.

CHAPTER 19

"What happened?" asked Morleo.

Cunedag did not wait to answer and spurred Bran down the dunes and dismounted, running across the sands towards the beached ship.

Several bodies littered the area, dragged away from the vessel by the receding tide and now being worked over by the crabs. He cursed as he recognised his own men, the clear signs of butchery on their bodies and wished he had armed them better than with the simple Roman daggers with which they had been forced to defend themselves.

"They were attacked while at anchor," said Morleo, inspecting the chain and anchor stone embedded in the sand. "What on earth persuaded the captain to put in here?"

Cunedag ignored him as he scrambled up and into the hold of the vessel, frantically searching for the cargo. "It's gone!" he yelled. "The bastards have taken it!"

He looked over the gunwale at the flat sands and rippling grass of the dunes that surrounded the cove. The desolate landscape had swallowed his hopes for claiming the crown from Brude.

"How had they known?" Morleo said, joining him in the hold, their boots splashing in the blood that pooled in the bilge, a clear sign of a fight to the death. The bodies of the captain and his crew were scattered about but of the attackers, there was no sign. "They must have been overwhelmed."

"But by who?" Cunedag said. "Who, by all the gods, knew about the shipment? This was no random attack by pirates. They were waiting for them."

"Something caused the captain to drop anchor in this cove," said Morleo. "If his body was not among the dead, I would be inclined to suspect some treachery on his part."

"You don't suppose it's that little prick, Philokal?"

"Could be. But I wouldn't have thought he'd have the balls to rob his masters. And even if he did, how is he supposed to get hold of the silver without raising suspicion?"

"Yes, that's the thing," said Cunedag. "The silver is hard to transport. This can't have happened more than a couple of days ago, so the silver is probably still north of the Wall. That means we have a chance of recovering it, though Modron knows where we are to start looking."

"It's clear that somebody involved betrayed us," said Morleo. "We need to find out who. That's the only way to find out where the silver went."

"Only a handful of people could have known," said Cunedag. "Our own boys are all here so it couldn't have been any of them and I trust our lads with my life in any case."

"And, as far as I can tell, the crew are all here too. Though, that doesn't mean one of them wasn't betrayed in turn. Something made them anchor here where they were attacked."

"It could be somebody below the Wall," said Cunedag. "Somebody who got wise to the shipment and tipped off someone in the north."

"We need to lure the traitor into the open," said Morleo. "Perhaps another shipment might tickle their greed a second time."

"There's no way Gemellus will send us another load of silver," said Cunedag. "I'll have a hard time explaining what happened to the first shipment as it is."

"It doesn't have to be a shipment of silver," said Morleo. "It just has to *look* like it is."

"A decoy?" Cunedag said.

"Aye. And we follow this one closely. When the thieves strike, we strike. I'm sure a prisoner might be persuaded to give the name of the man who betrayed us."

Cunedag grinned. "And when we get hold of him, I'll nail his balls to the Wall he endangered with his greed."

They rode on to Segedunum and planned their next move over wine and olives in a tavern. "We should send the decoy by road this time," said Cunedag. "Easier that way to apprehend whoever tries to steal it. Also, it would be believable that we tried to take a different route after the first load was stolen."

"I agree," said Morleo. "And we should ensure that the cargo looks like salt and in the same quantity as before. There's no point being too sneaky about it. We want to attract the attention of the same people who ordered the attack on the ship."

"And we'll accompany the cart ourselves," said Cunedag. "I'm not risking some poor trader's life again by setting them up as bait. We'll disguise ourselves and transport the cargo while our boys keep a close eye on the road to aid us when the enemy strikes."

"Best send a man north with your orders today," said Morleo. "It's a good three days to Din Peldur."

Cunedag ground his teeth in frustration. Every delay meant that he had less and less time to bring the fight to Brude.

It took a couple of days, but they were able to obtain empty salt sacks which they filled with sand and a cart with two foul-tempered old oxen. Cunedag had sent one of his men back north with orders to bring a turma south and camp in the woods between Segedunum and Din Guaire. It was along that coastal road that he hoped their enemies would attack. And he hoped their enemies were watching, or all this was for nothing.

The journey north was painfully slow. The oxen grunted and farted while the wheels of the cart ground and rumbled their way along the ruts in the track as it crossed the flat marshlands towards the distant woods where Cunedag hoped the enemy were planning on ambushing them.

He and his men, having left their horses at the fort in Segedunum, were disguised as common merchants, their cloaks concealing their spathas and daggers. Still, if they were ambushed by anything more than half a dozen men, the fight could easily go against them. It was with some relief when Cunedag saw Marcus trotting along the road towards them, similarly dressed in native tribesman style, sent to check that they were on their way.

"*Salve*, Marcus," said Cunedag, resisting the urge to return the young soldier's salute. There was nobody else on the road, but it paid to be careful.

"*Salve*, Sir! Good to see you."

"And you. Are our boys in position?"

"We have men in groups of two or three posted along the road at every half mile or so," Marcus replied.

"Any sign of anything unusual?"

"No, Sir."

"Then get back to your position and be ready."

"Remember, Sir, blast that horn of yours if there's any trouble and we'll be on them like hot pitch."

"You'll hear it. Now, be off with you. There could be spies on any stretch of this road. We don't want to give the game away. And don't salute me next time."

Marcus nodded and turned his horse around, galloping back along the road from whence he came.

They continued as the sun passed overhead and dusk deepened. They had passed a couple of riders from the Second Asturum disguised as travellers and had exchanged nods of recognition. Their presence on the road boosted Cunedag's confidence. One blast of his horn and their ambushers wouldn't know what hit them.

Night fell and talk turned to the possibility of stopping for the night. They were all hungry and the oxen needed a rest. They were about to pull off the track and make camp when the attack came.

The trees to the left of them erupted as tribesmen rushed the cart. Cunedag flung one side of his cloak over his shoulder and drew his spatha as one tribesman tried to clamber up the side of the cart. With a downwards swing, he embedded his blade into the enemy's head, wrenched it free with a spurt of blood and then booted the man in the face, sending his lifeless body tumbling to the dirt. As his men fended off the attackers in a likewise manner, Cunedag drew his horn and gave three short blasts.

The raiding party was about twenty men in total but even with those favourable odds, the attackers realised they had bitten off more than they could chew. These were no simple traders but iron-hard Roman soldiers who knew how to fight as a unit. Even without their shields, they mounted an admirable defence, facing the enemy on all sides, with the cart forming an advantageous high ground.

But it couldn't last. The enemy thankfully didn't have spears but there were enough of them that it was only a matter of time before the cart was overrun. Cunedag hacked through the wrist of a man who tried to scramble up behind him and kicked the severed member off the top of the cart to join its owner as he gave another three blasts on his horn.

His signal had already been heard as the thunder of hooves could be heard coming from the north. In the moonlight, Cunedag could see three riders coming down the track at a gallop, swords drawn.

The enemy had spotted them too and shrank from the mounted men, abandoning their assault on the cart. Several of them had been slain and more wounded. They knew they couldn't stand against what appeared to be disguised Roman cavalrymen.

One of the attackers put up a futile gesture of defiance and tried to take down one of the riders while his comrades vanished into the trees and was rewarded with a sword stroke that opened him up from belly to shoulder before he went down under the trampling hooves.

"Give me your horse!" Cunedag yelled to one of his men as he jumped down from the cart.

Swinging himself up into the saddle, he led the other two riders around the thicket from which the attackers had sprung while his unmounted men plunged into the foliage after their fleeing enemy.

Cunedag whirled his bloodied spatha around above his head as he saw the fleeing tribesmen desperately trying to cut across country. "Take some of them alive!" he bellowed to his companions as he swung his blade down and split a man up the spine, sending him reeling to land face-down in the tall grass.

The other riders passed the remaining tribesmen and blocked their escape while Cunedag brought up the rear, hemming them in. This was only a fraction of the men who attacked them; a mere three tribesmen. The rest were either dead or being chased through the woods by Cunedag's soldiers.

"Now then!" he said to the terrified captives who had utterly given up and were holding their hands up in surrender, their faces pale in the moonlight. "Let's have some answers from you scum!"

They dragged the prisoners back to the road and Cunedag sent riders north and south to gather his men. They made camp not far from the road and began heating up some knives to winkle the truth from the prisoners.

The miserable wretches were bound hand and foot and kept under close guard. Two more had been captured, the rest having been cut down and left for crow meat. The men Cunedag had sent to guard the road north had not yet returned but he didn't want to wait. He selected the strongest looking of the lot and had him tied to a tree as the knives in the fire began to glow red.

"You can spare yourself and your comrades a great deal of pain," he told the man. "Just tell me who your lord is and there will be no need for me to hurt you."

"Go fuck yourself, Roman!" came the stoic reply through gritted teeth.

Cunedag smiled. By their weapons and the canny trap they had set for the thieves, it was clear to these tribesmen that they were from below the Wall. "Would it surprise you to know that I am Votadini?" he asked the man. "Perhaps you are too. Who is your lord?"

"Fuck off!"

Cunedag sighed and plucked a knife from the fire. He held its glowing tip under the man's nose. "Tell us who sent you to steal the silver."

"You'll get nothing from me, Votadini scum! Whelp of the Romans!"

"Ah, so you are not Votadini, then?" Cunedag said. "Novantae?"

"Selgovae," came the pained reply, tribal pride breaking through his stubbornness.

"What?" said Morleo. "Selgovae warriors shaming the treaty my father has with Rome? I am Morleo mab Tasulus, your prince, you filth! Who is the lord you serve? Which of my father's nobles dares to threaten our peace with Rome?"

"Peace with Rome?" the man chuckled. "Rome desires slaves, not peace. And not all Selgovae chieftains are as weak and servile as your father."

An anger crossed Morleo's face that Cunedag had never seen there before and he took the glowing knife from Cunedag's hand and pressed it to the prisoner's breast, just below the left nipple. The man screamed and the stench of scorched flesh pricked their nostrils. "Speak, you dog!" Morleo yelled. "We can keep this up all night."

"Braga …" the man mumbled, hanging slack from his ropes as his body absorbed the pain.

"Braga of Din Guaire?"

"Aye, much good it may do you. Now finish me. Give me a warrior's death."

"No," said Cunedag. "We still have questions for you."

Screams and the stink of burning flesh hung in the air as Cunedag dragged everything the man knew out of him while his pale-faced comrades looked on in terror, wondering if they would be next. Braga had not come up with the plan to steal the silver alone. He had been recruited for the job by the leader of a Votadini warband who were somewhere in the area, sent by Brude, no doubt. These men had a contact in Segedunum, a customs optio, who had alerted them to the silver being transported north and had paid off the captain of the vessel, tricking him into putting in at the bay. There, Braga's men butchered everybody aboard and stole the silver which was now held at Din Guaire.

Satisfied that the man kept no more secrets, Cunedag had him cut loose, doused with cold water and tied up with the others.

"My father will punish Braga for his treachery," said Morleo as they ate their meal of dried mutton, hardtack and posca around the fire.

"We don't have time to call on your father for aid," said Cunedag. "We need to get that silver north as soon as possible."

"Din Guaire is a large fort," said Morleo. "And we are but twenty-five men. Even with the help of the other turmae and Tegid's men, we could not crack it."

"There has to be some other way," said Cunedag as he chewed thoughtfully on the leathery meat. "And where the hell are the rest of my men? They should have joined us by now."

The night passed and still the men posted north of their position did not come. With dawn breaking over the woods and a few hours' sleep behind him, Cunedag knew something was wrong. "Stay with the prisoners," he told Morleo. "I will ride north with three men and see what has happened to the others."

"You don't suppose they were attacked by more of Braga's men?" Morleo said.

"You, Selgovae traitor!" Cunedag said, aiming a kick at the man they had tortured. "Are there any more of your men loitering in these parts?"

"No," the surly man replied. "Of the twenty-two warriors who set out form Din Guaire, only we five wretches remain."

"Brude's men, perhaps?" Morleo said. "This traitor said that they were in the area."

"Watch them closely," Cunedag told Morleo. "I will return as soon as I can."

Galloping up the track, Cunedag and his two companions emerged from forest and looked out over the moors to the west and the grassy dunes to the east. The landscape was barren. To the north, the distant hump upon which Din Guaire stood could be seen against the sky, the white flecks of sheep grazing at its feet. There lay his silver, and he ground his teeth in frustration at it being so close and yet so unobtainable.

"Smoke, Sir!" said one of his men, pointing at a distant point to the west. "It's faint, too faint to be a settlement."

"You're right," Cunedag said. "Come!"

They turned off the track and galloped across the moors towards the vague plume of a campfire somewhere in the low hills. They dismounted as they entered a wooded glen, hobbled the horses and crept on foot towards a low ridge which screened the source of the smoke.

Crawling on their bellies, they moved along the ridge to get a view into a wooded dell where around twenty horses were tethered and as many men milled around a campfire, eating and talking in low voices. Nearby, Cunedag's three missing soldiers were tied up, their mouths gagged with a close guard watching over them.

Cunedag motioned to his two companions to move down off the ridge and out of sight. "We need to get back to the others," he said as they sat on their haunches. "The odds aren't greatly in our favour, but maybe if we come on them by surprise, we might have a chance of rescuing our comrades."

They hurried back to where they had left their horses but, before they could mount up, Cunedag became aware of several figures surrounding them on all sides. Limned against the sky, he saw at least ten tribesmen pointing spears at them and knew he had been a fool. They had ridden into this glen like hares into a trap. One of the tribesmen whistled and his comrades in the dell mounted their horses and rode over the rise to see whom they had captured.

"Cunedag mab Etern!" cried one of the mounted men. "To think my renegade brother rode into my trap with only two men!"

Chapter 20

"Murcho?" Cunedag called up. "Is it you?"

"Aye, Brother," said Murcho. "We have some of your men, though they remain tight-lipped as to what they are doing north of the Wall."

"These are Selgovae lands," said Cunedag. "And the Selgovae at least honour their treaty with Rome."

Murcho smiled. "Come, let us discuss matters in a more civil manner."

They were led to the dell where their bound comrades were being kept. Cunedag and Murcho sat by the fire, the crackling logs between them.

"It is good to see you, Brother, despite the circumstances," said Cunedag.

"Despite the fact that you are my prisoner, you mean," Murcho said.

Cunedag could see that he was affecting some bravado, likely for the sake of the twenty-odd warriors he commanded, but he could also see the nervousness in his little brother's eyes and the way he carried himself. Brude had clearly given him men according to his rank, but he was hardly experienced enough for the position.

"You are far south of our homeland, Murcho," he said. "What mission has Brude sent you on?"

"We have dealings with Braga of Din Guaire," Murcho replied. "Or at least, we did until he betrayed us."

"Oh?" Cunedag asked. "How so?" Murcho seemed agreeable to revealing everything to him. *Foolish boy*, he thought. *You'll play right into my hands.*

"We know about the silver shipments you are transporting north to fund your rebellion," Murcho went on.

"Braga supports the confederation against Rome, despite his king's reluctance. He was to capture the silver and turn it over to us, but greed has gripped his heart and he has kept the silver for himself. We had hoped to capture his men as they stole a second shipment but instead, we found Roman cavalrymen disguised as tribesmen."

"Braga no longer serves Brude?" Cunedag asked.

"He serves only himself. He hides behind the walls of Din Guaire like a crab in a shell, keeping the silver that was to fund the confederation."

"That must be irritating for Brude," Cunedag said.

"There's little our brother can do about it. Most of the Votadini warriors are with the main warband in the west. I lead only a small force to transport the silver north, but we are too few to take Din Guaire. Why are you laughing?"

Cunedag couldn't help himself. "Most of my soldiers would blame Fortuna while I might be inclined to see Modron's work but whoever it is, the gods have a fine sense of humour!"

"How do you mean?" Murcho looked affronted, as if his brother might be laughing at him.

"We traced the stolen silver to Braga and our business in these parts was to trap his men with a decoy posing as a second shipment only to be captured by you. You don't have enough men to take Din Guaire, you say, well, neither do we. But together …"

"Together?" said Murcho. "You propose a treaty?"

"For as long as it takes to bring Braga to task."

"But we both want that silver."

"Aye, but let us talk of that once we have taken it from Braga's cold, dead hands. As for the moment, we are presented with a rare opportunity. Two warbands with the same goal. The gods don't favour Braga this night."

"Even if we joined forces," said Murcho uncertainly, "we are still too few to storm Din Guaire."

"We need not storm it," Cunedag replied. "We have prisoners and a decoy shipment. They might be persuaded to aid us in getting within its walls."

"Cunedag, I ..." said Murcho, seemingly at a loss for words.

"You worry about what will happen once our task is complete," Cunedag said. "Is there any chance you might consider staying by my side. You must see that Brude's alliance with those Attacotti cutthroats will only end in ruin for the Votadini. I intend to take the crown from him, and I could use your help."

"I can't, Cunedag. I have pledged myself to Brude, our older brother who has the true claim to the crown. I'm sorry."

"Don't be sorry, Murcho. You are loyal and you honour your word. Those are fine qualities in a warrior and a leader of men. Whatever happens, you will still be my brother."

Cunedag knew that there was conflict within Murcho but for the moment, he had done all he could. The lad was hardly going to betray his king in front of his men. In time, he hoped to turn them all to his cause and recruit them into his growing warband, but earning men's loyalties was like tickling salmon. If you grabbed too early, you would lose the fish altogether.

The first order of business was the release of Cunedag's three men who had been captured by Murcho's party. Their bonds were cut, and they were given food while Cunedag sent for the rest of his men. They were twenty-six while Murcho led twenty and, although the Romans slightly outnumbered the Votadini, both sides knew that it would be a bloody and costly fight if it came to it. Besides, the love of brothers reunited, and the lure of silver ensured peace between the two factions … at least for the time being.

The Selgovae prisoners were herded into the dell and Cunedag took their leader to one side, his bonds cut but a close guard kept on him all the same.

"What's your name?" he asked the warrior.

"Gurust," came the reply. The man was clearly still in pain due to the burns inflicted on his body by the hot knife and Cunedag knew he had his work cut out for him if he was to win this man's loyalty.

"Well, Gurust. You can see that your lord's greed has undone him. This man here is my brother, the one Braga was supposed to deliver the silver to. He isn't happy. Not only that, but your lord has betrayed his king, Tasulus, who is the father of that man over there." He pointed at Morleo who drew his dagger and tested its sharpness for effect. Gurust visibly shivered at the memory of being tortured by the Selgovae prince. "Braga is finished, if not today then in a week or so when King Tasulus storms Din Guaire."

"What do you want from me?" Gurust asked.

"Only your common sense in not standing by your lord to be punished alongside him." Cunedag placed a friendly hand upon the tribesman's shoulder. "You have a chance, Gurust, to save yourself and the lives of your men. We want our silver back. And we need your help in getting within Din Guaire."

"Why not wait for King Tasulus's warband?"

"Because I need to get that silver north as soon as possible," Cunedag replied. "I must raise a warband before harvest if I am to claim my father's crown. You'll help me do that, won't you, Gurust?"

"Aye," the big warrior replied, seeing sense. "If I can, though I don't see how."

"Braga is expecting you to return to Din Guaire with a wagonload of silver, correct?"

Gurust gritted his teeth in frustration. "If we had not been tricked by a decoy, aye."

"Well, Braga need not know it was a decoy. In fact, my plan rests on him thinking he has stolen a second shipment of silver. No doubt he'll be greatly pleased with you. And I'm going to be right there to celebrate with you."

"How do you mean?" Gurust said.

"You think I'd trust you to wander into your lord's lair and risk having him send out every rider of his to cut us down? No, I and a dozen or so of my men will replace the ones you lost, and we shall escort the wagon into Din Guaire. Once inside, we will hold the gate open for my men who will storm the fort while it is caught off guard."

The prisoner looked bewildered at the audacity of the plan, but he knew that there was little else he could do but agree to it or die there in the hills.

Cunedag's own men, however, were more vocal in their opposition.

"You do realise that it's madness for you to wander into Din Guaire posing as a Selgovae tribesman," Morleo said to Cunedag once he had explained his plan.

"How so?" Cunedag asked. "You think my plan is no good?"

"Oh, it's a good plan, all right," the duplicarius said. "But if it goes arse up, then Braga will have a prince of the Votadini as a hostage and a powerful bargaining chip to smooth things over with Brude. Let me go, I'm Selgovae myself and will make sure Gurust and his men keep to their promises."

"But you're a prince too," said Cunedag. "And another valuable hostage Braga might use to get himself out of the spot he doesn't yet know he's in."

"He's right about that," said Marcus. "You know I'd volunteer, but I fear I may not pass for a British tribesman. My dark complexion rings too much of the Roman military."

"He's right," said Elffin. "And if he's required to open that foreign cesspit of a mouth, then he'd be done for. Let me go, Sir. A Briton is the only way, civilised Roman citizen I may be."

Cunedag smiled, despite his disappointment at the truth of Morleo's words. It would be folly for him to wander into the wolf's den and allow himself to be used as a bargaining chip but the readiness of his men to take his place made his chest swell with pride. They had a dangerous task ahead of them but, with such brave soldiers under his command, they had a fighting chance of taking the fort and making off with the silver.

None of them had slept in over a day but there was too much to do and too much at risk to rest now. Cunedag sent men south to strip the bodies of the Selgovae tribesmen of their arms and clothing and recover the wagon. Elffin and twelve cavalrymen dressed in Selgovae garments while Gurust and his two companions were made to swear on their ancestors that they would not betray the plan.

Morleo still had his doubts. "There are so many ways this could go wrong," he said to Cunedag as the men were preparing to set out. "The tribesmen we slew will have friends within the fort. What will happen when nobody recognises our lads?"

"It is a danger, I admit," said Cunedag. "Darkness will hopefully give us some advantage. By the light of the torches and the moon, our boys will look no different from any other Selgovae warriors, and I have given them orders not to converse with anybody. They need only survive a few hours until they have the opportunity to open the gates. And when they do, we will be on hand to charge the fort."

"We'll have to be bloody quick if we don't want the gates slammed in our faces," said Morleo.

"Aye, and again, darkness will provide adequate cover. We'll sneak upon the fort and hide in the long grass until Elffin and the others are inside, ready to strike at a moment's notice. It'll work, Morleo. Have faith in the gods who seem to be on our side for the moment."

"But for how much longer?" Morleo mused. Cunedag ignored him.

While they waited for darkness to fall, they ate a meal and Cunedag gave his men permission to sleep in short watches. Once the moon was high, the wagon and its contingent of fifteen men headed in the direction of Din Guaire while Cunedag, Murcho and their combined force of warriors waited in the hills.

"How is Mother?" Cunedag asked Murcho as they watched the stars come out behind the drifting clouds.

"Strong, as always," his brother replied. "Misses you, though. Brude has forbidden the mention of your name around Din Eidyn but I can tell she misses you."

Cunedag nodded. He had so recently been reacquainted with the woman who had birthed him and who should have given him his spear in his sixteenth year. To be cut off from her once more, not by Rome this time, but by the machinations of his jealous brother, must be as hard for her as it was for him.

"And Alpia?" Murcho asked hopefully. "She is well, I trust."

"Aye, the brains behind Tegid's rule, as you can imagine. Though she has a hot temper where our brother is concerned. He has driven a wedge into the heart of our family and pushed us apart, Murcho. I hope that you can see that he is the problem and not me."

Murcho gazed at the wavering grass, silver in the moonlight. "I don't blame you, Cunedag," he said. "But I cannot betray him. It is a matter of honour."

"I understand. Just know that when this is over, I will not hold a grudge against you, Brother. I just hope that you will not feel that you must fight a battle that is already lost out of loyalty to Brude."

The wagon had vanished into the gloom that shrouded the feet of Din Guaire.

"Time for us to make our move," Cunedag said.

They cut bushels of long grass and tied them to their arms and heads, turning themselves into something resembling an army of scarecrows. This, Cunedag assured them, would prevent them from being seen from the palisades as they approached the fort. They hurried off in the wake of the wagon, cutting away from the road and passing through fields of ripening rye and barley. When they neared the fort, Cunedag signalled them all to creep forward, like beasts through the tall stalks, their own camouflage blending them in perfectly.

They made their way around to the southern gate where they could smell the sea on the night air and hear the crashing of the waves on the shores beyond. Torches burned at regular intervals atop the wooden palisade and Cunedag could see the occasional glint off the helmed head of a sentry.

Holding his hand up to halt his men, he crouched in the field and watched as the wagon was admitted through the front gate to much muffled cheering behind the fort's walls.

"Damn fools don't know that Gurust is bringing them an empty wagon yet," said Murcho beside him.

"They'll get an even bigger surprise once Elffin gets that gate open for us," Cunedag growled.

They spent a nervous couple of hours lying in the tall straws, every man analysing the fort and guessing at its strengths and weaknesses. There were few sentries, but then, only a few were necessary. Nobody could launch an assault on Din Guaire without one of them hammering the alarm bell. It was what that bell could summon that was the real question.

Cunedag estimated about fifty to a hundred warriors if things were really set against them. That meant they would be outnumbered nearly two to one. They would have surprise on their side and most of the warriors would be sleeping with any luck. As long as they could get in, he was confident that they could take the fort.

"What if they don't manage to get the gate open?" Murcho asked Cunedag. "Do we sit here until dawn? We'll be a lot easier to spot when the sun comes up."

"I try not to think of what might happen if a man of mine fails," Cunedag replied. "I have trained each and every one of them to succeed no matter the cost. If they fail then we leave, before sunup, simple as that. But they won't fail."

Sure enough, before dawn touched the waves to the east, the great southern gate to Din Guaire began to creak open.

"This is it!" Cunedag hissed to his men. "On my signal, we rush the gatehouse, and I don't want any yelling. Tell your men that, Murcho. Ideally, we want to be inside the fort before they know what's hit them."

"Agreed," his brother said and passed on the message.

Cunedag rose onto his haunches, plucked up his spear and set off at a low run towards the slope that led up to the widening gate. Two score men behind him rose from the field like phantoms and swept towards Din Guaire, morphing into a column two men wide as they ran.

Already, Cunedag could hear cries of alarm within the fort as his feet pounded up the slope. *Shit!* he thought. Then, turning to yell at the men behind him; "In and at them, boys! Carve the bastards up!"

CHAPTER 21

They slipped in through the gate like water through a breached dam. Shadowed roundhouses and pig runs lay before them, illuminated by occasional torches. And some of those torches were moving towards them.

"Form up!" Cunedag yelled.

Aside from Murcho's men who had their small bucklers, they had no shields and sorely missed them as the Roman way of fighting is largely dependent on one man protecting his comrade's flank, even for cavalrymen when they fight on foot. Cunedag's men hastily assembled into a defensive line in any case and met the initial rush of tribesmen with their spears and their blades, yelling a concoction of Roman and British war cries.

Elffin and his contingent clattered down the ladders from atop the gate house and joined their comrades.

"Elffin, you marvel, you did it!" Cunedag said as he wrenched his spear head from the throat of a downed tribesman.

"Aye, but it was a close thing," Elffin replied. "It was noticed that we were not men of Din Guaire and we had to make up some half-baked story about being a hunting party from one of the Selgovae settlements further west who had helped Gurust and his men in their fight."

"Where are Gurust and his men?"

"God knows. They scampered off as soon as we opened the gate."

"If they take up arms against us now, I'll gut them personally!"

Every warrior in the fort must have been roused by the racket and came spilling out of their roundhouses, some tying up their breeches as they ran, half naked, while their women tossed them their weapons.

"Take the fight to them!" Cunedag yelled. "Close formations! Don't let them surround us!"

They wove their way between the roundhouses in small groups, dispatching any warrior who charged them.

There was a good deal of screaming from the inhabitants of the fort as the realisation that they had been breached set in but, through the hubbub, Cunedag could hear the bellowed orders of warriors as they tried to mount a last-ditch defence in the direction of the largest roundhouse.

"Surround the Great Roundhouse!" he yelled. "Herd them in there and we'll see if they're in a mood to negotiate!"

They enclosed the large, thatched building on all sides, cutting down the last stragglers of the fort's defenders who were too slow to follow their companions indoors. The wattle doors to the roundhouse were barred and barricaded and there was much shouting coming from inside as the defenders made fast the last building left to them.

Cunedag ordered his men to fetch torches. Then he addressed the occupants of the roundhouse. "Braga!" he bellowed. "Come out and surrender or we'll roast you alive inside your own roundhouse! Silver doesn't melt at such temperatures but, I promise you, your body's fat will be clinging to your charred bones come dawn if you do not yield!"

There was a brief moment of silence, then came a small voice from within; "What sureties do you give me that you will not slay me should I come out?"

"None but the word of Cunedag mab Etern," Cunedag replied. "And the surety that you will burn if you do not."

More silence followed until the main doorway opened and several warriors filed out, spears ready to fight to the death if they had to. A man in his early forties then emerged, grey of hair and with the golden torc of a clan chieftain around his neck.

"Braga, you despicable worm!" Murcho yelled. "Your greed has betrayed the promise you made to King Brude of the Votadini! Where is the silver you took?"

"Are you to lecture me on betrayal?" Braga fired back. "You, who ally yourself with your renegade brother who is trying to usurp King Brude? Have you traded one brother for another and now support Cunedag's rebellion?"

It was now Morleo's turn to chime in on the subject of a Selgovae chieftain's treachery. "Cunedag's claim is supported by Rome, Braga!" he cried. "I am Morleo mab Tasulus, your prince, or does Din Guaire stand apart from Selgovae lands in favour of a mad rebellion against Rome?"

"Your father is a coward, young whelp!" said Braga. "Even with all the north rising against the Roman oppressors, still he is content to be their client king. Well, not all Selgovae are as weak willed. Din Guaire stands against Rome as do many other chieftains besides."

"And yet you keep the silver intended to fund the confederation," said Murcho.

"Why not? Was it not my warriors who risked their lives in seizing it from the enemy? Let the Votadini and the Novantae and all the others find their own silver!"

"Enough of this tribal bickering!" snapped Cunedag. "Where is the silver?"

"In here, with me."

"Fetch it out!"

Two warriors were sent into the roundhouse and emerged with a large chest between them. They set it on the ground before Cunedag and opened the lid. Torchlight glinted off dozens of platters, cups and bowls, most either crushed or cut into fragments. Spoons and clipped coins depicting the faces of Valens, Arcadius and Honorius winked in the dull light. The sight of such wealth stunned the observers into silence.

"Return it to the wagon," Cunedag ordered. "We leave this place at dawn. Find food and drink and eat your fill. We have a long journey ahead of us."

"That's it?" Braga said, a little nervously. "You're just going to take the silver and leave?"

"I have no interest in you. Your betrayal of your king is a Selgovae matter, and I don't doubt King Tasulus will take it up with you in due course. Right now, I have more important things to attend to."

Braga watched in dumb silence as they loaded up the wagon and ransacked the homes of his people. Cunedag suspected that he was secretly jumping for joy at being allowed to keep his life.

They left Din Guaire and the corpses of its warriors with full bellies and skins of mead to pass around as they accompanied the wagon north along the coast. As the hills rose on the western horizon, Murcho wanted to head for them, skirting the territories that may now be loyal to Cunedag and his allies at Din Peldur.

"It seems the time is upon us," said Cunedag as they camped for the night. "This wagon is for Din Peldur to buy off the coastal chieftains for which it was always intended. And you have not the men under you to change its course, Brother, for my own outnumber yours."

Murcho's men tensed at the implied threat while the two brothers faced each other across the campfire.

"Would that I had brought more men with me from Din Eidyn," said Murcho, "you might not be so cocky."

Cunedag grinned. "Come with us, Murcho. It's not too late. It's never too late."

"You know where I stand, Brother," he replied.

"I know. I just pray to the Great Mother that we will never face each other in battle."

"As do I."

With morning light, Murcho and his men made to depart. There was some grumbling from the more outspoken of his warriors about returning empty-handed, but Murcho made them see that they had no other alternative. Refusing to fight one's brother was one thing, but there was no way they could overcome Cunedag's men and make off with the silver. They had lost it and that fact had to be admitted.

The progress north was slow as they made for Din Peldur, avoiding the coastal settlements Cunedag intended to buy support from. It would be folly to pass through those territories with a wagon of silver in case they ended up hostages of another chieftain whose greed matched Braga's. The silver would be cached at Din Peldur and then Cunedag would send separate payments to each chieftain. It was a laborious process but, after going through so much to get the silver north, he wasn't going to do anything to compromise it now.

Upon arrival, he joined Tegid and Alpia in the Great Roundhouse and began planning the next stage of their campaign.

"There's no way we can besiege Brude at Din Eidyn," said Tegid. "We have to draw him out into the open."

"And then snare him in a trap," said Cunedag. "But how to lure him?"

"The best way to cripple an enemy is to cut off his food supply," said Alpia. "And it is almost harvesttime."

"These are our people," said Cunedag. "Whether they support Brude's claim or no. I don't like starving my own people, especially as I may ask them to be my subjects in the near future."

"This is war, Brother," said Alpia. "See if they will still support Brude when their bellies and granaries are empty and winter approaches."

"I'm glad you're on my side, Alpia," said Cunedag with a grim smile. "I certainly wouldn't want you as an enemy."

As late summer ripened the grain in the fields, Cunedag took fifty of Tegid's mounted warriors from Din Peldur and returned to the coastal chieftains to buy their support. He took from them around two hundred of their best riders whom he began training as a crack cavalry regiment. Their ponies were small, hardy things and they were used to fighting as individual warriors and not as a single unit, but he was determined to forge them into the best semblance of a Roman ala as he could in the short time that was allowed to him.

Before long, the harvest began, and the fields began to be stripped of their bounties. As the granaries swelled, Cunedag knew it was time for him to make his move.

He took only his three turmae, leaving his tribal allies in the east. Warriors on foot were too slow for what he had in mind and the coastal cavalry still too undisciplined. He would strike hard and fast, snatching grain before melting back into the heather. It pained him to wage war on peasants who had little say in who wore the crown of the Votadini but, as Alpia had said, the way to hurt Brude was to cut off his food supply and his warriors lived off these lands.

They rode into settlement after settlement, looting granaries and stealing wagons to transport their stolen grain. Mounted Roman cavalry met no resistance, and the villagers merely looked on with sour faces, stifled curses on their lips as they watched their winter feed vanish.

"If you want to eat this winter," Cunedag told them, "fight for me, not Brude."

"All our warriors are up at Din Eidyn or with the war host to the west," one elderly man told him. "We are no fighters and yet you starve us all the same."

"Then pray to Modron that Brude comes out of his fortress to face me," Cunedag told him.

"This plundering sits ill with me," Morleo told Cunedag one evening while they were eating their rations around a campfire in the hills, the bulging wagons of grain guarded on all sides.

"And with me, Morleo," Cunedag replied. "I would much rather wage war on those who oppose me than starve their families."

"What if your plan doesn't work? What if Brude is content to remain at Din Eidyn and let his people starve?"

Cunedag stoked the embers of the fire with a stick. "When we were children, Brude and I were nearly gored by a boar. We got separated from my father's hunting party and the boar found us before we found them. Brude tried to attack it, and it slew his pony and injured him in the fall. I was also cast from my saddle, trying to save my brother's life, and we clung to each other with a single spear to defend ourselves as the boar charged us again. We were so scared. I remember being so sure that we were about to die but I held out my spear anyway, my hands shaking. I braced myself, planting the spear butt in the earth and looked into the boar's eyes as it came towards us."

"You skewered it?" Morleo asked.

"Aye," Cunedag replied with a smile. "Damn thing could have turned tail and left us alone and it would have lived to a ripe old age, but it was so enraged that it had nothing else in its mind but charging at us full pelt. I merely held my ground and the boar did the rest, impaling itself on my spear.

"Brude took all the credit for the kill, of course. We never were friends after that, but it taught me a couple of valuable lessons. One was never to trust Brude and the other was that his pride and his impatience will eventually be his undoing. What we are doing here, Morleo, is poking the boar, working it into a frenzy. And when it is foaming at the mouth, we shall merely hold our ground and let the boar do what boars do."

"Brude will be the boar this time," said Morleo.

"Aye. And we must hold the spear."

They worked their way from east to west, in a semi-circle that swept the lands below Din Eidyn with the aim of starving Brude out. It was slow progress due to the wagon train of looted grain they took with them which required constant guarding. It was only a matter of time before Brude realised what they were doing and tried to foil their plan. It was clear when one settlement they raided had no grain in its stores.

"What happened?" Cunedag asked the village elders. "Why are your granaries empty?"

"Brude's men came not two days ago and took it all!" they cried. "Between two brothers, we are starved!"

"Where did they take the grain?" Cunedag demanded.

He was met with shrugged shoulders of men resigned to their doom. "Westwards," was all they could tell him.

Another couple of settlements told the same story and it became clear that Brude was stripping his lands of their harvests as they were collected to stop them from falling into his brother's hands.

As they cast their net closer to Din Eidyn, they came upon a large, walled settlement which boasted a small host of warriors who launched arrows and spears at them as they approached.

"Brude must have garrisoned this one," Cunedag said to his men. "We may finally be drawing him out of his shell."

"It may be that grain from nearby settlements has been stockpiled here," said Morleo. "Awaiting transport to Din Eidyn."

"Aye, it seems a ripe target. We shall encircle the place and force them to throw down their arms."

He led one turma around to the south, following the wattle palisade while Morleo led the remaining two around to the north. Night had fallen and the darkness rang with curses and taunts from both sides as well as occasional arrows and slingstones.

Cunedag ordered ropes to be slung over the posts supporting the southern wall while most of the enemy's attention was on the two turmae harrying its northern gate. The ropes, attached to their saddle horns pulled taut and a large section of the palisade was ripped down.

With oaths of victory on their lips, they stormed the settlement, sweeping in through the opening in the wattle. The defenders knew they had lost and threw down their arms, having no desire to be butchered where they stood.

"Check the granaries!" Cunedag ordered his men as the warriors were disarmed.

Morleo and Marcus booted down the doors to the great thatched beehive structures that held the settlement's grain and emerged with grins on their faces.

"Full to bursting!" Marcus said. "There's enough grain here to feed five-hundred men!"

"Start loading it up."

The work had barely started before Elffin came running up from the northern gate. "Sir!" he cried. "Our sentries report riders approaching from the north!"

"How many?"

"They estimate a hundred or so."

"Damn!"

"Too much to hope for that Brude is leading the charge, Sir?"

"My brother isn't the heroic type. A hundred riders are enough to see us off but it's hardly his whole warband and I doubt he would set out from Din Eidyn with anything less. Torch the granaries!"

"Sir?"

"Do it! We can't take the grain with us this time. The only way to stop Brude getting it is to burn the lot!"

As blazing torches were hurled onto the thatched roofs of the granaries, Cunedag sent the wagon convoy with an escort into the hills. "We'll have to lead Brude's men on a chase," he said to Morelo as the blazing granaries lit up the night sky, sending glowing embers whirling up to rival the stars. "We must protect our grain, no matter what. Mount up and we'll see if we can't lose them in the hills."

Chapter 22

They galloped out of the settlement with the burning granaries at their backs like the fires of Hades snapping at their heels. Cunedag led them northeast while the grain convoy rumbled south, hoping that Brude's men would take the bait and follow the cavalry.

They did and, turning in his saddle, Cunedag could see the column of mounted tribesmen riding hard and fast around the northern side of the blazing settlement. Roman cavalry horses could easily outrun British ponies, but Cunedag wanted to draw them as far away from the grain convoy as possible and that meant leading them on a little.

They headed up one glen, only to turn and ride out again to enter another, giving the pursuing riders enough time to catch up. As the steep slopes of the hills rose up to green cattle pastures, the valleys deepened, and the foothills and livestock trails provided ample opportunity for Cunedag and his men to leave the tribesmen far behind them. Skirting the northernmost range of hills, they headed back south to catch up with the grain convoy which had meandered its way east into the safety of Tegid's lands.

They returned to Din Peldur where the grain was stockpiled and Cunedag wasted no time in setting the trap with which he hoped to snare Brude. His brother was clearly getting desperate now, knowing that he could not feed a warband nor contribute to the confederation with his rival for the crown so close to his doorstep, raiding every granary in his lands. He would be forced to mass an attack against Cunedag and Cunedag had every intention of choosing the battleground.

One bright morning, two weeks after Cunedag had burned the last of Brude's grain stores, three-hundred tribesmen marshalled in the pit of a deep glen on the western side of the hills which ran through its northernmost peaks. It was perfect for what Cunedag had in mind. Beyond the northern ridge, two of his turmae and a hundred riders from the coastal clans waited, screened from view by the steep, heather-strewn slopes. A similar force was hidden beyond the southern ridge, made up of one turma, the remaining hundred riders from the coast and sixty mounted warriors from Din Peldur and its surrounding lands including Tegid himself and Alpia who had kitted herself out in a mail coat and a wolfskin cloak.

Cunedag had tried to persuade his sister to remain at Din Peldur, but she was as stubborn as he was and, as they were to be facing their brothers on the field of battle, she wanted to be there alongside him to bring them to heel. In truth, he did not fear for her safety for she had always been a fine warrior, and he was secretly glad to have her with them.

"You do realise we have left the western approach to Din Peldur unguarded," Morleo said to Cunedag as they sat astride their horses and enjoyed the steadily strengthening sun on their faces.

"I know," he replied.

"If Brude's warband decide to skirt the hills and follow the estuary east, they could take it easily."

"They won't. Brude wants me dead more than he wants Din Peldur. If he thinks I am massing my forces in this glen with the intention of marching west, he will try to pin us in and destroy us right here."

"Another risk," Morleo pointed out. "If we are unable to overcome your brother's force, then this glen will be a tomb for those men down there."

"I am confident we can meet anything my brother throws at us," said Cunedag. "It may be a hard fight, but once his ranks are broken, Brude will cave and surrender. It's not like him to fight to the death on principal."

"I hope you're right," Morelo replied. "By all the gods, I hope you're right."

Alpia came riding up to them from where her husband's men were positioned on their left flank. "One of our scouts has come down off the ridge," she told her brother. "He sees a column of dust approaching from the direction of Din Eidyn."

"Are they headed for the glen or are they following the estuary?"

"Straight for us," she replied. "They've taken the bait."

"As I knew they would. Tell Tegid to wait for my signal."

Alpia nodded and galloped back to her faction, cloak billowing behind her. Cunedag dismounted and bade Morleo do the same. "Pick three good men and follow me," he told his duplicarius.

"Where are we going?" Morleo asked.

"To get a look from the ridge."

Morleo and three stout fighters hurried after him as he scrambled up the slope, wading through the heather. As they reached the ridge, they sank down onto their bellies and crawled along until they could see down into the valley where their infantry was clustered. To the west, where the hills sloped down to the rolling moors, they could see the approaching warband.

"I don't know if my brother is battle-smart enough to send out scouts," said Cunedag, "but somebody in his warband might be. We need to be ready to take down any that come up here. I don't want them warned that they are marching into an ambush."

Belly-down in the heather, they watched as the warband approached. The shifting clouds drifted overhead, and the glen seemed deceptively peaceful given the slaughter that was about to take place within its bosom.

"There's an awful lot of them," said Morleo as the various contingents of Brude's warband came into focus. On either side of the column of marching warriors, cavalry units rode, tribal standards fluttering in the wind.

"He does seem to have brought more supporters than I had thought," Cunedag admitted. "But we can still beat them."

"Wait, what's this?" Morleo said, his eyes wide.

The right cavalry flank had broken away from the enemy column and was making its way up the southern ridge. Before long, they would be upon them and would be able to spot Cunedag's massed cavalry behind the ridge.

"Damn him!" Cunedag hissed. "I thought he might send scouts but never an entire cavalry wing!"

"Those standards," said Morleo. "They look like …"

"Attacotti," said Cunedag, spitting out the word like a foul oath. "So that's why his ranks are so swollen. He's received help from the confederation."

"I suppose they want Brude to rule the Votadini as much as Rome wants you to," said Morleo.

"We must get back to the horses," said Cunedag, and they edged themselves off the ridge, keeping low until they were out of sight.

"Orders, Sir?" Morleo asked as they swung themselves back up into their saddles.

"Our only hope is to outflank the Attacotti," he said. "If we engage them, we'll be dragged into a lengthy battle and will never be able to aid our men in the glen."

Drawing his spatha, he bellowed orders and led his turma the length of the line, twenty-five cavalrymen beneath a billowing draco, to the far-left flank where his sister and brother-in-law waited.

"Follow me!" he roared. "The enemy will be upon us at any moment! Ride! Ride like the wind in the heather!"

A hundred and sixty riders moved to follow him, spears prickling the sky. But it was too late; the enemy were already cresting the ridge and had seen them.

"Ride! Ride!" Cunedag bellowed, sword held aloft.

With a churning of earth, the enemy cavalry began to descend the slope, horses slithering, hooves grinding the dirt. Cunedag led his warriors west, following the ridge of the glen, riding against time to round its southernmost fringe and fall upon the enemy's rear. But the Attacotti, given the advantage of speed, came thundering down the slope to slam into their right flank, crashing and rolling, spears bursting through mail and flesh, men and horses screaming as the two factions mingled in a bloody red slaughter.

Knowing that they must now stand and fight, Cunedag wheeled what was left of the front portion of his column around and came upon the enemy's right flank with a mad yell on his lips. As his riders gouged into the enemy flank, he caught a spear tip on the boss of his shield, feeling the rasp of metal as it slithered off the polished iron. Thrusting it to one side, he brought up his spatha and hacked through the shaft, leaving the enemy rider weaponless. A second hack to the man's neck all but severed his head, leaving him reeling in his saddle, blood gushing from the hideous gap below his chin.

All was confusion now with no semblance of factions or formations as the two hosts mingled in a hot, mad press of slavering horses, churning mud and the spray of blood. Anybody who was not recognised was hacked down. Bodies carpeted the ground, trodden on by the panicked horses. Many men had been unhorsed by the sheer shock of two cavalry forces slamming together and now fought it out on foot, standing atop the bodies of their comrades as they hacked and slashed at each other.

Cunedag was deeply worried. Not that they were outnumbered by the Attacotti – he was confident they could win through – but every minute they spent fighting them was a minute his warriors in the glen faced the brunt of Brude's force with no cavalry support. If they could not disentangle themselves from this fray, then the men on the other side of the ridge would be slaughtered and the battle lost.

The press of battle was suffocating and Cunedag fought for purchase on Bran's back, his thighs screaming as he gripped his mount's sides to avoid being knocked to the churning chaos below. He parried and blocked and slashed with his spatha, his ears ringing with the clash of steel and screams of the dying all around him.

Another sound reached his ears; the sound of men at some distance yelling war cries. Through the red mist of slaughter, he looked up at the ridge and saw another contingent of mounted warriors charging down the slope towards them. He did not recognise them and cursed. The enemy were receiving reinforcements. That meant that they were done for and so were the men in the glen for there was no way they could fight through to them now.

But, as the newcomers ploughed into the fray, Cunedag could see that they were attacking the Attacotti and not his own men. Could it be true? Were Brude's forces turning on each other?

And then he saw his brother, Murcho, bloodied spear raised high in salute, bellowing his name.

"Murcho!" Cunedag yelled back. "You stand with us at the last?"

"Aye, Brother!" Murcho yelled back. "If only to save your life! And it wasn't too hard to convince my men to attack these Attacotti scum. We never liked them."

The Attacotti knew they were beaten now, pressed between two units who were intent on butchering them. But, among all the Gaels, the Attacotti were counted as the most ferocious and battle hungry and surrender was not in their vocabulary. They stood their ground and died on their feet, crushed between the forces of the Votadini brothers.

"What changed your mind, Murcho?" Cunedag asked as he brought Bran up close to him, extending his arm to grasp his brother's.

"You might say I came to my senses," Murcho replied. "Brude knew that you would try to trap him with cavalry and so he sent his own wings to outflank you; the Attacotti south while I led the left flank north. He gave orders that you be cut down. He's terrified of you, Cunedag. I tried to reason with him, make him take you prisoner, treat you as family but … well, our brother has become decidedly unreasonable these days."

It was then that Cunedag saw the purple bruise around his brother's eye, barely concealed by the cheek guards of his helmet. He gritted his teeth. "His bullying days are over, Murcho," he said. "Let us finish this."

"Aye, you are the better man to lead the Votadini, Cunedag," Murcho replied. "I always knew that, and I am only sorry that I did not have the courage to stand by you until now."

"There is nothing to apologise for. You rode to our rescue and will forever have my thanks. What's more, you left my riders to the north untouched, and they must be awaiting my signal to charge as we speak. The battle is yet to be saved! Come! Ride with me and let us knock our brother off his perch!"

Cunedag's dismounted men quickly found horses and mounted up and within moments, they were pushing their tired animals up the ridge to see how the rest of the battle fared.

Atop the ridge, they were afforded a view down into the glen and it was a heart-rending one. Cunedag's men held the gap like heroes, but he could see that the cost had been high. The dead carpeted the glen and the sound of shields slamming together and steel clashing against steel was outmatched only by the roar of oaths and screams of the wounded.

"Keep the formation tight!" Cunedag shouted to his men. "We hit them from behind and break their assault!"

Across the glen, they could see the sun glinting off the helms of the other two turmae and their coastal allies as they emerged atop the north ridge. The poor bastards must have been in agony watching the battle in the glen, just waiting for the signal to join. Well now, by all the gods, they had their signal and, as Cunedag and his men began their charge down the slope, so too did they.

If any of Brude's men had thought to turn their heads and look behind them instead of at the steadily dwindling force blocking the narrowest part of the glen, they would have seen two plumes of destruction rolling down the slopes to the north and south of them. As it was, it took them until the last minute to realise that their doom was upon them.

The two cavalry charges almost met on the floor of the glen just as they scythed into the rear ranks of Brude's warband. Men screamed as blades and spears cut a bloody harvest. Hooves trampled bodies and splintered bones. Cunedag roared and swung his already tired sword arm, cleaving the helms and splitting the skulls of any who tried to bring him down.

By the time they had worked their way well and truly into the rear of Brude's column, Cunedag decided that enough Votadini had died. He had no desire to rule over a kingdom of widows and orphans.

"Men of the Votadini!" he bellowed. "Hear me! I am Cunedag mab Etern! Throw down your weapons! You are defeated! All who surrender will receive mercy! Throw down your weapons!"

Many stood back, uncertain of what to do and, while some fought on, their thunder had been stolen. It was over and the realisation of this radiated from the rear of the host to its front ranks who still pressed against the men from the coast.

And then, almost as one, the defeated began to drop their weapons. Spears, axes and blades fell to the ghastly mixture of mud, blood and shit that squelched underfoot and clung to the fetlocks of the horses. Cunedag pushed Bran through the horde of surrendered warriors who parted for him like wheat bending in the wind. Up near the front, some damn fool was making a spectacle of himself, swinging his sword about and daring all to fight him.

"Traitors!" he bellowed. "Fight on, you bastards! I am your king!"

It was Brude, unhorsed and caked in mud and blood. A circle of his own men surrounded him, staying out of reach of his wildly flailing sword. "You dare to disobey me!" he howled. "Fight on! Fight on!"

"Peace, Brother," Cunedag said. "Have not enough men died? It is over."

Brude looked up at him with wild, wide eyes. Alpia appeared at Cunedag's side and Murcho on the other. The three of them looked down on their defeated and disgraced brother. Their broken king.

"Murcho, you treasonous bastard!" Brude yelled. "I'll have you skinned and boiled alive! You dare betray me?"

"He is no traitor, Brude," said Alpia. "You are!"

"Throw down your blade, Brother," Cunedag said.

"I take no orders from a usurper! Kill him! I command it! Kill all three of them!"

Cunedag sighed and moved Bran in close to him, neatly sidestepping a swing of his blade. Before Brude could recover his balance, Cunedag slammed the sole of his boot against his forehead, knocking him senseless into the mud.

Chapter 23

They rode out of that vale of slaughter and breathed the fresh afternoon air deeply as the wind swept across the hills, cleansing their nostrils of the stink of the dead. Cunedag rode immediately for Din Eidyn to claim his father's seat and crown. The defeated trailed in the wake of the column of horsemen, unarmed but now his followers, nonetheless. After all, who else did they have to follow now but Cunedag?

The only prisoner was Brude who was given a horse to ride, though his hands were bound.

"What is to become of your brother?" Tegid asked Cunedag as they marched west.

"He will be banished," Cunedag replied. "It is too dangerous to allow him to remain in these lands."

"It may be that he is too dangerous to be left alive," said Tegid. "He has allies in the west, remember. He may call upon them to aid him in his war against you."

"I will not execute my brother in cold blood," said Cunedag. "Besides, within weeks I expect the Roman army to be marching north to put an end to this damned confederation. Let Brude see where his allies are after that."

The return to Din Eidyn was a victorious homecoming the old hill fort had not seen in generations. Brude had proved to be an unpopular king and, once word had got around that he was defeated and that Cunedag was to be their king, the atmosphere was joyous. The cellars were flung open and meat and mead were brought out for a welcoming feast. As they rode in through the main gate, Cunedag saw his mother standing at the gateway to the upper enclosure, tears in her eyes at seeing all four of her children returned to her alive.

He dismounted and she embraced him first, caring nothing for the blood on his armour that stained her fine dress.

"Thank the Great Mother that you are returned to me," she said squeezing him hard. "And thank you for sparing Brude's life. He was not fit to wear your father's crown, but I couldn't bear to see him slain by your hand."

"I would not take a son from you, Mother," he told her. "Not after we have already lost so much."

"It is over then? You are to become king?"

"It would seem so. I must rally the chieftains to see me crowned as soon as possible. Rome is depending on me to hold the Votadini lands and aid them in the war to come."

"So, we are to be a vassal of Rome," his mother said.

"No more than we have always been," Cunedag replied. "Rome holds the lion's share of this island. Only a fool would stand against them. The Novantae, the Attacotti and the tribes of the highlands are soon to find that out but, by the grace of all the gods, the Votadini have now been spared the fate that will swiftly be meted out to them."

"Because of you, my son," said his mother. Tears fell from her eyes as she touched his cheek fondly.

"Well, I did have some help," he replied. His mother embraced Alpia and Murcho in turn and even Brude who stood shamefaced and humiliated. Despite everything, it truly felt like a family had been reunited.

While Din Eidyn prepared itself for the crowning of a new king, Brude was provided with a pony and some provisions and sent on his way one cold morning. There was no sendoff for the usurped king of the Votadini. Cunedag didn't want a big scene, partly because he didn't want to risk fostering the idea that his brother was a martyr, but partly to spare Brude the shame. The eldest son of the late King Etern slipped away westwards with barely anybody noticing.

Later that same day, riders were sent out to every clan chieftain in the Votadini lands, summoning them to a tribal meeting at Din Eidyn, the subject being their new king. Most arrived looking a little fearful that they would be held to task for their support of Brude and Cunedag took some small pleasure in their discomfort. He addressed them all in the Great Roundhouse, beneath the red cloak of his ancestor, Padarn, and several eyes looked to it, knowing its significance. Rome had always ruled through the kings of the Votadini, for as long as anybody alive could remember at least.

Cunedag was surprised that Brude hadn't taken the cloak down but then, Brude hadn't been the shrewdest of men. Cunedag would keep Padarn's cloak, as his father had done before him. Symbols were useful and, now that he had returned to his ancestral lands to rule them as a king with the support of Rome, he found himself thinking more and more about how useful they could be.

The chieftains came, one by one, to kneel at his feet and kiss his sword as a sign of their loyalty to him and he placed his hand on the head of each. He spoke no words of forgiveness for their support of his brother. Brude had been the rightful king after all, but he had been a poor one and, if anybody present had any qualms about the right of succession, they kept as quiet on the subject as Cunedag did.

Once the oaths of loyalty were complete, the kingmaking ceremonies began. Old Gonar the druid came up to the fort to officiate over the rites and Cunedag was pleased to see him after so many years. He was little changed from how he remembered him; perhaps a little whiter of hair and lined of face, but he was still the same old wise man who had been old when his father had been a boy.

Cunedag stood naked but for a loincloth before all as Gonar painted the sacred symbols of kingship all over his body in red ochre. The Votadini may have given up the practice of running into battle naked, their bodies adorned with warpaint, but their kingship ceremonies had more than enough about them for the Romans to still consider them 'Pictish'. Once Gonar had placed the gold band of kingship on his head and the gods had been invoked to bless his rule, six chieftains bore Cunedag around the hall three times on a broad shield while everybody present chanted his name.

At the kingmaking feast that night, the venison sputtered and crackled over the peat fire and the mead was poured liberally. Cunedag sat in his father's high seat and gazed at the cream of the Votadini, sitting side by side with his cavalrymen, as they ate, drank and tried to put the bloody events of the past few months behind them. They were whole once more and stronger than ever, yet dark clouds boiled on the horizon, Cunedag knew it and he was sure they did too. Their new king was tied to Rome and Rome's wars would now be their wars.

Murcho, having drunk a little too much mead, was giving an account of the Attacotti whom Brude had allied himself with. Before the battle, he had accompanied Brude on a diplomatic mission to Alt Clut, the Attacotti stronghold, and had much to say regarding their evil practices.

"Their chieftain is all but a slave to their high druid, a fearsome old sorcerer called Blathmac," he told his enraptured audience. "Far from our good friend Gonar, here, this Blathmac is feared by all for his dark magic. It is said that the Attacotti indulge in vile and unnatural rituals that are known only to themselves. I tell you, the sooner we defeat this confederation, the sooner we can drive them from Albion's shores and back to the sea!"

There was a hearty cheer at this and Cunedag noticed Gonar observing the boy across the smoky roundhouse with a grave and thoughtful expression as he nursed his mead horn. Cunedag wondered what the old man was thinking. By all accounts, these Attacotti were even considered degenerate outcasts in their native Erin which was perhaps why they had come to these shores, and he wondered just how much Gonar knew about their alleged dark practices. He supposed they would all find out before the year's end.

"Have you given any thought to taking a wife yet?" Alpia asked Cunedag, disturbing his gloomy thoughts.

"No," he replied. "I have barely placed my arse in father's chair, let alone given any thought to wives."

"I am sure many of the chieftains here would gladly offer a daughter," said his mother. "But I advise you to cast your net a little wider. The Votadini are short on allies. Only the Selgovae stand with us against the confederation. I believe King Tasulus has a daughter as yet unmarried. And you are good friends with his son, after all …"

"Aye, my sister is comely, though I say so myself," said Morleo. "And my father would be proud to have you as a son-in-law. We would be brothers twice over!"

"Little use in marrying the daughter of one who is already an ally," said Alpia. "Better he look to a highland tribe as yet unaffiliated with either Rome or the confederation. The Venicones, perhaps. Or even the Taexali."

"We don't know where they stand," said Tegid. "They may have thrown their lot in with the Caledonii and the Epidii. And I wouldn't like to be the messenger sent to find out, for he may well return without his head."

"No more talk of marriage," said Cunedag. "I can't think about that now. We have more pressing concerns that need my immediate attention."

But he was lying to his family. He had been giving considerable thought to marriage, though he was reluctant to speak of it. There was but one woman he wished for his marriage bed and there was a whole world that stood between them. Besides, he doubted if she would be amenable to swapping the luxuries of bath houses and fine palaces for a smoky roundhouse in the gloomy north. She'd probably laugh in his face if he asked her.

"What are these more pressing concerns, Brother?" Murcho asked, his voice slurred.

"The shortage of grain with Kalan Gayaf approaching," Cunedag replied, referring to the end of the harvest and one of the most important festivals of the year. Kalan Gayaf marked the beginning of winter and the end of campaigning and was usually a time of feasting and full granaries. "I wish to redistribute the grain we took. Give it back to those chieftains whose lands we took it from."

"The gods know," said Tegid, "there is little left to go around. Especially after we burned Brude's stockpile."

"An ugly business but a necessary one. We would not be feasting in our father's hall tonight had we not drawn Brude from behind these walls. But I rule all the Votadini now and I will not let them starve if it is within my power. Besides," he added grimly, "our worries may be for naught in any case."

"How so?"

"Soon every warrior will be drawn from every settlement under my rule to aid the Roman army as it marches north. How many mouths will need feeding come Kalan Gayaf? We may have defeated Brude, but he was an incompetent fool compared to our true enemy. Canaul waits in the west with thousands of tribesmen, and he is a far more formidable foe than my brother was." He grinned at the uneasy faces around the roundhouse as they overheard his words. "Drink deeply tonight, comrades!" he said, raising his mead horn. "We still have a hell of a war ahead of us!"

Part IV

"Why should I speak of other nations when I myself, a youth on a visit to Gaul, heard that the Atticoti, a British tribe, eat human flesh …" – St. Jerome, *Against Jovinianus*

Chapter 24

The mist of late autumn cloaked the hills like a funeral shroud, clinging to the rock of Din Eidyn which poked out of it like an island. Cunedag, leaving the fortress alone, made his way down the eastern approach and was enveloped by the mist as he headed towards the crags of the great peak a mile distant that towered higher even than Din Eidyn. At the foot of those crags, where they rose from the grassy hump like the bones of a slain giant, Gonar the druid lived.

Gonar's house was little more than a lean-to of timber and hide with a roof of mouldering thatch. Smoke always drifted up from a hole in the blackened straw to be caught by the wind and carried away over the crags.

Cunedag dismounted and approached the hovel. "Gonar!" he called. "Your king has come to see you!"

The hide curtain twitched and was pulled aside to reveal the wizened old face of the druid.

"Barely two days on the throne," Gonar said, "and already he has need of my help!" his cracked and twisted lips split into a grin. "Come inside, young Cunedag, and warm yourself by my fire."

Cunedag tried to mask his disgust as he stooped to enter the hovel and saw the collection of human heads dangling from bits of twine, skin shrivelled like raisins with painted pebbles pushed into the vacant eye sockets. Gonar was proud of his collection; each one an enemy or criminal of some note whose soul he now commanded.

He sat down on an old wolf pelt opposite Gonar, the peat fire and the bubbling pot of some pungent liquid between them.

"Soon the Votadini must ride south to war," Gonar said.

"Yes. Such are the obligations of their kings."

"And now you have come seeking guidance from me. How best to defeat your enemy, is it?"

"Yes."

Gonar sucked his rotten teeth. "The Attacotti are the driving force behind the confederation. The Novantae would never have dared rebel against Rome themselves, and the tribes of the highlands would not have dared come south while the lowlands remained loyal. The Attacotti are the key, they always have been."

"Remove the Attacotti and the confederation falls apart, you mean?" said Cunedag. "But how?"

"There is a key within a key. One man holds the Attacotti in their grip. You have known this for a long time now."

"Blathmac."

"Aye. Never underestimate the power of the druids." He gave Cunedag a proud wink. "Julius Caesar did. His successors did not, and the groves of Ynys Mon are littered with the bones of my kindred. How else could Rome have taken the lands below the Wall and keep them for a dozen generations? Not by letting the druids live. Kill Blathmac and you kill the dream."

Cunedag stared into the flames, deep in thought. "Not an easy task," he said. "The man is like a ghost. He'll be somewhere deep in enemy territory."

Gonar chuckled, a dry, sick sound. "The gods do not give us easy tasks, my boy. Else we would have no legends. Find Blathmac and kill him."

Cunedag nodded and got up to leave, his lungs craving fresh air.

"Oh, and Cunedag?" said Gonar as he pulled aside the hide curtain.

"Yes?"

"A favour. When you do kill Blathmac, bring me his head?"

Cunedag grinned and let the curtain fall behind him as he turned back into the whiteness that obscured the crags.

The mist was little better a week later when Cunedag sat astride Bran with two hundred riders at his back as he stared down into the glen, unable to see its floor.

"Damn this murk," said Morleo at his side. "We could be surrounded and not know it until they were upon us."

"It is well we are here to meet our allies and not our enemies," said Cunedag.

"Aye, let us hope they know us for who we are and not mistake us for a Novantae raiding party."

Cunedag had received word that Britannia's new comes, Ambrosius Aurelianus, was at last preparing to set out to crush the confederation. He had sent a contingent of five hundred Taifal cavalrymen north to join forces with the Votadini. Together they would form a massive cavalry flank while the Sixth Victrix marched from the Wall with the aim of catching the enemy in a pincer manoeuvre. If the confederation could be lured into attacking the Sixth, they would find themselves smashed by an almighty hammer from the north.

Above Cunedag's host, a red banner fluttered; the banner of the new king of the Votadini. Upon it, in gold stitching, was the image of a dragon. The dragon had long been the tribe's symbol and was found engraved on standing stones reared by people that none now remembered. The red cloth had been cut from the cloak of Padarn that had hung behind the throne of the Votadini for two generations. A Roman cloak emblazoned with a Pictish sigil; The symbolism was intentional on Cunedag's part. The draco of the Roman legions given a native twist. His dynasty was to be one of both Roman and British heritage, just as he was.

"Look!" Morleo said, pointing down into the glen.

Emerging from the mist like spectres, the first line of horsemen could be seen astride their massive stallions, mail coats on man and horse making the whole column seem like a massive, scaled beast. The billowing draco standard above them only added to the effect and Cunedag could hear the wind moaning through its bronze mouth. Here, on this hillside, dragon would meet dragon.

Cunedag led his men down the slope and greeted their allies in the glen, Briton and Sarmatian, united against Rome's enemies. Neither commander dismounted, even though Cunedag was a king and, as tradition dictated, was the senior of the two.

"Well met, Briton," said the Taifal commander in heavily accented Latin. "I am Asaros, commander of the Equites Honoriani Taifali iuniores."

"King Cunedag of the Votadini."

There was a slight bow of the head on the part of Asaros, but otherwise the man showed the usual Roman disregard for kingship.

"Come," said Cunedag. "Our camp is not far from here. You must be tired and in need of refreshment from your journey."

"I would not say no to a cup of wine," Asaros replied, "but we Taifali are used to riding long distances. The length of this entire island is naught compared to the territory of one tribe where I come from."

"Haughty fellow, isn't he?" Morleo said to Cunedag in British as they followed the curve of the glen towards their camp.

Cunedag said nothing.

While the Taifals brushed down and fed their horses, Cunedag and Asaros shared a jug of wine in Cunedag's tent.

They talked of horses mostly and the dealings of the Romans in the south.

"This new military leader of yours is something of a firebrand," Asaros said, grimacing a little at what passed for wine in the north.

"The comes?" Cunedag said. "Yes, I've heard he is both ambitious and young."

"A Roman soldier to the bone and one of the good ones," said Asaros. "What Ambrosius Aurelianus lacks in experience, he makes up for in energy. Some of the prefects and tribunes don't like him but the real military men, the ones who do the actual fighting, see him as a breath of fresh air."

"Does he give any indication of when he intends to march north?"

Asaros shook his head and held out his cup for Cunedag to refill. "We must wait like the viper in the bushes."

"In the meantime," said Cunedag, "I wish to ride westwards and harry the enemy while we have both the time and the horses. The confederation mostly consists of infantry. We can cause some havoc and weaken them before they march south. Disrupt supply, put the fear of the gods into them."

"Well, I won't disagree to that," said Asaros. "My men get irritable if they're not kept busy."

Cunedag nodded. He said nothing of his true reasons for wanting to ride west as he didn't know how this foreigner would react to the notion of hunting the hills for a druid. "What is your homeland like, Asaros?"

Asaros leant back in his chair and took a deep gulp of wine. "My people are from Oltenia, sheltered in the bent arm of the Southern Carpathians where the Danube winds its way into the great Black Sea. That sea, I tell you, is the size of your whole island! I feel like I barely have room to move here in Britannia. In my homeland, the plains flow north, above the Black Sea into Sarmatia where one can ride for five days and the only sea you will encounter is the sea of grass bending in the wind beneath the open sky. This misty island of yours is like a prison. Your tribes fight each other over a tiny rock caught between two crashing seas. And for what? Control of muddy villages and crumbling Roman cities?"

"You are rather contemptuous of our small island which you may lay down your life defending," said Cunedag, a little affronted by this foreigner's summation of Albion.

"Of course I am contemptuous of the place I may meet my death for it is not a place of my choosing. I would rather die on the plains of my ancestors, beneath a warm sky, fighting for the honour of my people, not the greed of Rome. You think I choose to ride with the legions? Ha! My people are but slaves under Rome's heel, just as the Britons are. We, who were once free, are now dependant on our conquerors to save us from the Huns to the east; another people who are ever envious of that which does not belong to them."

"A wise man once told me that we cannot change the past," Cunedag said. "Only decide how to deal with the present."

"That was a wise man indeed."

They spent the next few days training and Cunedag got the feeling that the Taifals were keen to show off. He remained envious of their stallions but when they started showing him what they could do astride them, he became envious of their entire warrior culture.

Most impressive was their skill in the saddle with a bow and arrows. Approaching their target at a gallop, they would put their horse into a right turn, drop the reins and then, standing in their stirrups as to minimise the rise and fall, loose an arrow at their target with profound accuracy. By carrying spare arrows in their left hand resting against the stave of the bow, they were able to use their right hand to pull new arrows on to their bowstrings, shooting off one after another with both speed and precision.

Cunedag could see why Rome was so desirous of having these Sarmatian peoples as part of their cavalry. If only he had the time, he would train all his men to ride like the Taifals but he felt that there was not enough time in the world for men accustomed to British ponies to adapt to the fighting customs of men of the great eastern plains. Some things you had to learn from infancy, he suspected.

A few days later, they rode west, following the remains of the Antonine Wall which was grown over with grass now where sections of it had not been torn down by the natives. They passed the tumbledown remains of wooden forts and watchtowers, green and rotten with age.

As they entered Attacotti lands, Cunedag sent out scouts. Even though they were a strong cavalry force, it would not do to run into the whole warband. It wasn't far across the border when they came across the first sign that the confederation was on the move. A camp on the banks of the Aber Clut had been abandoned. Flattened, yellowed grass, burned out campfires and empty shelters were all that told them that a large band of warriors had been encamped there, and recently too. There was also a sickly stink about the place, of something rotten.

"Attacotti?" Asaros asked.

"This far north? Most likely," said Cunedag. "Or their Caledonian or Epidii allies."

"Why have they moved? This here is a good place for a camp."

"Must have gone south. Perhaps the warband is making its move."

"Yet we have not heard from the comes," said Morleo.

"Perhaps they think to attack the Wall again," Cunedag replied. "Last ditch attempt of the season."

"They'd be mad to!" said Morleo. "Surely they know Britannia has been reinforced from the continent now?"

"And yet they are still here, feeding their warriors, stripping the land bare while their women and old folk reap the harvest in their homelands. They would not remain on the warpath if they were not planning something."

"Cunedag!" cried Murcho from the centre of the camp. He and his men were investigating the wreckage left behind by the departed. Some sort of a dais had been constructed in the middle of the camp out of fresh cut logs that were deeply stained. Detritus surrounded the platform and, upon inspection, it was clear where the awful stink was coming from. The detritus was made up of body parts, clothes and bones.

"What, by all the gods, happened here?" Cunedag said as they approached the massacre.

There must have been the remains of at least a dozen people there. In many cases, the flesh had been stripped from the bones. One thing that was noticeable was that there wasn't a single head among them.

"Human sacrifice," said Murcho, holding his cloak to his nose to screen the nauseating smell. Flies rose angrily at their approach and dissipated into the fetid air.

"This is more than just sacrifice," said Cunedag. They had all heard of the northern tribes offering living victims to the gods on the eve of battle, even the tribes closer to Rome had done it in days past. But these victims had not had their throats cut or been drowned in cauldrons as was the custom. These people had been cut to pieces.

"There's more bones here than flesh," said Morleo. "Clothes too, discarded in a pile over there. These people were stripped of both cloth and flesh. But why?"

"I have heard of such a people in my own homeland," said Asaros. "A tribe to the east who eat the flesh of men in their religious rites."

"Even the Attacotti can't be that mad," said Cunedag.

"I wouldn't put it past them," said Morleo. "Haven't we always heard that they practise dark rites and human sacrifice? This druid of theirs, Blathmac. I've never heard of a man spoken of with such fear. Now we know why. They're maneaters!"

Confirmation of this horrible truth came when they found a pit full of refuse including what looked like human bones, boiled and picked clean.

A couple of men vomited while everybody else stood around looking stunned, not knowing what to do.

"Let us leave this place," said Cunedag. "The evil that has been done here has left a stain on the land that will not heal anytime soon."

The others didn't need telling twice and they left the stink of death and dark aura of horrible sorcery behind them.

Chapter 25

They turned south, following the Aber Clut as it wound its way through the hills. The land resembled one stripped by the passing of a warband and they found little game or grain to feed themselves with. Farms had been pillaged and their inhabitants solemnly tried to repair their lives or had simply moved on in search of new ones.

Cunedag continued to send scouts west to check for signs of any other factions of the confederation on the move. If they were indeed following the trail of the Attacotti, then he hoped they were moving alone. If they were small enough in number, there would be a chance of cutting them off from the rest of the warband and hopefully wiping them out.

On the second day, they had entered Novantae territory, and the scouts reported a Novantae camp on the other side of the hills to the west. Cunedag guessed that the Attacotti were somewhere in the Clut valley to the southeast of their position and, as long as their presence was not detected, they had a chance of driving a wedge between the two enemy factions. But they still had no idea how large the Attacotti warband was.

As they camped for the night, more scouts returned with news that a small Attacotti raiding party was pillaging a nearby settlement on the border between Novantae and Selgovae territory. That meant that the main warband could not be far off.

"I want the third turma to follow me," Cunedag ordered his men, "and thirty Taifals under you, Asaros. It's time to show us how good you are against real enemies. We'll see if we can't catch those bastards with their breeches down and take a few prisoners."

They mounted up and set off, following the river through the bald hills that lay spread beneath the starlight like slumbering lions. It wasn't hard to find the settlement for it was lit up by the torches of the looters which were reflected in the rushing water of the nearby Aber Clut and the screams of its inhabitants could be heard across the river.

"This is a Selgovae settlement," said Morleo through gritted teeth.

"Then we will avenge it," said Cunedag. "We cross the river here, boys and fall on them like wolves. Cut down anybody who assails us but remember, I want prisoners!"

Hooves sent up silver spray as they galloped across the ford in a long column of sixty riders. The wattle palisade of the settlement screened their approach and any sentries the settlement boasted were either dead or fighting for their lives somewhere within.

Cunedag led his men around to the settlement's northern gate which the defenders had futilely barred against the Attacotti. It lay in ruins along with the bodies of a few tribesmen who had mounted a brave defence.

They didn't slow their pace as they rode through the settlement and fell upon their enemies. They were easy to spot. Few men of fighting age had been left alive and the Attacotti were glutting their appetites on the screaming women and laden storehouses, eating, drinking and raping at their leisure.

Cunedag hurled his javelin, skewering an Attacotti through the back. Arrows thrummed from Taifal bows, striking several targets who fell, screaming to the mud. They rushed out of the southern gate before the Attacotti knew what had hit them and turned sharply to give the settlement another pass.

This time, what remained of the Attacotti were ready. They dropped whatever they were doing and assembled on the main street that ran through the settlement, shields and bucklers overlapping, spears held ready.

They hadn't a chance against a cavalry charge and scattered as Cunedag led his men through them like a hot knife through butter. He swung his spatha, hacking open a man's chest and trampling another under Bran's hooves as the enemy melted into the settlement to take cover.

"Dismount!" Cunedag roared. "Dismount and form up!"

They sent their horses on through the northern gate and huddled together, shields and swords drawn. Some of the Taifals kept their bows, arrows nocked, ready to deal death to any Attacotti warrior who dared show themselves. Cunedag split them into four groups and, reminding them all once again that he wanted prisoners, they swept through the settlement to each of its corners. After checking every building, three Attacotti tribesmen chose death rather than capture and met their fates on the ends of Votadini and Taifal swords while two more threw down their weapons.

"Bring them in here," said Cunedag, indicating the nearest roundhouse. He knew from experience that he had the stomach for torture if it came to it, but he preferred not to have an audience. Besides, the quicker he removed them from the sight of the outraged villagers, the better. These people would tear them limb from limb, given the chance.

He had the prisoners bound to the posts supporting the roof with the firepit between them. If he was forced to torture one of them, he damn well wanted the other to watch.

"Heat up some irons," he said to Morleo. "Do we have anybody who speaks Gaelic?"

"Not that I can think of," Morleo replied.

"You don't need an interpreter," said one of the Attacotti in the heavy accent of Erin. "I speak British."

"Good, then we'll start with you," said Cunedag, drawing up a tree stump to sit on. "How large is the Attacotti warband and where are they currently camped?"

"If I tell you, how will you know that I speak the truth?"

This is a cocky one, Cunedag thought. "Because I plan to keep you alive until I know if your information is good or not," he replied with a smile. "That way we won't be in danger of being sent into a trap because you'll be the first to die if we are. Now, whether you choose to spend your time in my company in agonising pain or not, is entirely up to you."

The man swallowed and looked at Morleo who was placing a variety of blades and pincers into the glowing embers of the fire one by one, like a surgeon laying out the tools of operation.

"Fine," he said. "They are camped a dozen miles or so southeast from here. The remains of a Roman road lead away from the Clut to a point where three rivers meet. An old fort is there. That's where they are encamped."

"How many men?"

"We numbered two thousand when we left Alt Clut," he said. "We picked up more warriors on the way. Must be near to three thousand by now."

"Is the druid with you? Blathmac?"

The mention of the name caused a look of fear to cross the prisoner's face. "Aye," he said, his voice barely more than a mumble. "Blathmac is with us."

Cunedag cut the prisoner's bonds and handed him a charred stick from the fire. "Draw the layout of the camp for me," he said, pointing at the dirt floor of the roundhouse. "And point out where Blathmac is likely to be found."

The Gael gave him an incredulous look but set to work all the same, scratching out a layout of the rivers, roads and encampments to be found less than a day's march to the southeast. When he was finished, Cunedag had a good idea of an area of land where three rivers converged with a Roman road running north to south. The main portion of the warband was encamped to the south behind the overgrown earthworks of two Roman marching camps. North of that was a stone fort containing two barrack blocks which the Attacotti chieftains had commandeered and billeted their household warriors. Blathmac, the prisoner claimed, was in the fort where he had claimed the old praetorium as his sleeping quarters.

Cunedag tied the prisoner up again and he and Morleo left the roundhouse, leaving two men to guard the prisoners. Outside, they found the village in the middle of another uproar as Asaros's men had started the work the Attacotti had begun by raiding the granaries and helping themselves to sheep and chickens.

"What are you doing?" Morleo demanded. "These are Selgovae lands! These are our allies!"

"Then they should not be so averse to feeding us and our horses," Asaros answered, biting into an apple. "My men are hungry. How are we to fight Rome's enemies on empty bellies?"

Morleo turned to Cunedag in exasperation.

"He's right, I'm afraid," Cunedag said. "We have been on the march for several days now. Our own supply wagons grow light. We must relieve these people of some stores or we will not be able to win this war."

While the granaries were emptied and the requisitioned supplies sent north to feed the rest of the warband, Cunedag called a meeting in the main roundhouse.

"We have learned from our prisoners that the Attacotti are camped less than a day's march down the road from here." He drew an approximate copy of the map the prisoner had provided in the dirt of the floor. "We can safely estimate their numbers to be around three thousand."

There were some curses from the assembled warriors at this.

"Have we received any word of Roman forces setting out from the Wall, Sir?" Marcus asked.

"No," Cunedag replied. "But the harvest is almost over. They will not wait much longer. The final battle is almost at hand."

"Our orders were to come down from the northeast and hit the enemy's left flank," said Morleo. "But we are directly behind them. If the Romans march up from the south, we will not be able to break through their lines and aid our allies. Do we ride east?"

"We remain here."

"But if the Attacotti turn back, we can't possibly hold them, Sir!" Elffin said. "Our horses could outrun them, certainly, but our baggage train couldn't."

"I do not believe they will turn back," said Cunedag. "This is the final move of the confederation. The Attacotti await their allies before they intend to hurl themselves against the Wall with the hope of smashing through it, whatever the cost to their numbers. We can severely weaken them here and now."

"Why do you pursue these Attacotti with such vengeance?" Asaros asked him. "I detect something more personal than a desire to fight Rome's battles for them. Why risk so much when our job is merely to assist the Romans when they march north?"

Cunedag had been dreading this moment. It was time to come clean, both to Asaros and to his own men. "There is a druid with the Attacotti. A powerful one by the name of Blathmac."

"Druid?" Asaros enquired.

"A spiritual leader. A priest of sorts. He holds the Attacotti in a grip of fear and they follow his orders without question."

"Ah, yes, the power priests hold over people must not be underestimated."

"This Blathmac is the man behind the entire confederation, I am sure of it," Cunedag continued.

"How can you be so sure?" Morleo asked.

"It has always been the Attacotti who were the driving force behind this rebellion. The Novantae and the Caledonii and all the others wouldn't have acted had not these settlers from Erin unified them in their hatred of Rome. And Blathmac is the advisor to their chieftains, maybe even their chieftain himself. And I want to kill him."

There was a chuckle from the assembled men at this. "We'd all like to do that, Sir," said Marcus. "We'll get our chance when we wet our blades against his warriors in battle."

"I want to kill him before the battle starts," said Cunedag.

That silenced them.

"Tonight, I will lead a ten-man unit behind enemy lines and cut off the head of this vile serpent. The Attacotti will crumble after that and perhaps even the entire confederation."

"You're not serious, Sir!" Marcus protested. "You just said that the enemy is three thousand strong!"

"Which is why we can never defeat them in battle," Cunedag insisted. "We must use subtlety and strategy. I want volunteers. I will order no man to follow me on so dangerous a mission."

"What exactly is the mission, Sir?" Elffin asked. "Sneak into the enemy camp, kill the druid and sneak back out again, all the while avoiding any sentries or polite conversation because not one of us could pass for a Gael if we are forced to open our mouths?"

"That's more or less it. A contingent of our boys will be waiting on the riverbank with our horses so we can make fast tracks back to safety once the job is done. I also want thirty of Asaros's men to cover our escape. Their bowmanship and fast horses will keep anybody off our heels. I will send our baggage train into the hills where it will be safe if we incur the wrath of the entire Attacotti warband. As Elffin said, we can easily outrun them if they decide to pursue us north, but I doubt they will."

Elffin sighed. "Well, Sir, as you quoted my confident words so succinctly, I suppose I had better volunteer for this mad mission."

Cunedag grinned. "Thank you, Elffin. I knew I could count on you."

"You can count on me too, Sir," said Marcus. "Though the gods know I can't pass for a Gael."

"This won't be like sneaking into Din Guaire," Cunedag said. "Their warband is large enough for some unknown faces to avoid suspicion, even swarthy ones like yours and the shadows of night will aid us. I aim to avoid speaking with any of the bastards if I can help it. I don't know any more Gaelic than any of you."

"And you'll need your duplicarius to keep these fools in line," said Morleo.

Cunedag clapped his foster brother on the shoulder, grateful that he had such good men under his command.

"I'm with you too," said Murcho.

"No, Brother," said Cunedag. "Two royal figures endangering themselves is enough. I need you here and if I do not return …"

"Do not even say it!" said Murcho. "You are so newly crowned it is ill-luck to talk of succession in the same season you became our king. Just make damn sure you return to us."

Cunedag smiled at his brother. "Aye. I will."

The mission, as Elffin had stated, was indeed a mad one. But Cunedag knew that the damage done to the enemy would be crippling if they could only pull it off. The gods would be with them in the final battle if they were able to slay such a blasphemer as Blathmac, he was sure of it.

More volunteers came forward from the third turma and Cunedag assembled a team of ten. He had them strip their Roman armour and put on the garments salvaged from the Attacotti warriors they had slain, those that showed no bloodstains at least. Their clothing was little different from that of British tribesmen but their shields, painted with various swirling patterns, would do well in convincing anybody from a distance that they were Attacotti warriors.

The only vocal resistance to the whole plan came from Asaros. "I don't like this, Briton," he told Cunedag as they were making the preparations that afternoon. "My men and their horses are valuable to me. Too valuable to waste on suicide missions when our job is merely to support the Romans in battle."

"Nothing will be a greater support to the Romans than killing Blathmac," Cunedag said. "And besides, if this is a suicide mission, then we are the ones risking our necks. All you and your men have to do is shoot a few arrows at the enemy and then retreat. Think you can handle that?"

Asaros grunted at the implied question of his courage and said no more.

"Are you so sure the Taifals will be there to cover our escape?" Morleo asked as they bedded down to catch a few hours of sleep in the waning light of dusk. "I don't trust that Asaros any further than I could throw him."

"They'll be there," Cunedag replied with more confidence than he truly felt. If they weren't then their retreat from the enemy camp would be a hot one.

Chapter 26

They were awoken by one of Cunedag's men after night had fallen. Rousing themselves, they mounted their horses and, with a small escort and thirty Taifal riders, set out along the road south.

It was a clear night and Cunedag cursed the absent clouds for their lack of cooperation. On a night such as this, they would easily be spotted as approaching the Roman fort was the hardest part of the whole plan. Once inside the Attacotti camp, he hoped they could easily mingle with the enemy and worm their way into Blathmac's quarters but the woods that grew so close to the road petered out as they neared the fort and there was a lot of open ground to cover.

The road ran across a small bridge over the westernmost of the three rivers before it joined the other two upstream. Even at that distance, they could see that it was guarded. The shaggy heads of two tribesmen could be seen moving about as they guarded the road north.

"We need to take care of those two," said Cunedag, "or we'll never make it down to the fort."

"We'll have the whole warband after us if their bodies are found," said Morleo.

"We'll have to risk that. Besides, I intend to be quick enough that their bodies won't be discovered until we're long gone. Those sentries probably won't be relieved until dawn. Asaros, do you have men that can make that shot at such range?"

"Not at such range, no," he admitted. "Even for Sarmatian bows, it is too far. We would have to ride closer to make the shot."

"Then send out your riders and be damn sure you get both sentries. If one of them runs screaming towards the camp, this whole mission is done for."

Asaros barked orders in his own tongue and two of his men unslung their bows and nocked arrows to their strings.

"Hadn't you better send more than two?" Cunedag asked him.

"Two is all that is needed, trust me. Besides, more than two would be easily seen from the bridge."

They watched as Asaros's two riders galloped from the cover of the trees towards the bridge. It wasn't long before they were spotted, and the guards could be seen jumping up, alert and ready to challenge the strangers.

They never got the chance. Two arrows sailed through the night from the formidable Sarmatian bows and Cunedag watched in awe as the two sentries stumbled and fell, pierced by feathered shafts.

"Bloody impressive, it has to be admitted," he said to Asaros as the riders came galloping back.

Asaros smiled.

"All right, men," Cunedag said to his ten volunteers. "Now it's our turn. We ride for the bridge and stow our horses below it before continuing on foot. Asaros, you wait under the cover of these trees and be ready to ride out if you see anybody pursuing us."

They broke from cover and rode fast towards the bridge, fifteen of them; Cunedag and his ten volunteers plus four men to guard the horses and have them ready for their escape. The river was low at that time of year and there was plenty of room beneath the bridge to hide the horses. Dismounting, Cunedag led his men up the embankment and across the bridge, stepping over the dead sentries as they headed towards the lights of the enemy settlement.

Hide tents and cookfires lay spread across the valley and men milled about, lounging around the fires or wandering around in twos and threes, drinking, laughing and utterly oblivious to the imposters in their midst.

Cunedag and his men tried to look like they were men on an errand and headed straight for the crumbling walls of the fort, hoping that nobody hailed them or invited them to drink or dice. They reached the fort with nothing more than a couple of curious glances cast their way and Cunedag was thankful that the enemy were so numerous for they could never hope to stroll through a small camp where everybody knew one another.

The gate to the fort presented a problem. Although the entire fortification was a ruin, the Attacotti had seen fit to post sentries at the main gates, though warriors seemed to be making their way into the fort unhindered.

"We're not going to get in that way," Cunedag murmured to his followers. "Not without being looked at too closely. Let's look for another way in."

That the fort was in ruins made guarding its gates a little futile. The wall wasn't even standing in some parts and the ditch that surrounded it was overgrown and filled with rubble. It wasn't hard to find a suitable gap where a stubborn tree had made room for itself, thrusting up through the wall.

They slipped in, single file, and found themselves on ground that was more familiar to them than the Attacotti. It was a small fort with only two barrack blocks, but the layout of Roman forts was almost uniform throughout the empire. The via principalis led from east to west, past the praetorium and the principia, just like at Cilurnum and every other fort on the Wall.

The abundance of Attacotti warriors strolling about made the place seem utterly barbaric compared to the tight discipline Roman forts were usually accustomed to. Again, it was a boon to their plan as Cunedag and his men were able to melt into the crowd without being challenged.

The hub of activity seemed to be the principia which was in an even worse state of decay than the fort's walls. The roof was utterly gone and most of the buildings had less than two walls each. Most of the pillars of the forecourt still stood, supporting nothing now but the starry sky into which the embers of a large fire whirled.

The crowd of warriors was thickest in the ruins of the complex, all with their backs to them, focused on some spectacle and the shouted voice of somebody in authority as they yelled a stream of Gaelic over their heads.

Cunedag and his men stowed their shields against a pillar and pushed their way through the throng to get a better look. In the centre of the forecourt, a large cauldron bubbled over a cookfire. Next to it stood a man in a long robe that must have been white once, a long time ago. Now it was filth-smeared and reddish brown to the elbows with dried blood which contrasted with the fresh blood that slicked his gnarled hands which were upraised to the stars. A long, brown beard streaked with grey into which had been woven ornaments of bone and iron, hung nearly to the man's waist and a wreath of autumnal leaves and antlers crowned his shaggy head.

The man had to be Blathmac, there was no doubt about it.

But what dragged Cunedag's eyes away from the extraordinary druid was the grotesque scene behind him. On racks, as if they were meat hung up to cure, were the bodies of two people, a man and a woman. Their naked flesh was streaked with gore which ran down from several horrific wounds and Cunedag could see that large chunks had been cut from them.

The crowd was going wild as Blathmac's words rose in crescendo. He seemed to be calling on the gods to witness something or perhaps accept a sacrifice. Picking up a long-handled ladle, he began to stir the cauldron, scooping up chunks of meat and letting them splash back into the foaming broth. Cunedag had a good idea of what kind of meat it was.

The crowd began to jostle its way forward and some sort of procession began as warriors lined up in a somewhat disorderly queue. One by one, at a gesture from Blathmac, the warriors came forward and knelt at the druid's feet. They watched as a chunk of meat was plucked from the cauldron and fed to a kneeling man. As he chewed, eyes closed and arms outraised in devotion, Blathmac dipped his forefingers in a bowl of blood that rested on a pedestal near the slaughtered victims. Placing his bloody fingers to the forehead of the warrior, he painted the image of a crescent moon. When the man had swallowed his meat, he stood and, to the roaring cheers of the crowd, stepped aside for the next warrior to receive his portion.

"We're going to need some sort of a diversion," Cunedag murmured to his men, wary of being overheard. "There's no way we can get to that bastard druid with all these people around. Marcus, take Lepidus and Sitracos and start a fire somewhere. We'll try and nail Blathmac in the confusion. Meet on the northern side of the fort and we'll see if we can't escape this hellhole in one piece."

Marcus nodded, wisely remembering not to salute and led his two companions off. Cunedag turned back to the scene and began to plan his attack. They could pretend to protect the druid, get close to him as everybody else panicked. With any luck, he would scamper to his quarters and all they need do was follow him …

He nodded to his men, and they pushed their way through the crowd, approaching the ghastly scene, ready to make their move when all hell broke loose. The crowd was boisterous and rowdy, like they'd all had a bellyful of mead before the horrific rites had begun. Cunedag supposed that even these mad cretins needed to addle their brains to partake in anything so monstrous.

They were jostled about as people pressed forward, somehow eager to get their taste of man flesh and whatever magical properties Blathmac had convinced them would aid them in the battle to come. They were dangerously close to the druid now and Cunedag tried to hold his ground but was dragged forward like a man caught in a strong tide. Unable to do anything about it, he and his men found themselves in the line of supplicants before the glowering gaze of the mad druid.

As the man in front of Cunedag received his rites and departed, Cunedag felt Blathmac's eyes land upon him like slabs of granite. There was no backing out now. He had to play along, though his stomach recoiled at what he would be called on to do. With legs of water, he stepped forward and knelt at the druid's feet.

The meat was offered and, heart hammering, he opened his mouth. Blathmac pushed the horrific morsel in. It was hot and Cunedag closed his eyes, trying not to think that this was a piece of human buttock or breast or arm muscle resting on his tongue.

Blathmac said something he did not understand but he knew he was going to have to start chewing. He fought the urge to grimace as his teeth sank into the tender meat and he chewed it up as best he could. Blathmac's fingers daubed his forehead in cold, congealing blood, marking him as one who had received the gods' blessing. He swallowed the meat, knowing that he would vomit if he didn't desperately focus on not doing so. At a word from the druid, he rose and took his place alongside the other marked warriors.

One by one, his seven remaining men followed suit, and he watched their faces with pitying pride. Not one of them gagged or in any way showed themselves reluctant to eat human flesh and, with pale faces, they came to stand by his side, none of them quite believing what they had just done.

Before long, there were cries of alarm from the western portion of the fort and smoke could be seen rising behind the shattered walls of the principia. As Cunedag had hoped, chaos erupted in the forecourt. A fire within a fort was always a serious matter and this fort was overcrowded and lacked any kind of discipline. If not dealt with immediately, the whole place could go up in flames.

There was a surge of movement in several directions as some fled while others headed through the west wing of the principia to combat the fire. Cunedag and his men held their ground while several of the other warriors who had been marked by the bloody crescent, joined the mob. Blathmac, his face enraged at the disruption to his ceremony, turned in a swirl of hair and robes, and headed east towards the small praetorium.

Cunedag and his men hurried after him, but they weren't alone. Several other warriors seemed keen to protect the druid, and nobody spoke as they hurried through the ruins and into the next building.

The praetorium was one of the few buildings in the fort that still had most of its roof, though thick clumps of moss grew on the cracked tiles and Cunedag wouldn't have put much stock in the strength of its timbers.

They followed Blathmac up a sagging staircase which creaked and groaned alarmingly under the tread of so many warriors and found themselves in what had once been a grand room with arched windows overlooking the principia and the coil of smoke to the west.

There were four unknown warriors with them who needed to be dealt with and, just as they turned to look at Cunedag and his companions, questioning looks on their faces,

Cunedag drew his sword and ordered Elffin to bolt the door behind them.

Recognising them as a threat, the four warriors drew their weapons and stood between them and Blathmac who watched on with curiosity.

Cunedag batted the blade of the nearest man out of his hand with his spatha and then ran him through, his blood raining down on the mosaic floor. His men dealt with the remaining warriors with ruthless Roman efficiency, hacking them down. Only Blathmac remained and the old druid showed no fear at being cornered by eight enemy fighters.

"Who are you?" Blathmac said in accented British. "What is your purpose here? You are no men of mine."

Cunedag wiped the bloody crescent from his forehead and pointed the tip of his spatha at the druid. "Very perceptive of you, Blathmac. We are here to kill you and end your reign of terror. As to who we are, you may as well know who it is that sends you to Annun. I am Cunedag mab Etern. These are my men, Roman soldiers from below the Wall. The Wall you and your wretched tribe will never breach!"

A grin revealed a mouthful of rotten teeth as the druid leered at them. "Cunedag mab Etern, King of the Votadini!" he said. "Slave to Rome, betrayer of his own people! Your brother did you a disservice, for you are far braver than he claimed. To sneak into our camp with a mere seven men – a tad more, perhaps, as I assume that fire yonder is your diversion."

"You knew my brother," Cunedag said through gritted teeth. "Was it you who twisted his mind and made him betray his people's allegiance to Rome?"

"Your brother's mind was twisted long before I met him," said Blathmac. "I had high hopes for him, but he failed me at the end. He was not strong enough to rule his tribe or remove the threat to his crown and came crawling back to me after being ousted by his brother. But he still had his uses. Royal flesh is the most sacred of all and his meat has fed our warriors, giving them the strength to overcome our oppressors!"

A cold hand of ice gripped Cunedag's heart. He had never liked his brother but to think that he had suffered a similar fate to those poor wretched he had seen stretched out on those racks in the principia, chunks carved off them like carcasses in a butcher's shop …

"You murdered my brother and fed him to your men?" he asked Blathmac.

"Aye," said the druid with a nauseating grin. "Clearly I backed the wrong brother. You hold the Votadini in your palm and command more respect than Brude ever did. Join me, Cunedag, and ensure your people's place in a bright new future where Rome serves us rather than the other way around."

"My brother may have been weak and easily led," said Cunedag. "But he wasn't utterly mad as you are."

The druid's face grew thunderous. "You won't leave here alive and each of you will scream for death when I have you on my altar. Throw down your weapons and submit, King of the Votadini!"

At his words, as if summoned by magic, there came a hammering at the door.

"Sir, we have to get going!" said Elffin.

"The gods are on my side!" Blathmac screeched. "And all who stand against me will drown in their own blood!"

Cunedag cut his fanatical torrent short by ramming his sword up to the hilt in his guts. Blathmac doubled over, a gasp of pain escaping his lips which then began to drool blood. Cunedag ripped his blade free and, as Blathmac sank to his knees, swung it around to connect with his neck.

The druid's head tumbled from his shoulders in one clean sweep. Blood jetted from the severed neck before the lifeless body slumped forward. Cunedag seized the severed head by the hair and looked out of the window. The fire burned ever hotter beyond the walls of the principia, and he hoped it would be uncontrollable enough to wipe out a good portion of the Attacotti camp. But they needed to be long gone by then.

Gaelic voices and heavy blows sounded on the other side of the door as the dead druid's followers desperately tried to get in. Cunedag grabbed some sackcloth from the detritus of Blathmac's belongings and wrapped his grisly trophy up in it.

"This way," he said to his men. "Follow me."

Chapter 27

Cunedag clambered out of the window and, by hanging from one hand, dropped to the street below. The entire fort was in chaos as people ran in all directions, some with pails and skins of water to douse the spreading flames and others merely trying to escape. Cunedag led his men towards the gap in the wall through which they had gained entry, but they still had a large enemy camp to get through before they reached their horses by the river.

On the north side of the fort, they found Marcus and his two fellow arsonists loitering in the shadows. "Good work setting that blaze," Cunedag said to them. "It should keep them occupied for the rest of the night."

"Damn fools just left barrels of pitch and straw lying around," said Marcus. "The fire practically lit itself."

The entire camp had been roused by the coil of smoke and whirling embers rising from inside the fort and most stood around not quite knowing what to do. That made their desire to move north quickly somewhat problematic. Everybody's eyes were on the fort so moving in the opposite direction would quickly draw attention. They kept to the shadows as best they could, waiting for groups of curious onlookers to pass before moving on.

They had almost reached the bridge when they saw that their way out of the camp to the north was blocked. Several warriors, some mounted, were clustered around the bridge, inspecting the two dead sentries.

"Shit!" said Marcus. "There goes our way out!"

"What about our men and horses below the bridge?" Morleo wondered. "They've been discovered, surely?"

"Well, we can't get across that way," said Cunedag. "We'll have to wade through the river upstream and hope we don't get spotted."

They hurried towards the riverbank not far from where it converged with two other rivers and slid down into the water. Holding their swords above their heads, they waded through and helped each other up the bank on the other side. Poking his head above the grassy slope, Cunedag looked across the open ground to the trees where Asaros and his men were waiting.

"A hell of a lot of ground to cover on foot, Sir," said Marcus by his side.

Cunedag looked west and could see that there was nobody beneath the bridge. "I wonder where our bloody horses are," he murmured.

The enemy tribesmen on the bridge were still milling around and looked to be guarding it for the night. The horsemen would ride them down in moments if they were spotted.

"Keep low and stay together," Cunedag told his men. "We have no choice but to run for the treeline."

"What if they spot us, Sir?" Elffin asked.

"Run bloody fast."

It wasn't much of a plan, but they had little choice. Cunedag only hoped that Asaros would stay true to his word and ride out to rescue them should the need arise.

They got to their feet and, Cunedag in the lead, hurried across the grassy field, stooped like apes. Blathmac's bloodied head banged against Cunedag's thigh as they ran, weighing him down. They hadn't got halfway before Morleo warned them that they had been spotted.

"Riders crossing the bridge!" he breathed.

"Keep going!" Cunedag told them. "Have they seen us?"

"It certainly looks that way," said Morleo.

"Then run!"

They straightened and pelted with all their might towards the distant treeline. Gaelic curses could be heard behind them and the thunder of hooves gradually drowned out the pounding of their own feet.

Cunedag risked a glance over his shoulder and swore as he saw five Attacotti warriors bearing down on them, spears raised, ready to skewer them in their paces.

Arrows sailed over their heads, striking two of the riders. Cunedag glanced back at the treeline and gasped in relief to see a line of Taifal horsemen galloping towards them with the men and horses he had left under the bridge bringing up the rear.

The Attacotti veered away, alarmed at the sudden and deadly precision of these new enemies. The Taifals, led by Asaros, yelled war cries in their own tongue and loosed more shafts at them while the Votadini riders reached Cunedag and his men with their horses.

Swinging up into their saddles, they drew their weapons and joined the Taifals in giving chase to the Attacotti who were now heading back towards the bridge. "We don't have time for this," Cunedag said. "We must break away and head back north before the whole damn camp is on our trail."

He had little cause to fear that the Taifals would be drawn across the bridge and into the enemy camp chasing their quarry, for three more arrows from those deadly eastern bows felled the enemy riders in their saddles and, before their bodies hit the grass, Asaros and his men were wheeling back towards the trees.

"I can't thank you enough, Asaros," Cunedag said, once they were riding back towards the settlement upriver. "Your swiftness and accuracy saved our lives. That was a bit of a tight spot, I don't mind admitting."

"They were not the first men we killed for Rome's cause this night," Asaros replied. "Your men under the bridge were discovered and made a break for the trees. Riders from the camp followed them and we let them come to us. They found more than they were expecting in these woods."

"I did wonder what happened to our horses," said Cunedag, patting the side of Bran's neck, grateful that he had come through unscathed.

"And this druid of yours?" Asaros asked.

Cunedag held up the bloodied sackcloth. "The head of the serpent has been cut off," he replied. "And the Attacotti warband will be in its death throes without it."

Dawn had broken by the time they returned to the settlement on the river. After a quick breakfast, they rode north to rejoin the rest of the warband. Cunedag held Blathmac's head up before them and they cheered wildly, feeling like a serious blow had been delivered to the enemy.

"That was a great risk you took, Brother," said Alpia when they were alone together. "Sneaking into an enemy camp with a handful of men? A prudent king would not be so quick to gamble with his own life."

"I will not ask my men to do something I would not do myself, Alpia," he told her.

"You forget that you are not just a cavalry commander now," she chided him. "You are our king and the second one we've had in a year. What if you were killed on one of these mad excursions? What of the Votadini then?"

"You worry too much, Sister."

"And you not enough!" There was an anger in her words that surprised him. He was not used to warriors under his command speaking to him like that but his sister had ever been one to speak her mind and showed no sign of holding back, even though he was now her king.

"Perhaps you are right, Alpia," he admitted. "I have ridden with my men under the draco of a Roman turma for many years now. It comes hard for me to sit back and send warriors into danger when, as a decurion I should be leading the charge."

She smiled. "I understand, Cunedag, and nobody respects your courage more than I. Just try to remember that you are responsible for more than the men in your turma now. We can't afford to lose you."

The next day, they rode northeast, around the hills and then curved south, following the rugged terrain over moors and through wooded valleys, crossing the southern uplands and made camp for the night. It was a few hours before dawn that Cunedag was awoken in his tent by one of his men who had come to report that the scouts had returned with somebody.

Throwing on his cloak to keep out the morning chill, Cunedag hurried from his tent to where his scouts were waiting at the edge of camp. A stranger in Roman armour was with them along with his horse, a dun mare with the brand of the legions on its flank.

"My king, we came across this man ten miles southeast of here," said his scout. "He claims to be under the command of the Comes Britanniarum."

"Speak, friend," said Cunedag, "for I recognise a fellow soldier of Rome. I am King Cunedag of the Votadini."

The Roman seemed to be put a little at ease at the revelation that he was among allies. "Sir, I am a scout with the Sixth Victrix. We have been looking for you. Riders have been sent north to locate your warband for the hour of battle is almost upon us. The Roman army is camped twenty miles southeast of here at a bend in the river. The enemy are massing to the west of them, thousands strong."

"There is an Attacotti warband camped in the valley on the other side of those hills to our west," said Cunedag. "We were able to deal a serious blow to them by killing their druid, but they may yet join with their allies to the south."

"Ambrosius Aurelianus, the Comes Britanniarum, desires that you move your men southeast to guard our right flank," the scout said.

"We will be on the move come daylight," said Cunedag. "You had best return to your unit and report that we are on our way."

"Yes, Sir." The scout saluted and mounted his horse.

Cunedag sniffed the cold air, knowing that he would get no more sleep that night. War was on the wind and the final battle was at hand.

Alpia came to him as he was wolfing down a hasty breakfast in between giving orders for the camp to be struck. "Are you still so committed to continuing south to join the Romans in their war?" she asked him, helping herself to a ladleful of porridge from a sputtering cauldron.

"It's not just their war," he replied. "This confederation must be smashed if there is to be peace in the north once more."

"Father would have been content to deal with our enemies as they came to him, not pursue them south into the lands of other tribes."

Cunedag frowned, surprised by his sister's reluctance. "I am not our father," he said. "I have pledged myself to Rome's defence."

"Yourself, aye," she replied. "But the rest of the tribe?"

"We are allies of Rome, Alpia! Allies help each other."

"My understanding of it was that Rome sent you north to break Brude's control over the tribe so the Votadini wouldn't stand against them. You succeeded. Must we sacrifice so many of our warriors fighting Rome's war for them? Why not return home and defend our own borders?"

"I don't understand you, Sister," he said. "You who have been one of my strongest supporters. You helped me win my crown and now you don't want to fight under me?"

"I didn't say that!" she snapped, her anger at his words getting the better of her. "I just question your judgement in leading all the warriors of our tribe into a battle so many of them might not survive."

"You don't think we can win!" Cunedag exclaimed. "Alpia, you are not accustomed to the might of the Roman military. Stilicho has sent enough men to—"

"Again, you mistake my words for cowardice!" Alpia growled.

"Alpia, I would never—"

"I would fight to the death under you, Cunedag! As long as I believed in the cause."

"How can you not believe in this cause? Supporting Rome is the only way we can win."

"We? Or Rome? This confederation has no fight with the Votadini, only with Rome. Your devotion to the people below the Wall was fostered in you from a young age but try to see things from our perspective. We want no war with Rome, but we want no war with the other tribes either. Be sure that what you do is best for the tribe and not just best for Rome."

Cunedag had had enough and his anger boiled over. "You forget yourself, Alpia. You might be my sister, but you are still my subject and your counsel is neither wanted nor asked for."

Her face turned stony at this, though her eyes blazed like hot coals and she stormed away from him without a word.

The following evening, they reached the edge of the Roman camp where the southern uplands sank down to the grassy plains above the Wall. It had rained for much of the day and the men were soaked through and the ground was muddy.

Below them, the Roman camp stretched for miles. The Sixth Victrix were encamped in tidy lines, with trenches and embankments dug before them, the blue haze from the cook fires hanging over hundreds and hundreds of drab tents pitched in neat rows. Cavalry were camped on each wing and Cunedag saw the standards of the alae First Sabiniana and Second Asturum along with various other limitanae units from the Wall.

To the west, there was little sign of the enemy but dim lights in the trees and smoke rising above the pines. The confederation had chosen to keep to the cover of the woods while the Romans blocked their path to the Wall.

There was cheering as the Votadini warband approached, the arrival of yet more cavalry boosting the spirits of those who held the plains against untold odds. Cunedag ordered camp to be made on the slopes above the Roman lines and set his dragon standard where all could see it, though it hung limply in the drizzle.

Both Candidius and Titus Gemellus came to greet Cunedag that evening and he was warmed by the company of his old commanders. They drank spiced wine and discussed tactics in his tent while the rain continued to drum down on the waxed goatskins.

"By Christ, I am glad we put our stock in you, Cunedag," said Gemellus. "By uniting the Votadini and allying them with us, you have stripped the enemy of one of their factions."

"And I have the head of the man who may well be the instigator of the whole rebellion preserved in a barrel of salt," said Cunedag.

The two men gaped at him and, with a chuckle, he explained the events of the last few days. By the time they were on their second cup of wine, spirits were high, and all three men were confident of their chances of success over their enemies.

But the following morning, accompanied by yet more rain, a blow to their spirits arrived from the northwest. Emerging from the glen from which the river flowed, came a couple of thousand tribesmen who spread their tents at the valley mouth. The Attacotti had arrived.

Their appearance spurred their allies to come out of hiding and the defenders watched with grim faces as the confederation emerged from the forest like a sweeping tide flooding the land. There must have been five thousand all told, arrayed according to tribal allegiances with none of the disciplined formations of the Roman army. They relied on the advantage of sheer numbers and there was no doubt that there were more of them than the defenders.

Horns bellowed in the misty morning air like the lungs of a beast woken from its slumber. Helmets were strapped on, shields and spears lifted, and battle lines formed. Cunedag mustered his men on the slopes, guarding the right flank. Just across the plains from them stood the Attacotti, every one of them surely sore with the loss of their druid. They were no longer so sure that the gods were with them. Their fate was now clouded but they were prepared to hurl themselves against the spears of the Romans in vengeance if for nothing else.

The Romans let the enemy come to them and they came in a surging, painted horde of howling, roaring death. Arrows and javelins sailed overhead, finding their marks in shields and flesh, cutting men down in their paces moments before the front lines of each side collided in an almighty slam of wood and iron. The sound echoed across the plains and rolled up the slopes to where Cunedag waited for his signal.

The line of battle wavered like a writhing snake beneath the drifting clouds and men pushed and shoved, each side bracing themselves in the slippery mud as they hacked and stabbed at each other.

"Why haven't the Attacotti engaged?" Morleo asked. "They're just standing there. What are they waiting for?"

"Their courage, perhaps," said Cunedag.

"We could crush them now," Murcho said. "Before they decide to join the fray."

"Aye, we could," said Cunedag. "And leave ourselves exposed at the rear of the enemy. We wait for our orders."

But it was a hard wait. No orders reached them requesting their support on the right flank, but the sounds of slaughter seeped up from the plains as they watched men fight and die over mere yards of mud.

"A rider comes!" said Morleo.

Sure enough, a foaming mount carried a young soldier up the slope towards them. He flung out a salute. "The comes requests that you charge the enemy's left flank, Sir!" he said.

"That would place us between the bulk of the enemy and their Attacotti allies on the slope over there," Cunedag replied.

But the man was just a messenger. He had no authority to discuss orders, merely to relay them. He shrugged apologetically and rode off. Cunedag swore. Cavalry was no good if it wasn't on the move. And if the Attacotti decided to charge while they were engaging the enemy's left flank, they could drive their spears into his men and horses like skewering fish in a barrel.

"Asaros!" he bellowed.

The commander of the Taifals rode over to him. "Take your men along the ridge up there and rain down arrows on the Attacotti. See if you can't get them to remember why they are here. Do not engage them hand to hand. Ride back here and, with any luck, they will follow you."

The Taifal nodded and galloped back to his men.

"Disobeying orders, Brother?" Alpia said. "How very un-Roman of you."

"Who says I'm disobeying them?" he replied. "Merely interpreting them as best I see fit. The comes wants us to engage the enemy's left flank? Well, those Attacotti bastards are on their left."

They watched the Taifals ride up the muddy slope and vanish behind the clustered trees on the rise. They did not have long to wait before they could see frantic movement among the Attacotti as arrows rained down on them. Shields were raised high and those who weren't quick enough fell where they stood. The host seem to shift as it moved down the slope, sacrificing higher ground to get beyond the range of the Taifal bows.

And then they charged.

Driven to desperation by the sudden attack from above their position, they threw their caution to the wind and broke into a run towards the raging battle on the plains below, despite the Votadini cavalry waiting on the slopes like a cat ready to pounce on a mouse as it leaves its hole.

"I suppose anything is preferable to standing in the rain like targets for Asaros and his boys," said Cunedag with a grin. "Ready, men! On my signal!"

As the Attacotti passed their left flank, Cunedag raised his spear and urged Bran down the slope with a roar on his lips.

The roar was taken up by every one of his warriors and they must have sounded like a peal of thunder rolling down the slopes as they charged, hooves drumming and churning up sods of earth, spears lowered, shields braced for impact. The Attacotti hadn't even reached the battle before Cunedag led his men into them, intercepting them and preventing them from aiding their allies. Men screamed as they went down under hoof, spearheads tore into flesh and ruptured mail links and blood spurted up shields as the Votadini cavalry ripped through the Gaelic host.

Chapter 28

By the time they had passed through the front ranks and wheeled around for a second charge, the Taifals had returned and were galloping down the slope, draco billowing above, with the war cries of their homelands on their lips to slam into the next few ranks.

Cunedag grinned to see his eastern allies finally wet their blades in the blood of his enemies. They were magnificent archers in the saddle and were proving themselves to be deadly horsemen at close quarters too. The front few ranks of Attacotti warriors had been utterly wiped out and the dead lay strewn underfoot as their living comrades stumbled about, not knowing whether to advance or hold their ground.

Their chieftains bellowed orders while those with bows and slingshots tried to take aim at Cunedag's riders as they charged again. That was enough for most of them and there was a general retreat as they trampled over their dead in their attempt to get away from the iron-hard horsemen who showed no scrap of mercy.

They were finished, their courage broken, and the Votadini roared a victory cheer as the Attacotti turned tail and fled the battle, heading for the glen from which they had emerged.

"Do not pursue!" Cunedag bellowed, holding his bloodied spear aloft, red droplets flying from its tip. "Stay with me! Our allies need us on their right flank! Form up!"

They let the Attacotti run and marshalled themselves to charge the enemy host on its left flank as they had originally been ordered to do. Cunedag sent the Taifals ahead to soften up the mass of tribesmen with their arrows and sow confusion before breaking away and heading up the slope, while the brunt of his cavalry ploughed into them.

As Asaros led his men away, the Votadini rolled over the enemy ranks like a bloody tide, sweeping them away from the front line of Romans the way cavalry was designed to. Cunedag thrust his spear through a man's chest and wrenched it free, his arm already aching from having done the same thing a dozen times already. But the battle was far from won and the enemy showed no sign of giving up as their Attacotti allies had done.

The Votadini fought on, hacking, stabbing and slashing. Many had lost their spears now and fought with their spathas and long British swords as the enemy surged around them on two sides. The Romans were now massing to the south to press against the enemy Cunedag and his men forced and herded before them.

The rain continued to pelt down on them, and every warrior ran slick with water, sweat and blood. It got in their eyes, ran down behind their armour, and made their clothes sodden. The ground underfoot was a ghastly concoction of blood, mud, shit and entrails, churned up by the hooves of the horses, plastering the shapes of dead warriors.

"Cunedag!" a voice to his left bellowed.

Titus Gemellus, the dux himself, was near to their position, mounted and surrounded by his personal guard.

Cunedag raised his blood-slicked sword in salute.

"We have them penned in!" Gemellus cried. "Our cavalry on the left flank are driving them into the centre where there is nowhere for them to go but in retreat, but they're not retreating, by God!"

"Aye, they know they can't win," Cunedag called back. "But they'd rather die than retreat. Their honour is at stake."

"Try and take down some of their leaders!" Gemellus said. "Break their resolve!"

Cunedag glanced over the heads of the swarming host and could see mounted men in the distance, at the rear of the enemy ranks. Chieftains and kings, directing the battle, sending men to their deaths. They would ride away before it got too hot for them, and, if Cunedag could reach them, it would give him great pleasure to send them to the otherworld along with all the other souls they had sacrificed that day.

But it would be cavalry against cavalry and that was always a bloodbath for both sides. Horses slamming against horses generally knocked most men out of their saddles and all the advantages of a cavalry charge were stripped away, leaving nothing but a bunch of men hacking at each other on foot. There was only one advantage he could think of that might see more of the enemy unhorsed than his own men.

"Asaros!" he bellowed, reining Bran around and out of the fray.

The Taifals were engaged on their right flank, having circled around to aid their allies. Cunedag forced his way through to them and hailed their chief. "Asaros! Disengage! Take your men up the slope and wait for my orders!"

The Taifal commander nodded and Cunedag returned to his men and began the laborious process of extracting them from the battle. Roman infantry swarmed in to take their place, mostly fresh troops from the rear ranks who thrust at the enemy with their spears, forcing the enemy closer towards the middle, packing them in tighter and tighter so they could barely swing their blades.

Sweating, bloody and riding exhausted mounts, the Votadini made their way up the slope to join the Taifals. Their losses had been slight, but they had dealt a devastating blow to the enemy. Now it was time to finish them once and for all.

"I want the Taifals to lead the charge around the rear of the enemy ranks," Cunedag told his warriors. "We hit their cavalry hard on their left flank and try to sever their leadership from the rest of the warband."

"Cavalry against cavalry, Sir?" Marcus asked, uncertainly.

"The Taifals have stirrups," Cunedag pointed out. "They have a distinct advantage over us and the enemy. A rider with stirrups can easily unhorse one without."

"Once again, we Taifals have to show you Britons and Romans how to wage war from the saddle," said Asaros with grim humour. Cunedag did not begrudge him. He was sending an ally into battle ahead of him and it sat ill with him to do so.

"We will be right behind you, pace for pace," Cunedag replied. "Your job is to break their formation while we plunge in after you. It's the only way to ensure half of us aren't immediately unhorsed."

The horns blared and the standards were held high as Cunedag's cavalry formed into a long, iron-hard column much like a spear with the Taifals as its razor-sharp point. On Cunedag's word, they set off, winding their way around the haze of slaughter before them.

The confederation's leadership saw them coming but had little room to manoeuvre. Such was the disorganised rabble of their warband that there were nearly as many men behind them as there were in front of them and the Taifal vanguard carved their way through the rear lines of warriors, knocking them aside and trampling those directly in front of them.

Desperately trying to turn to meet the oncoming threat, the enemy leadership jostled each other but had no time or space before the Taifals were upon them. Cunedag could see horses being hurled forward, spilling their riders under the impact of the hammer blow of the Taifal charge. Not a single Taifal was unhorsed but, by the time the Votadini joined the fray, there were more enemy on foot than there were mounted. Panicked horses bucked and bolted over the heads of warriors, trampling some in their desperation to escape the slaughter.

Cunedag and his riders rode into the chaos of the enemy ranks, butchering all before them. They focused on those who remained mounted but the sheer number of warriors on foot amid the panicked, riderless horses made it difficult to reach those at the rear.

The enemy had spears which were deadly against cavalry and the fetid air rang with the screams of both horses and men as they were skewered. Cunedag hacked through shafts as they were thrust at him and blocked others with his shield. Others were not so fortunate, and he roared with anguish as he saw Elffin, his loyal draconarius, punctured in the abdomen, lean forward in his saddle and tumble to the ground, the dragon standard of the Votadini swaying and going down with him.

It was a terrible blow to them. Like the Roman legions, the native tribesmen put much stock in the symbolism of their tribal standards, treating them with a reverence akin to sacred objects. The standard must survive, no matter what.

Tears in his eyes, Cunedag fought with even more ferocity to reach his downed comrade and to rescue the dragon banner, but the enemy were numerous and crowded him like wheat in a field, ready for his scythe and he could not reap his bloody harvest quick enough.

"My king!" Tegid yelled to him over the din of slaughter. "The enemy leadership is fleeing!"

Cunedag had already seen the cluster of nobles turning their mounts now that the warriors in front of them had surged forward to meet the attacking cavalry. The craven bastards were fleeing and leaving their men to their fates! He could even see Canaul among their number, his estranged foster brother who had once lived under the same roof as him. Now was the chance to end this rebellion once and for all and, if he did not act quickly, he could see it slipping through his fingers.

"Disengage!" he roared to his men. "Pull out! Follow my lead!"

Hauling on Bran's reins, he forced his mount through the press of warriors and made for open ground. The enemy leadership was making tracks towards the woods from where they had emerged. As Cunedag broke free from the battle, he glanced over his shoulder and could see Tegid, Alpia, Morleo and a few others struggling to keep up with him. There was no time to wait and form up. He had to stop the enemy chieftains from getting away or this war would never be over.

He pushed Bran harder than he had ever pushed him before. The animal was already exhausted after multiple cavalry charges that day and he foamed and panted as his hooves drummed on the earth. "A little further, Bran, just a little further!" he encouraged his loyal horse.

He was nearly parallel with the enemy now. Tartan cloaks billowed behind them, and the British ponies struggled to comply with the lashing reins of their masters.

Canaul was close to Cunedag. He could almost reach out and touch him. All the upheaval of the past few months boiled in Cunedag's gut as he rode close to his foster brother, knowing that he was instrumental in Brude's betrayal and ultimate death. With an oath, he drove Bran into the flank of Canaul's horse and, with an animal scream, the pair of riders went down in a tumble of kicking limbs and clashing armour.

Both horses seemed to be unhurt and got to their feet and galloped off. Cunedag, groggy from the blow of his helmed head striking the earth, rolled over and came up, gripping his spatha, but stumbled like a drunkard. Canaul was little better and both men faced each other, blades ready and hatred in their eyes. Both tore their askew helmets from their heads and tossed them to one side.

The rest of the enemy leadership had reined in their mounts and circled around to defend the fallen prince of the Novantae. Cunedag's men had caught up to them now but both factions were reluctant to engage each other. Not when two of their leaders stood face to face, on foot and clearly intent on single combat.

"You should have let me go, Cunedag," said Canaul. "Now I will kill you and the Votadini will mourn the death of yet another king."

"Your rebellion is over," said Cunedag. "And as for killing me, I am no longer a stripling living in your shadow at Eboracum. I have become twice the warrior you'll ever be."

Canaul laughed. "Boastful for a man living in chains. I offered you your freedom, Cunedag, but you chose slavery instead. There really is no helping some people."

"Look around you, Canaul! See what your rebellion has brought to your people! I thank the gods for aiding me in saving the Votadini from a similar fate!"

"Better to die a free man than live as a slave, though only a man with honour would understand that."

"Then die a free man, you pitiable fool!"

Cunedag lunged with his spatha, but Canaul was ready for him, batting his blade away with his own and driving in with his own attack.

The watching warriors had formed a circle around the pair and were yelling encouragement to their champions. Such a fight was one for the bards to sing of; two foster brothers, one who fought for Rome and one against it. Two branches which had grown from the same root, gone different ways, joined together now on the field of battle to end their feud once and for all.

"Kill him, my son!" yelled one of the enemy chieftains as Canaul hacked and slashed at Cunedag and Cunedag knew then that the king of the Novantae was watching. He had to defeat Canaul, not just for himself, but to force the enemy into submitting to Rome's rule. The outcome of this battle now depended on him.

But Canaul was a demon with a blade and seemed to have limitless energy. Cunedag was exhausted from fighting all morning and the muddy ground seemed to suck at his feet, hindering his legs as the tiredness in his arms slowed his sword strokes.

Their blades rang and slithered as they fought on. The crowd cheered and bellowed as the rain continued to pelt down. This was war in the old way, from before the Romans had come to this island. The single combat of chieftains to determine the fate of a whole tribe went back to the dawn of ages.

Canaul's blade nicked Cunedag's mailed shoulder, and he grunted as he felt the pain through the iron links. He stumbled, planted one foot wide to steady himself, then thrust his blade at stomach height.

Canaul, his own blade swinging wild after catching on Cunedag's mail, was too slow to block and the tip of Cunedag's spatha punched into his own mail, slightly to the side, splitting some links and grazing his ribs.

He hacked down on Cunedag's sword hard, and Cunedag felt the ring of the blow vibrating up to his elbow. Canaul brought his sword up in an overhead arc with the aim of landing its crushing edge on Cunedag's unprotected head.

Cunedag held his spatha up with both hands, gripping the tip, newly wetted with Canaul's blood in his left and holding the weapon like a barrier, blocked the savage chop which nearly drove the strength from his arms. Knocking Canaul's blade aside, he slammed the pommel of his spatha into his opponent's face, hearing the splintering of his nose.

Canaul roared in pain and stumbled backwards, blood gushing from his nose and mouth. His sword hung limply to one side, its weight dragging his right arm down. He was open for the kill. Cunedag had a rare chance to end this, and he took it.

With a roar, he whirled his sword around his head and swung it at Canaul's neck. The edge bit deep, hacking through flesh and shattering the collarbone. If it had been a little higher, it would have severed Canaul's head from his body but, as it was, it crunched in deep, lodging itself between Canaul's shoulder and breastbone.

The onlookers roared, some in elation and others in dismay as Canaul, prince of the Novantae, sank to his knees, his sword slipping from his grip to land in the mud. Cunedag planted his boot on the chest of his defeated foster brother and wrenched his blade free with a nasty sucking sound.

Canaul slumped onto his back in the mud, life still clinging to him. Unable to move, his eyes darted about wildly, glancing from Cunedag to his father who looked down, despondently. There was nothing the king of the Novantae could do. His son had fallen.

Cunedag stood over Canaul. "You made your choice and stood by it, Brother," he said. "May the gods honour you for your courage. You die a free man."

He dropped his sword into a reverse grip and held its point over Canaul's throat. Lifting it as high as his screaming muscles allowed, he brought the tip down into his defeated opponent's gullet. The blade slid in noiselessly. Canaul choked. Blood poured from his mouth as he arched his back and then died.

The assembled chieftains, to their credit, did not try to flee. Enough of Cunedag's mounted warriors had arrived to all but encircle them and make any attempt at flight futile. They all dismounted, Canaul's father included, and formally surrendered to Rome.

The battle which had been raging on the front lines further east, came to a standstill. Many of the enemy had thrown down their arms when they had seen their chieftains fleeing and, once word of the death of Canaul and the surrender of the chieftains reached them, the battle was over.

Victories in war are always bittersweet as Cunedag was fast learning. They had lost many men that day, none of which pained him more than the loss of Elffin, his brave draconarius. He sought out his body where it lay beside the fallen dragon standard and nearly wept to see Elffin's lifeless hand still gripping the shaft. He wasn't even Votadini, but he had died holding the new dragon standard of Cunedag's kingdom. He had died for Rome and he had died for Cunedag.

Taking the muddy and blood-stained standard from his grasp, Cunedag handed it to Marcus who stood by his side, teary-eyed at the loss of his dear comrade. "He was a joyless old stick-in-the-mud," Marcus said, "but he was my friend and I'll miss him."

Cunedag folded Elffin's hands across his chest and closed his eyes for him. "Be at peace, Elffin of Britannia," he said. "Go with your god."

"Brother," said Alpia, approaching him as she cleaned her sword. "I apologise for my words to you yesterday. It was not my place to question my king."

"But it is your place to question your brother," he told her with a small smile. "I apologise for my words also. I will always value your honesty and your courage."

"Rome won the day," she said as she gazed around at the dead who carpeted the ground for as far as the eye could see. "And we share in their victory. The north is secure, as you said it would be."

"Aye, there'll be few who'll stir up trouble now. At least for a generation or so."

"Will it always be like this? War after war, generation after generation, never learning, never changing?"

"I don't know," he said. "But I do know what Gonar would say. He'd say that is for future generations to decide. All we can decide is what to do with the time the gods have given us. Not even they can ask more of us than that."

He left Tegid and Alpia to oversee the disarming of the enemy chieftains with Asaros and his Taifals on hand should anybody have any last-minute thoughts of heroism. He rode back to the front lines to report to the Roman leadership.

He found Gemellus with Ambrosius Aurelianus at the rear of the ragged and exhausted lines of the Sixth Victrix. He had not yet met Britannia's new military commander and was surprised by the youthful smoothness of the man. He had expected a grizzled warhorse like Candidius or Gemellus, but this Aurelianus seemed to be barely older than himself, clean shaven and with the bearing of the Roman aristocrat.

"King Cunedag," said Aurelianus. "You have served Rome proud this day. She owes you her gratitude. If the rumours are correct, it was you and your men who pursued the fleeing enemy leadership and forced them to surrender."

"Too many men have died this day to allow them to escape, Sir," Cunedag replied.

"Indeed. And in doing so, you made up for disobeying my orders earlier today when I told you to attack the enemy's left flank."

The comes's eyes were severe and Cunedag knew he was on dangerous ground with this stickler for Roman discipline.

"From where we were standing, Sir," he said, "the Attacotti reserves *were* the enemy's left flank."

The Roman's hard eyes softened, and he allowed himself a small smile. "There is that independent mind of yours I have heard so much about," he said. "The liberal interpretation of orders is not a trait the Roman military looks fondly upon, though it is not uncommon among its *foederati*. Your training as an auxiliary cavalryman no doubt stood you in good stead today, but it was as a king of your people that you won through, not a soldier of Rome. You have proved yourself a loyal ally, King Cunedag. I'd say your days as a cavalry commander are over, though that is very much Rome's loss and the north's gain."

Chapter 29

A week later, Cunedag and his men were honoured with a ceremony in Eboracum. It was a cold, blustery day and the standards on the parade ground were whipped about by the winds of late autumn.

Ambrosius Aurelianus commended the third, fourth and seventh turmae of the Second Asturum for their success in aiding their commander in claiming his throne and for their bravery in the final battle. Then, he presented Cunedag with a bronze diploma signifying his honourable discharge from the Roman army. It was a symbolic thing recalling the days when the enlisted *peregrini* class could be awarded Roman citizenship for their service. The military had dispensed with such things ever since Emperor Caracalla had granted Roman citizenship to all the inhabitants of the empire, but Cunedag was now a king of a nation beyond Rome's borders, and yet deserved to be recognised as a Roman.

After the ceremony, when the soldiers were enjoying jugs of wine, Ambrosius Aurelianus had a private word with Cunedag. "Now that you are free to rule your kingdom, will you be returning to the north immediately?"

"Yes, Sir," Cunedag replied. "There are many things that require my attention. The war was not a welcome thing for my people."

"It never is. Tribes such as the Votadini will always be the first to suffer when Rome's enemies attack. But you can count on Britannia's support if the Picts try such a thing again. So long as we can count on you for one thing."

"Sir?"

"Keep the bastards on the other side of the Antonine Wall where they belong. It's not Rome's frontier anymore, but it is yours."

It was a bittersweet celebration. The men Cunedag had served with for years and years were no longer his men. He bade them farewell with a heavy heart, knowing that it would be a rare occurrence if he ever saw any of them again. That included Morleo who, as the youngest of several brothers, was unlikely to follow in Cunedag's footsteps and succeed his father as king.

"My life is with the limitanae," he told Cunedag as they shared a jug of wine. "I may be a prince, but I'll never be king and that suits me just fine. As long as the next decurion of the ala isn't some bone-headed fool from down south."

"I had thought it would be you," Cunedag told him in all honesty.

Morleo shook his head. "I'm happy enough to relay orders and leave it to some other poor sod to come up with them."

They both laughed and, the following day, with slightly sore heads, they feasted at Colias's house along with Gemellus and several other high-ranking Britons of the north. It was an event Cunedag had been greatly looking forward to. Vala had been on his mind more or less constantly since he had last seen her, even when he had a kingdom and a war to win.

She sat opposite him, her hair done up in ringlets, looking even more beautiful than he remembered. Or perhaps it was the brutality of war that made him appreciate the fairer things in life. He cared little which. All he knew was that he wanted her.

The men talked of the various goings on in Britannia and how it was picking itself up from the chaos of the summer. Much talk was given to Stilicho's appointment of a new governor of Maxima Caesariensis, one of the four provinces of the diocese. His name was Vitalinus and he was spoken of with curiosity that was not unlaced with suspicion.

"His father, Vitalis, was a powerful chieftain from some western territory," Colias told them. "A power-hungry family if ever there was one."

"Wasn't Vitalis the man who married the daughter of Magnus Maximus?" Gemellus asked.

"That's the one," Colias replied. "He had hoped to weasel his way into the royal family of the new emperor, but those hopes were dashed by Maximus's defeat and execution."

"But this Vitalinus is too old to have been born to the purple, as it were," Gemellus said.

"Indeed. Vitalinus was the product of his father's first marriage. There *was* a son born of his father's union to Maximus's daughter. A lad called Brutus."

"The name of Britannia's first king," said an amused Gemellus. "The man wasn't exactly subtle."

Colias smiled. "No doubt young Brutus was groomed to become the successor to his namesake and ruler of the whole island under Emperor Maximus. But the lad mysteriously died not long after Maximus's defeat, leaving it to young Vitalinus to succeed his father and he is no less ambitious than his father was. We must keep our eyes on these southerners, old friend. They are not as bluntly honest and trustworthy as our northern allies like King Cunedag." He smiled at Cunedag and raised his glass to him.

Cunedag raised his glass in reply to accept the slightly ham-fisted compliment. Colias was drunk and Cunedag ached to be alone with Vala.

He got his chance at last as the meal wound down and a poet was brought in to recite some dull effort for a bloated and drunken audience. The lively theatrical dances of the old days with their erotic and pagan undertones had been banned by the church but even the strictest Christian households were hard pressed to show much enthusiasm for the replacement entertainment. For Vala, it was apparently too dull to bear and Cunedag watched her slip out into the gardens.

He got up to follow her and, surrounded by the moonlit bushes, he wrapped his cloak around them both against the chill evening air. She snuggled into his arms and he could smell the perfume in her hair and wanted that moment to never end.

She looked up at him, their lips barely two inches apart and stroked his hair. "You've let your hair grow long," she said. "I like it. Not sure about the beard, though. Very unbecoming of a Roman soldier."

"I am a Roman soldier no more."

"No, I suppose not. But I hope you're not expecting me to bow my head and call you 'lord' now that you rule a tribe."

He smiled. "Not at all. I may be a king, but you are still my foster sister."

"I'm not sure I like that arrangement any better."

"What do you mean?"

"Come on, Cunedag. You know as well as I that we see each other as more than that."

As always, her boldness and habit of driving straight to the point with more accuracy than a Taifal arrow flummoxed him.

"You have been more than a sister to me for quite some time," he admitted. "My thoughts dwelled on you often even when I was facing the worst of dangers. My memories of you were a great comfort to me during the fighting."

"I can say the same of you, though I must confess that boredom was my enemy rather than Picts and Attacotti. I often thought of how you rescued me and my mother from Canaul and looked after us during those awful days north of the Wall. Well, it's all for naught in any case. Father has found me a suitable husband. Fabius Lepidus, the son of a tribune with the Sixth Victrix. We are to be married in the spring. He's a nice boy but dreadfully dull."

"Are you saying you'd rather marry me?" It was meant as a joke, despite feeling like he had been punched in the gut by Vala's news.

"Yes."

"Are you being serious?"

She frowned at him, her face offended. "I wouldn't joke about that, Cunedag. I have loved you for quite some time and I was under the impression that you loved me. If that isn't the case, then damn you for making a fool of me."

"I do love you, Vala," he said. "With all my heart."

"Then we are a tragic pair, are we not? Doomed lovers worthy of Ovid or Senneca."

"Tragic? To hell with this Fabius Lepidus of yours. I'll have a word with your father."

Vala gave him a sad smile. "Father would never allow us to marry. He loves you as a son and respects you as a king, but you are just not Roman enough for his precious daughter."

"Leave it to me," he said with a smile. "Am I not currently a hero of Rome?"

Two days later, Cunedag put his case to Gemellus and pointed out the sense in a union between the Votadini and a high-status Roman family, preferably one involved in the governance of the province. As Governor Colias had a daughter of ripe marrying age, wasn't that the perfect opportunity to strengthen ties across the Wall?

Gemellus wasn't fooled into thinking that Cunedag was purely thinking of diplomacy, but he was keen on the idea in any case and even took it to the comes himself. With Aurelianus's support, the notion was put to Colias who, as expected, was appalled. His outrage was matched only by his wife's who, despite her affection for her barbarian foster sons, saw them as barbarians, nonetheless.

But, with the urging of Aurelianus, Colias was made to see the strategic sense in marrying his daughter to a tribal king who had deep ties both to Rome and his own family. So what if his precious daughter had to go and live in some muddy hillfort and spawn babes with Pictish names? The Votadini were Rome's barrier against the howling wilderness and Cunedag had proved to be a strong and loyal leader already. Despite his wife's tears of despair, Colias reluctantly agreed to the wedding.

They were married in the governor's palace two weeks before Kalan Gayaf. Vala wore dried flowers of yellow broom and autumn leaves in her hair and, as they recited their vows before a burning brazier, Cunedag knew he was the luckiest man alive. A garment of Vala's childhood was burned on the flames to symbolise her transition to adulthood and then she and Cunedag each took a bite of a mustaceum; a cake made from wheat, honey and wine.

Once the gifts had been presented to the happy couple and the celebrations were well underway, Cunedag took Vala to a room in the upper portion of the palace lit with candles and spread with dried petals. There, on a silk couch, he made love to her, and they held each other until the dawn shone through the arched windows.

They journeyed north to Din Eidyn the following day, eager to reach the royal seat of the Votadini before the festival of Kalan Gayaf was underway. They rode in a carpentium for much of the way, with Cunedag occasionally riding ahead on Bran which he had been gifted by the Second Asturum, the brand on his flank cancelled out. The wounds of war were slowly healing in the countryside as families did what they could to brace themselves for winter. The rest of the harvest had been reaped and preparations were underway for the festival.

Towards the end of their journey, they quickened their pace and travelled through the night to ensure they reached their destination before the 'spirit night' that preceded the harvest festival. It was on that night that the people lit large bonfires and stayed indoors to avoid the shades of the dead that were said to roam the countryside after dark.

Cunedag had been nervous that Vala would regret marrying him once she saw the place that was to be her home for, although Din Eidyn was a large and well-quipped Votadini fortress, it was hardly a palace with the luxuries she was used to. But Vala surprised him, beaming at the crowds that lined up to greet their new queen and accepting their compliments with grace and charm. Even when confronted by the alarming spectre of Gonar the druid, she did not baulk.

Gonar was greatly pleased with the head of Blathmac which Cunedag had brought him, preserved in its barrel of salt, and had come to bless their union and invoke the gods to safeguard their reign. Vala, Christian in name, accepted this pagan gesture without complaint, showing that she was going to make a fine ruler of a tribe with many loyalties: Roman, Briton, Christian and pagan.

The war was over, Rome's frontier had been protected and Cunedag had defeated more enemies in the past six months than he cared to list. He had left this fortress eight years ago as a hostage. Now he ruled it as a king with a Roman wife who would no doubt bear him many sons. Life was good. The hard times were over. Peace and prosperity lay ahead of them like the long table in the Great Roundhouse which was currently being laden with the harvest feast.

A bright future lay before them, and, as he watched his wife smiling as the lys broke out into singing and dancing, he swore to all the gods he could name that he would allow nothing to disrupt them.

Cunedag returns in *The Pictish Crown*: book two in the *Dragon of the North* trilogy.

If you enjoyed *Defender of the Wall*, please consider leaving a review on the platform you purchased it and following the author on social media to keep up to date with new releases.

Printed in Great Britain
by Amazon